The Seaside Café Metropolis

The Seaside Café Metropolis

A Novel About Dining Under Complicated
Circumstances, with a Nod to *La Bohème*

Antanas Sileika

CORMORANT
BOOKS

Copyright © 2025 Antanas Sileika
This edition copyright © 2025 Cormorant Books Inc.
This is a first edition.

No part of this publication may be reproduced, stored in a retrieval system or transmitted, in any form or by any means, without the prior written consent of the publisher or a licence from The Canadian Copyright Licensing Agency (Access Copyright). For an Access Copyright licence, visit www.accesscopyright.ca or call toll free 1.800.893.5777.

The publisher and the author expressly forbid the use of this book in any manner for the purpose of training so-called artificial intelligence systems or technologies, and reserve this title from the text and data mining exception in accordance with the European Parliament directive.

 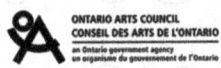 

We acknowledge financial support for our publishing activities: the Government of Canada, through the Canada Book Fund and The Canada Council for the Arts; the Government of Ontario, through the Ontario Arts Council, Ontario Creates, and the Ontario Book Publishing Tax Credit.

LIBRARY AND ARCHIVES CANADA CATALOGUING IN PUBLICATION

Title: The Seaside Café Metropolis / Antanas Sileika.
Names: Sileika, Antanas, 1953- author
Identifiers: Canadiana (print) 20250165929 | Canadiana (ebook) 20250166089 | ISBN 9781770868106 (softcover) | ISBN 9781770868113 (EPUB)
Subjects: LCGFT: Novels.
Classification: LCC PS8587.I2656 S43 2025 | DDC C813/.54—dc23

United States Library of Congress Control Number: 2025905102

Cover and interior text design: Marijke Friesen
Manufactured by Copywell in Woodbridge,
Ontario in August 2025.

Printed using paper from a responsible and sustainable resource, including a mix of virgin fibres and recycled materials.

Printed and bound in Canada.

EU RP   eucomply OÜ
Pärnu mnt 139b-14, 11317 Tallinn, Estonia
hello@eucompliancepartner.com, +3375690241

CORMORANT BOOKS INC.
260 ISHPADINAA (SPADINA) AVENUE, SUITE 502,
TKARONTO (TORONTO), ON M5T 2E4

SUITE 110, 7068 PORTAL WAY, FERNDALE, WA 98248, USA
info@cormorantbooks.com / www.cormorantbooks.com

To invite people to dine with us is to make ourselves responsible for their well-being for as long as they are under our roofs.
— Jean Anthelme Brillat-Savarin, *The Physiology of Taste*

They [bohemians] are the race of obstinate dreamers ... They live, so to say, on the outskirts of life.
— Henri Murger, *The Bohemians of the Latin Quarter*

For Alma

–1–

Apple Compote

IF BOHEMIANS ARE said to live on the outskirts of life, you could say I was living on the outskirts of the outskirts.

For the Moscow-mandated lesson in hygiene, I had assembled all thirty-six of the restaurant staff. We stood around a massive stockpot sitting on a low table by the ovens. The kitchen staff were in whites and tall hats, the front of the house in skirts and white blouses or jackets and ties, and the cleaners in grey coveralls. Colour television would have been wasted on this spectrum. As for me, I stood with my clipboard, ready to rate the performance.

Inga's plan was to demonstrate how to fill a dessert bowl effectively by holding it above the stockpot of apple compote below.

We hadn't gone in for stewed fruit all that much back home, but in the USSR, apple compote was a common dessert dish. First, Inga explained, no one was to spit, sneeze, or cough anywhere near the stockpot. She recounted these prohibitions in exquisite detail; eyes rolled among the staff, feet shuffled, sighs multiplied.

Having finished her admonitions, she took the glass dessert bowl in one hand and a massive, long-handled ladle in the other. She paused dramatically without looking up at us, composing herself like a pianist before a tricky piece of music, say a Stravinsky or a Chopin. Alternating moments of uncertainty and determination flickered across her face as she prepared to start her performance.

Moscow was keen to modernize the restaurant processes and staff, and we were following the latest directive dreamed up by some gnome of a bureaucrat in some airless office among thousands of similar ones. It had taken only two, Marx and Lenin, to give us the theory, but it took thousands more to work out the details, and tens of thousands more to issue instructions to every niche of Soviet life.

For perpetually-striving Inga, it meant much more than fulfilling a directive. It meant proving herself worthy and perhaps rising one step in the centralized restaurant grading system and earning eight more rubles a month.

First, she dipped into the stockpot with the ladle, then she paused halfway to the bowl to make eye contact with her audience. Assured of our attention, she poured the juice and fruit into the dish. As she had planned, the drips ran back into the vast stockpot below. It was a brilliant tactic to avoid waste, but she was working the wrong lesson. This was supposed to be about hygiene.

The apple pieces splattered drops over the side of the dish, and some of the enormous ladle-full ran over Inga's chubby hand as well.

"See?" she said. "Not a drop wasted because there is no spillage that doesn't fall back into the pot."

Inga was always a couple of lessons behind. She was still thinking of the government-mandated course we had run on reducing food waste. And even I had to admit, she had wasted no food.

She was delighted with herself. Beefy chefs watched stone-faced while some of the more eager but stupid junior apprentices nodded along with her, not having noticed how the excess compote washed the back of her hand before falling back into the pot

The Seaside Café Metropolis

below. The more observant staff would be sure not to eat fruit compote again.

I had never eaten fruit compote in Canada, but one adapts to local tastes. As a former resident of the land of Jell-O, who was I to judge?

Still, I actually did have to judge her performance. Each dish of compote set out on a tray on the cafeteria side of the restaurant would have sticky sides. It would leave a ring beneath it that might dry in so hard the dish could not even be lifted from the tray.

I remembered a local saying: *We tried and we tried as hard as we could, yet the result ended up the way it always does.*

Hopeless.

The technique, Inga, my life, and the whole damned country.

Poor Inga, broad in the chest and hips, dressed in her whites and a tall paper hat, was looking at me for support, but something in my expression must have given my thoughts away. I saw her face begin to crumple toward one of her regular crying fits. Sometimes she just could not cope when all her best intentions did not match her limitations and the Lenin Prize for Kitchen Workers remained an unattainable dream.

I was the one who should have been weeping. I would need to point out the error of her ways to the others, and then console her as she cried in my office. What she really deserved was demotion to a third-class restaurant or student lunchroom, but I was not permitted to hire or fire my staff. They were assigned to me by the party representative.

Just as I was formulating my response, she set down the ladle and bowl and licked off the back of her hand where the juice had run over it. Then she wiped her fingers on her apron.

I shuddered, and a couple of the more hygienically knowledgeable staff smirked.

My life had come to this. I'd gone from riches to rags in a few short years. I blamed my mother for my present condition. My late father too, for the effect he had had upon her. And if I was apportioning blame, why not add General Francisco Franco of Spain for being instrumental in my father's death?

The double kitchen doors burst open, and a pair of men in grey suits waddled in as if they were penguins that owned the place. Former KGB types, it seemed, or cut from that primitive cloth. Real KGB types didn't look like thugs anymore, and the ones that used to work for the KGB and still looked like that had to take menial jobs.

"We're having a training session here," I said. "No outsiders allowed."

"Is this the Vilnius Soviet Ministry of Agriculture's First-Class Restaurant?"

"Bravo. You've found the place. The second-class cafeteria is right next door. You might like the lower prices over there."

They looked at one another as if considering it, then turned back to me.

"Are you Emmet Argentine?"

"Brilliant."

"Why do they call you 'the Canadian' if your last name is Argentine?"

"Because I'm a Canadian."

They shrugged as if they were a pair of marionettes hung on the same string. "You are to come with us."

My staff began to sidle ever so slightly away from me. I loved many of them and tolerated the rest, and I'm sure they felt the same about me. But solidarity is a fragile thing, and only people who live happily in the West imagine it holds true in the rest of the world. If I were being taken off to the gulag, it would not do to have been too close to me.

"The assistant deputy minister of agriculture himself is having lunch with a delegation from Smolensk this afternoon," I said. "When do you need me to come?"

"Now."

It was 1959, and the old days of summary nighttime arrests were past, although arrests still happened, and people tended to be nervous. True dissidents were still in jail. The gulag labour camps still had many, many unwilling residents. We did live under tyranny, but most citizens were now harassed in other ways.

I could have protested, but I was being saved from dealing with the tearful Inga. And stuck in Vilnius, in the Lithuanian Soviet Socialist Republic, I considered myself in jail already. So why should I worry even if they did turn out to be sinister government functionaries?

"I'll get my coat."

"We're just going up the street."

I insisted on getting the coat. Old-timers had told me to take as much as possible with me if I were being hustled away, just in case the short interruption turned out to be a long one. On the way out, I stuffed a few bread rolls into my coat pockets.

I told the staff to proceed with preparations for lunch and to pay special attention to the assistant deputy minister and his guests from Smolensk.

I walked out the door between the two men and onto Lenin Prospect. It was the main street of Vilnius, with the old cathedral (now a concert hall) down at one end and a miserable department store straight across the way. The store was called the Univermag. In other words, it was supposed to be a universal store, a department store that had everything, and occasionally it did have decent products, but never at the same time and never when you needed a particular item. At the moment, the store was full of baby strollers in the shape of an automobile, the Gaz M-20, a model discontinued the year before.

But real automobiles were rare. For some of the kids, that stroller might be the only chance in their lives to ride in a car that wasn't a taxi, and those were rare enough anyway.

In the other direction, it was a long walk up the road past crumbling nineteenth-century wedding-cake buildings to a bridge that crossed the river. An old lady in a head scarf was sweeping cigarette butts off the sidewalk into the gutter, and a passing dump truck with poor ignition was blowing diesel smoke into the air. It was a weekday midmorning, so the streets were pretty empty with everyone at work.

The building they took me to was not more than a few hundred metres up the road. I'd barely paid attention to it because it had been covered by hoardings for a very long time. No more. Now I saw the new place was more or less done, a fine five-storey structure with workmen visible through the picture windows facing the sidewalk. We went in.

The front part was a café with strange triangular tables, like nothing I had seen before in the Soviet Union or anywhere else, like something out of the future. Who could imagine that a table could have only three legs? The idea must have been stolen from stools. I was surprised the tables weren't illegal.

As we went in deeper, we passed a middle section empty of tables and chairs but with a small fountain in the centre and a standing bar off to one side. Very cool. This place was getting better and better. At the back was a very large restaurant with eight tall booths down the left side for those who wanted privacy, a stage at the end, and many more tables set throughout. Light poured in through sheer curtains from a bank of windows on my right. It was a room that could easily seat a hundred and fifty people.

The Seaside Café Metropolis

This was much finer than anything I'd ever seen in Vilnius, including some of the best hotels and Communist Party dining rooms, which tended to favour red damask, gilt, and dark wainscotting. But this place had a high ceiling and impressionistic wall mosaics with a nautical theme in bright colours — sailboats and the seaside and a pair of stocky nude women sitting on the sand with their backs to the viewer as they stared out to sea.

I felt like I'd dropped into the modern world for the first time in five years, and not just any modern world. Public rooms in the Soviet Union were of three kinds — dowdy, heavy, or pompous. This place was light and airy and fresh. It felt not exactly like Toronto, but maybe better, more like New York.

My grey-suited escorts led me to an elegant man who was seated in one of the booths. He was youngish, with romantic, upswept black hair greying at the temples, and his suit looked better than anything I'd seen in my Soviet time. He was smoking a BT, a Bulgarian cigarette brand, one of the better kind, hard to get. The man motioned to the grey suits, and they disappeared.

"Coffee?"

"Sure," I said.

He nodded toward the seat across from him, and I slid into the booth.

"What is this place?" I asked.

"Welcome to the Seaside Café Metropolis. Like it?"

I looked around myself to examine the place more slowly.

"I love it. But why this particular name if there is no seaside here? And let's face it, Vilnius is not exactly a metropolis. When I think *seaside*, I think sand dunes and beaches. When I think *metropolis*, I think New York City or Chicago. I mean, people who've seen Prague tell me it's like Vilnius, but even Prague is not a metropolis. Anyway, you see my point."

He shrugged.

"It's a bit of a fantasy, isn't it? The word *metropolis* received grudging approval from the Pan-Soviet Board of Food Service Institution Names, but frescoes of skyscrapers on the walls would have been too bourgeois, too American. We could have the word, but the board forbade metropolitan images for the frescoes. As for the word *seaside*, even people who will never get to a beach want to dream of one, don't they? So why not combine two dreams into one?"

"Two dreams or two lies?"

"Does it matter? A dream is just an unreality you hope for, isn't it? A form of deception? People seem to have no problem living with lies."

Well, I had slipped a few fabrications into my stories from time to time too. I liked everything I saw, even if they were building a kind of café appropriate for the Emerald City of Oz instead of the city of Vilnius. As long as no one pulled aside the curtain, we'd all be happy.

"Will this be open to the public?"

"Oh yes. New winds are blowing through here, you know. I'm the architect who designed this place, and now I've been asked to make it operational. My name is Dominic Valaitis. I've heard of you. Are you Argentinian?"

"Canadian."

His face fell. "I might have made a mistake. We heard you were an Argentinian trained in a first-class hotel restaurant."

"My last name is Argentine, but I'm a Canadian, and I was trained in a very fine hotel in Toronto, Canada. One of the best, really."

"What hotel was that?"

"The Royal York. It's part of a chain of railway hotels. Very grand. Over a thousand rooms, and a kitchen that would make you faint with envy if you ever saw it. World-class food and service that a Swiss *maître d'hôtel* would admire."

"And what did you do there?"

"I practically grew up in the kitchen. My mother was a dishwasher and a maid, and my father was dead, so she had no place to put me. I liked the restaurant kitchen, and I knew when to stay out of the way, so the staff doted on me. By the time I was ten, I was helping out, and I advanced to line chef well before I was out of my teens. I loved the kitchen, but I found my real calling at the front of the room."

"What sort of talent was that?"

"The talent to create atmosphere — to make the customers happy; to respect the kitchen staff, and above all the chefs; to serve the best food, and to do it in style; to be attentive without being obsequious; to have handsome wait staff who aren't clumsy but don't show off with fanciful pretensions; to know my regular clients and never to betray them if they come in with partners who are not their spouses; to demand a certain style of dress and to place beautiful men and women in places in the restaurant where others could enjoy looking at them; to referee fights between couples; to know birthdays, and to present complimentary glasses of champagne when appropriate. Of course, there is much more to it than this, but that gives you some idea."

Dominic considered what I had said. He butted one cigarette and, in no great rush, lit another one before going on.

"Very impressive, I suppose. And do you now get a chance to practise your skills in the Ministry of Agriculture's so-called first-class restaurant?"

He was smiling. It was tempting to say something dismissive about my current workplace, or to make the incident with Inga into a derisive anecdote. But it's never worthwhile to make an amusing or cutting remark about a place you will be going back to.

"The place where I work is not exactly humble because we serve deputy ministers of state and sometimes the minister himself, who is not exactly a friend, but he does know me by name. It might be better than you think. And here is the important part. Since my restaurant is under the umbrella of the Ministry of Agriculture, I know where to get beef when no one can get beef. I can find caviar both red and black when required. I know what is imported in food and spirits, and I know which Georgian wines are sublime and which Kazakh ones should be poured down the sink."

"Kazakhstan is a Muslim republic."

"Exactly. Imagine."

"Can you get your hands on Dvin?"

"Armenian cognac, of course. The five-star brand, not just the three."

"We have heard rumours that there is French cognac now being imported too."

"The rumours are true. The brand is Camus. I can give you the address of the warehouse where it's found, but not everyone can get it. Sometimes I can, though, within limits."

"Do you think your talents are being wasted in the place where you work now?"

"I do my duty. I work with joy wherever I am placed."

"You seem to have adapted well here, not only learning the languages but the local habits as well. Your English accent lingers but is actually charming. So how did you end up in Vilnius?"

I got this question all the time. Nobody believed that any sane person from the West would come to a city still suffering from damage since the last war. And on top of that, a city in the Lithuanian Soviet Socialist Republic, ruled over by Moscow. Not exactly a place with a high international profile.

"I came here to help build socialism."

He said nothing.

"With my mother," I added.

"It was her idea?"

"We think alike." It was so easy to lie.

"How many guests did you serve in this hotel of yours back in Canada?"

"It depended on the room. A hundred in the café, up to two hundred in the restaurant, many hundreds more for banquets."

"I was looking for someone to add a little Latin flair to this place when it opens, and I was hoping an Argentinian might do it."

"I'm Canadian."

"Yes, so you have said. Do Canadians have flair? I've never heard that said of them. And I'm not sure a railway hotel is what we had in mind. We are interested in creating café culture, something this city needs. Canada must be too cold to have cafés. Do you even know what cafés are?"

I thought of the gritty Barney's Café on Queen Street West in Toronto where I sometimes used to buy coffee and bran muffins. I thought of Kresge's café counters with glass displays under which devil's food cake was sold by the slice. I thought of scrambled eggs on brown toast.

Luckily, he couldn't read my mind, and I had done a little reading.

"Les Deux Magots in Paris is a popular café in the Latin Quarter, but the existentialist intellectuals prefer the Café de Flore. In Budapest, the Café Gerbeaud has tabletops painted by famous artists, and a monkey amuses the patrons. At least it did before 1956. One tries but often fails to find a place at the Montmartre in Prague. Closer to home, we have the Tulip in Kaunas, which still retains some of the feeling of the pre-war Konrad Café that occupied the same spot."

"Your range of knowledge astonishes me. What is the essential element in these cafés?"

"Atmosphere. A café must be elegant but not snobbish, bohemian but not vulgar, well supplied but with a limited and sophisticated menu."

"Music?"

"Yes, but not too loud and not traditional. No gypsy violins!"

"Dancing?"

"Absolutely not. Intellectuals will want to have discussions, and dancers are distracting. But let me ask you something. How is it that a place like the Seaside Café Metropolis was even allowed to open?"

It was a slightly provocative question, one that implied we lived under some sort of totalitarianism, or at least oppressiveness, and we all knew we were supposed to be a happy proletariat together.

My architect became thoughtful for a moment and sipped his coffee.

"There are wheels within wheels in every society, and we happen to find ourselves on a progressive wheel at the moment."

He thought some more.

"Would you object to it if we called you the Argentinian?"

"You can call me anything you want if the kitchen is any good and I can hire my own staff."

"And what about that first name of yours? What is the origin of *Emmet*? Were you named for someone?"

"Yes. My mother was an admirer of Emma Goldman, the revolutionary, so she gave me the male version of the name. And Emma Goldman was born in Kaunas, and that is part of the reason we ended up in Lithuania."

"Ah." He smiled. He had finally found a way to categorize me. Politically, I was a useful idiot, but the stress lay on *useful*.

The Seaside Café Metropolis

MY MOTHER LIVED in a poorly ventilated basement room with a view of the sidewalk from a window near the ceiling. She could have got a better place by virtue of her propaganda value as an immigrant to the Lithuanian Soviet Socialist Republic, the birthplace of Emma Goldman. But she'd insisted she didn't need anyplace better than the room a single worker had rights to, and the authorities had obliged with this underground hutch in the medieval part of the city. I'd thought she had underplayed her hand at first, but later I found whole families lived in these types of rooms, so maybe it wasn't as bad as I had imagined.

I went down a few steps and could hear her coughing from outside the perpetually unlocked door. She claimed that anyone who robbed her could only be the sort of person who needed what she owned more than she needed it herself. Luckily, she was so far off the beaten path and the door itself looked so miserable that it would never occur to a thief that there was anything of value on the other side.

Inside, she was smoking a cigarette and drinking coffee at a small, wobbly wooden table with two chairs. She had folded a piece of cardboard to balance the table legs, but it kept slipping out. The ashtray was overflowing, and there was bread and jam and butter that I had put on the table that morning, but the loaf was uncut and the jar unopened. She liked a warm room, so the lump of indolent butter lay in a partially melted pool. Her bed was unmade.

She hadn't lived all that differently back in Toronto, where her room in our shared apartment was always a mess. I don't think she ever washed a dish after my father left when I was around eight. She made fun of me for drying the dishes when she said they'd dry themselves if I left them long enough.

As for cooking, well, she never cared for it, so that was up to me. I didn't mind. It turned me into a pretty good cook, not that she ever mentioned it. She would have had us live on scraps brought home from the hotel, which were sometimes quite good, but unpredictable. I saw my first shrimp in a lake of leftover ketchup and horseradish sauce, and I thought it was the most exciting discovery of the month. There were no shrimp in the stores in those days, at least not in the kind of stores where working-class people shopped. To ask for shrimp in our corner grocery store would have been a sign of pretentiousness. And in Canada, there was no greater crime. Who did I think I was?

My mother needed care and protection, mostly from herself. Who else was going to provide it if not me?

She butted out her cigarette and gave me a look.

"So the fascists got what they deserved in Hungary," she said. Where she'd pulled this from, I didn't know. She was probably brooding. The failed Hungarian revolution had happened three years earlier. At the time, I'd hoped the revolution in Hungary would stir things up and loosen the system enough that I could get us out of this place. But no such luck. And anyway, she would not have agreed to leave.

My two tyrants were the Soviet Union and my mother, and she was turning out to be as unbending as the first. I'd thought my mother would come to her senses once she saw the way people lived in the Soviet Union, but her idealism and loyalty blinded her to the proof right before her eyes. She loved the Soviet Union the way a mother ought to love her son, wholeheartedly. Maybe she loved the USSR more. Maybe a little too much.

Having made her bed here, unmade as it was, she was going to sleep in it.

As for me, I was loyal to her, and that was my failing. She had always lived on the verge of disaster. Back in Toronto, she was always fighting with the landlord, the city, her bosses, and any other figure of authority who was not a member of the party.

Communist Party people got a pass. I often had to intervene in her squabbles with authority, to calm things down, but I can't say she seemed to appreciate it very much. I had tried to keep her out of trouble, but she'd dragged me down into it with her, and that was how I'd ended up where I was.

My mother's greatest strength was her determination to live in a manner consistent with her beliefs. This way to hell was certainly paved with her good intentions. She was a socialist, so she was going to help build socialism after failing to start a socialist revolution among the workers in the Royal York Hotel. She was filled with passionate intensity in spite of repeated bouts of bronchitis, a bad skin condition that left her hands and scalp all cracked, and some unspecified pain she would not describe and whose existence I divined only by her occasional wincing.

"I've got good news," I said, slipping into the chair across from her and slicing myself a piece of bread. The soft butter kept trying to escape from my knife, but I finally managed to spread some of it on the bread and to add plum jam on top. I made an open-faced sandwich for her too and set it in front of her, but she ignored it. She didn't offer me coffee. She believed able-bodied people should help themselves and politeness was just a bourgeois pretension.

The loaf was the local black rye sourdough. I missed the white bread of my childhood and youth, but I had to admit the dark bread had more body. Everything was so grey in Vilnius that black bread was appropriate. Although Canadian Wonder Bread was spongy and caused constipation, the coloured balloons on the bag would have added a little brightness to the room we were in.

She didn't seem all that impressed when I told her that I was going to be the new director of the Seaside Café Metropolis. It was bad enough that I worked in a high-end ministry commissary, which she considered an unseemly trough for bureaucrats. But now, worse, I would be working in a place aimed at the intelligentsia, a place that aped the styles we had left behind.

To her, there were degrees of commitment to the cause, and living in the Soviet Union was just a first step in our shared commitment. Of course I should have been leading us on the path to deeper commitment. The way she saw it, her leadership got us here, and now it was my turn to step up in socialist activism. Instead, it looked like I was going to disappoint her once again.

"What would your father say to this?"

It was her favourite refrain. I wasn't even a teenager yet when my father died in Spain in 1938, fighting with the Mackenzie-Papineau Battalion of volunteers from Canada. He'd been gone almost two years at that point. Before he left, he'd held my chin firmly, looked into my childish eyes, and told me to take care of my mother and never to forget he was fighting for a good cause.

How could I forget when my mother kept reminding me of it? As far as she was concerned, my interest in food and dining were a poor substitute for fighting for social justice.

My father and the Mackenzie-Papineau Battalion — the Mac-Paps as they were fondly known — were going to defeat the Spanish fascists and install communism, or anarchism, or some such anti-capitalist system, even though they couldn't agree among themselves what that system would be. I suspect my father was a Trotskyite, and he would have been killed by the communists if they had won, the same way they destroyed the anarchists. It was more important for them to be pure than to win the war.

My mother spoke fondly of the Mac-Paps, and some of the veterans who survived used to visit her. When I was young, they would tell me about my father's courage and his commitment to socialism. As I was growing up, I wished he'd been a little more committed to my mother and me.

The Seaside Café Metropolis

I didn't subscribe to any political thought myself. I just wanted to be left alone to pursue my dreams. I loved the Royal York Hotel, with its soaring lobby ceiling. I loved the rush of guests who came through the tunnel from Union Station across the street. I loved Oscar Peterson, who played jazz piano there. And I would have loved to remain, but I was cursed with an obligation to my mother and my childish promise to my father to take care of her. It wasn't an easy job. In 1954, a whole year after the death of Stalin, my mother decided that the Soviet Union needed her help to get back on track after the loss of its great leader.

Why did I go with her? I was a grown man, and she was a grown woman. I couldn't stop her from making bad decisions, but I decided I might be able to prevent her from suffering too badly for having made them. Besides, there was a certain pastry chef who decided she didn't want to see me anymore. Nobody would care if I left.

It was only after we ended up in Vilnius that I came to realize I could not stop my mother's suffering. Instead, I joined her in her suffering. And there was no way out of the Soviet Union, which had welcomed us with open arms and then closed those arms around us to keep us from ever going back.

Khrushchev's 1956 speech about Stalin's crimes made no impression on my mother. She pretended the words had never been spoken. The crushing of the Hungarian Revolution that same year reassured her rather than making her think twice.

Now I was being handed the helm of the Seaside Café Metropolis and asked to build an oasis of civilization in a city where a slice of fatback and onion on a piece of black bread was considered a simple delicacy. Maybe I couldn't go back to the world I had lost, but I could rebuild the manners and fine dining that would stand as consolation for all that had vanished from my life through my foolish support of my mother.

Better yet, a café like the one they had planned would eventually attract some sort of visiting diplomat or dignitary who would help me get out of the Soviet Union and back to the Royal York Hotel where I belonged.

Apple Compote

2 glasses dried, firm apples
Cinnamon
Cloves
1 glass sugar
3–4 glasses water

Combine all the ingredients. Boil for about twenty minutes. Some apples are firmer than others, so test doneness frequently. Remove cloves. Serve warm or at room temperature. Dumplings may be added if the previous course had consisted of a light meal of chicken or fish.

Serves four normal people.

−2−

Chicken Kiev

I DREW UP plans for opening day.

In Canada, we had billboards, newspapers, radio ads, and skywriters to advertise new cafés and restaurants. Sandwich-boarded people walked the sidewalks bearing their posters front and back. Paid magazine stories featured restaurant chefs and dining room designers to help build anticipation. Where I was living in the Lithuanian Soviet Socialist Republic, anyone wearing a sandwich board would have been arrested. Or if not caught by the police, then followed by fascinated crowds as if he were the Pied Piper, leading those huddled masses longing to be free to drink decent espresso.

In Soviet Lithuania, you didn't need to bring them in. You needed to keep them out if you had a popular place, always preserving a table or two for an unexpected party official, KGB operative, visiting Russian officer, or gangster who might threaten to harm your child if you treated him badly. Luckily, I didn't have a child. I did have a baby, and my baby was the Seaside Café Metropolis. I didn't have to worry much about gangsters except for street toughs who did not typically come into a place like ours but who sometimes circulated in alleys and niches like trolls, waiting for an opportunity.

We could fill the place easily enough, but we had to fill it the right way. The café had to have atmosphere and a little glitter. People only want what's difficult to get. I needed the café and restaurant to be attractive and chic, and the door had to be watched by thugs because the harder it was to get in, the more people would want to try.

I found out the names of the two grey penguins who had escorted me from the Ministry of Agriculture restaurant, discovered they were bachelor brothers, John and Joe. These simple men thought little, worked hard, and spent their leisure hours singing in a choir that turned out to be the retired KGB collaborators' choir. They were especially good with melancholy tunes and marches.

John and Joe were perfect to staff the door.

The kitchen was downstairs at the back of the building, so I hired waitresses for their strong legs and for their slightly icy demeanour, the better to carry heavy plates up and down the stairs and handle the older male customers with wandering hands.

Julia was fierce enough to be the head waitress at the back of the café by the stage. She was tall and dark and beautiful and had once placed on the All-Soviet women's high jump team, so she had the legs required to work the stairs all day. She could smile readily enough if necessary, but she had a look that could sober even the drunkest of men.

Julia had left a bully of a husband and sometimes needed to bring in her little daughter, Ona, to draw pictures at the butcher block when it wasn't being used, or occasionally in my office. I didn't mind. It was nice to have a kid in the place to moderate our devotion to our craft.

Angela was the head waitress at the front, another type of creature altogether, softer, fairer, more inclined to joke with the younger people who would sit at the street side of the café.

The Seaside Café Metropolis

The basement was a peculiar place because it contained, in addition to a rather fine kitchen, storage area, and cold room, an unusually long and broad corridor with a locked door and beyond it a staircase. Sometimes we put a child's chair under the staircase there for Ona, with a second one she used as a desk to draw upon.

Useful though the space was for the child, I couldn't divine the purpose of the mysterious door. We had a separate one for deliveries at the dock upstairs and yet another that led up to the restaurant proper, so this corridor and its strange door seemed superfluous.

I had queried my boss, Dominic the architect, about this locked door, but he said it had to do with operations of the building and I didn't need to concern myself with it.

I was down in the cellar, chatting with my head chef, Niko, an ebullient, elfin Georgian with curly hair and a keen sense of culinary history. Unlike some chefs I had met in the past, he retained a lively interest in developing new dishes.

Niko's backstory was grotesque in the manner so common in that part of the world. After training in the finest restaurants in Georgia's seaside city of Batumi, he made his way west during the war through battlefields, past vindictive commissars of one kind or another, all the way to Byelorussia, where he lived for a time. He sharpened his skills while cooking for the German high command in occupied Minsk. As Jews were slaughtered outside his kitchen, soldiers fell by the thousands and civilians died of hunger, Niko survived because a certain German officer appreciated good food, especially if it was delivered under difficult circumstances.

By virtue of his serving the Germans instead of dying of starvation like a real patriot, Niko was declared a Nazi collaborator when the Red Army surged back. He fled Byelorussia as the fortunes of war changed in the east, aiming for the Savoy Hotel in London. But he moved too slowly and only got as far as Lithuania before the borders closed.

Dealt an unlucky hand by fate, he made the best of it, having seen so many others whose fates were even worse.

I trusted Niko. His history was far more dramatic and fraught than mine, but we were both outsiders in Vilnius, and we both loved food as our shared emotional homeland. Niko loved the kitchen, and he was loyal to his personnel once we had hired them. I asked him how the kitchen staffing was going because I'd given him wide reign to employ staff we could rely on.

"We have a dedicated crew, but a few of them are new to kitchens."

"Isn't it a little risky to hire amateurs at this point? We need to start off with high standards, and we don't get a second chance to make a first impression."

"Experience and training are part of the equation, but motivation shouldn't be underestimated. I have an electrical engineer who has a small child at home and an ailing wife. If he knows how to electrify a town, I am sure he can learn how to peel vegetables. He is an intelligent man who has been unemployed for three months."

"Why is that?"

Niko gave me one of those looks so common in the Soviet Union. It meant I should have known better than to ask. The man was unemployable. Either he had escaped illegally from the gulag or he had offended the regime in some fashion and was on the verge of being punished further now. There were different levels of punishment, not necessarily the gulag. You could become unemployed, and it was illegal to stay that way. If no one would hire you, you were classified as a vagrant and could be arrested.

"What's his name?"

The Seaside Café Metropolis

"Genius Nagle."

"That sounds funny if I spell it out in English. He calls himself a genius? Or did his mother do that to him?"

"Short for Eugenius."

"Ah. Anyone else I should be aware of?"

"A sharp youngish graduate from a technical school. Her name is Lucy — a little older than most graduates, who are usually just out of their teens. Also two more single mothers who will need to let their children in here sometimes when school is out."

"Young apprentices!" I could replicate my childhood experience by having some of the kids learn restaurant skills the way I had, right on the kitchen floor. I would just need to think of something if there ever became too many of them.

I started discussing chicken Kiev because we had served it as a so-called Russian specialty back at the Royal York Hotel, but Niko, for all his culinary knowledge, had never heard of the dish.

"How can it even be called a Russian dish when Kiev isn't in Russia?" asked Niko.

"Most westerners have only the foggiest notion of European geography east of Germany."

"So Ukraine is terra incognita to them?"

"Oh, yes."

"So, they know nothing of Georgia and its national dish, khachapuri?"

"That's right."

"What about something closer to the middle of Europe? Say a Czech drink, a Pilsner?"

"A prime minister once said that Czechoslovakia was a far-away country about which the British people knew nothing. As far as North America is concerned, we're all Russians."

"And to think we all idolize the West. We are like foolish lovers whose feelings are not returned."

Niko was a slight man, both short and slim, which had helped him hide away to escape his postwar fate. His escape also explained his sympathy for people with complicated backgrounds. I did not mention to him that we in the West did not believe in complicated backgrounds. We believed only in heroes and villains. My mother considered Joseph Stalin one of the greatest heroes of all.

Niko was now curled over a pad of cheap Soviet paper, the kind that tore if your pencil was too sharp. I was sketching out the construction of chicken Kiev.

He shook his head. "There is no such dish from Kiev. You must be mistaken. You are thinking of the Pozharsky cutlet."

"How is that made?"

"Minced chicken is mixed with butter and cream before being shaped, breaded, and fried. The additions make the cutlet very tender."

"No, no. In chicken Kiev, the chicken is a filet that is beaten until thin and then wrapped around a knob of very cold butter. The final shape resembles a small blimp."

"The shape you describe is a Zeppelin."

He was referring to a traditional Lithuanian food. "No, no. That's a potato dumpling filled with ground meat. I am talking about a chicken cutlet around a knob of butter."

"But the butter will melt when the chicken is cooked."

"Exactly."

"And what will keep the butter from running out during the cooking process?"

"You use cold butter, almost frozen, and the chicken is chilled too and wrapped tightly around the butter. Then you coat it all with breadcrumbs and eggs to seal the butter inside as you fry the whole thing."

Chefs have a reputation for being temperamental, and rightly so because they work under pressure, but a real chef is interested in food, and great chefs have open minds. Niko was just such a great chef. He thought about what I had said. He was traditional but not hidebound.

"How did you come to have chicken Kiev in Canada?"

"Canada is a land of immigrants. The dish must have immigrated."

"But I grew up much closer to Kiev than anyone at this Royal York Hotel in Toronto that you speak of, yet I have never heard of chicken Kiev until now."

"Some things are a mystery."

"And now I have learned this from an Argentinian."

"I am Canadian."

"So you say. I understand. We all have our secrets. The knob of butter in the centre of the chicken is a kind of secret too."

"Yes. You can flavour it with garlic and parsley if you like."

"Still more surprises."

We agreed to develop the dish. I walked down the basement hallway away from the kitchen, and as I walked by the mysteriously locked door, on impulse I turned the handle and the door opened.

The room inside was surprisingly large — we could have had a private dining room with twenty people seated there — but it had many small workbenches and electrical apparatus including wires and vacuum tubes, various kinds of tools, speakers of all sizes, and other materials I didn't even know how to identify. Sitting at a desk with papers heaped upon it was a dry stick of a man with thick glasses, one who looked up at me as I stood there, amazed by the room and its contents. His collar was too big for his neck.

"Close the door behind you."

"What is this place?"

"I said close the door."

He had the air of someone whose orders were followed promptly. It was slightly childishly defiant of me, but I did not close the door all the way. The latch did not click. He noticed it. Good.

"We are logistical support. We'll take care of the electrical wiring and sound. Sit down. I've been expecting you."

"I don't know who you are."

"Piotr Zorin. Logistics Department of the Ministry of Communications. We'll be working together. There is an important matter I wanted to talk about with you."

I did as he asked and took the opportunity to mention some of my concerns. "I am particularly interested in the heating because it gets too hot in here sometimes, and if we have a full house and people are drinking, they'll begin to sweat. Not very attractive, especially on women."

"We don't do heat. That's another department."

"Ah, I see. Well then, I have been wondering about the lighting. There are not enough switches, so the place is too dark or too light, and I can't get just the right luminescence."

"*Luminescence?* What are you, a poet?"

"I'm just talking lighting."

"We don't do lighting."

"Well, what do you do then?"

"Sound."

"Excellent. The microphones and speakers onstage need to be finely calibrated."

"Are you an idiot, my Argentinian comrade?"

"What?"

"Are you not aware that the bourgeois countries would like nothing better than to destroy our nation? That we are involved in perpetual struggle?"

"I've heard it said. What does that have to do with me?"

"Don't play the fool. For all I know, you are a foreign agent who is planning sedition. But one thing is sure, some of the people who gather here will be planning it. Places like this ape the luxuries of the West and attract just the sorts of people who would like to replicate the decadent Western models."

"I think you'd get along well with my mother."

"What are you talking about?"

"Do you mean counter-revolutionaries might come here?"

"Exactly."

"Wouldn't they be more likely to make their plans in private places? Out in the countryside somewhere? In ruined basements where they store the cloaks and daggers?"

"Practically insolent! Are you trying to teach me my job?"

"No. I'm sorry. I just don't know how I can be helpful to you."

"That's more like it. I want to discuss your opening day."

"November 7, on the anniversary of the October Revolution. Funny, eh?"

"What is funny? Nothing about the revolution is funny."

"I mean the dates. Don't you find it odd that the October Revolution is celebrated in November?"

"I'm sure there is a good reason. In any case, that opening day is not possible. Not all of my supplies will have arrived by then."

"What supplies are those?"

"None of your business. But since you ask, copper wire and microphones."

He looked at me steadily. I had to admit that all the subtleties of living in this culture sometimes escaped me. So much was unsaid, and one was supposed to catch the drift of things by intuition. Whole herds of elephants remained unmentioned in the rooms around here. But his message was so clear, even an amateur like me could get it. He needed to plant listening devices in my café.

This was an affront to my sensibilities. Of course I knew most phones were bugged. Of course I knew many hotel rooms and even private apartments were bugged. But my café, my precious Seaside Café Metropolis? I felt like I had gone all out to buy a fine dress for my daughter's first dance, only to find out her date was a pimp.

"Do you think that is necessary?" I asked.

His fist came down on the table. That was my answer.

I studied Comrade Zorin for a while. He wore an ordinary grey suit, and his shirt looked like he had borrowed it from his older, bigger brother. He was a little scrawny, this fellow. His hair was cut short, as if he were just entering the army, and his eyeglasses magnified his eyeballs somehow. The only human touch on the man was his tie, a rather elaborate paisley creation that looked as if it had come from another era, say the twenties. So our man, for all his Soviet bureaucratic swagger and sensibilities, was trying to have a little panache of his own.

"Will we be working together for long?" I asked. "Or will you just be installing the devices and moving on?"

"I or some of my team will always be with you, Argentine. I will be your guardian angel."

"Though I walk through the valley of death?"

"What?"

"What I mean to say is, thank you for that. Your words make me feel thoroughly protected. But if I may say so, perhaps I can be helpful to you. You seem a bit lean, too lean, really. Maybe you could try some of the dishes we're going to prepare here."

"Your observation feels a little insolent. Of course I expect to eat here and to take leftovers home to my family. But don't think I consider it any sort of favour."

"No, no. I just wanted to see what you thought of some of our new creations. So how long do you think you have to wait for your supplies?"

"I don't know. They will arrive when they arrive."

"Can you give me some idea?"

"No."

"If I open on Revolution Day, the streets will be full of people ambling along after the march. The opening here would be a kind of celebration of the revolution and an advertisement for the café."

"An advertisement? That sounds capitalist to me."

"Well, yes, it does a bit. Why don't you tell me what kind of wire and microphones you need? For that matter, maybe some small speakers as well. I have some very good friends in the Ministry of Agriculture who have some friends in the Ministry of Communications. Maybe we could speed things along."

He didn't like it, but he didn't dismiss the offer out of hand. I needed to rush him if I wanted to open on October Revolution Day, but I also wanted to make a few adjustments to his project.

YOU CAN CALL it synchronicity, you can call it serendipity, you can call it coincidence. Call it whatever you want. Sometimes the thing you need appears, and you recognize you need it without ever having gone out to look for it in the first place.

All the finer restaurants had music, but I had not given music a great deal of thought. I had imagined light classics from philharmonic musicians on their days off, or Russian pop, occasionally a little local Lithuanian folk music. I had been concentrating on food, layout, and servers for so long that I had let slip the thought of music until I was on my way to my mother's basement room and heard a tune come sliding suggestively out of another basement window not all that different from my mother's. The sound wrapped itself around me and pulled me in close as I walked.

"My Funny Valentine," an instrumental, was coming up onto the sidewalk. This in a country that had barely ever heard of Frank Sinatra, let alone Chet Baker. Even I had barely ever heard of Chet Baker, but if you heard him once, you remembered his sound. I could hardly believe my ears.

How was it possible that someone was playing that tune in a provincial capital of the Soviet Union? I found my way down some steps into that cellar and tried the door, but it was locked, so I knocked. The music stopped. I knocked again.

"Who is it?" someone asked from inside.

"An admirer."

"Go away."

I knocked again but received no answer, so I went back outside to where I had heard the sound in the first place and looked at the low window of the room. It was a very low window — I would have had to lie on the sidewalk to see inside, but luckily it was slightly ajar and I didn't need to do that. I crouched and brought my mouth close to the opening.

"Your looks are laughable, not photographable," I called/sang into the window, in English, of course. The shuffling that had been going on stopped. I heard nothing more.

I called/sang again, "Is your figure less than Greek, is your mouth a little weak."

"What do you want?"

"I want to know if you know Oscar Peterson."

"Never heard of him."

"Then your jazz knowledge is pitiful. Let me in, and I'll tell you something about him."

There were four kids down in that cellar, not much older

than twenty, if that, but they were students at the university and therefore forbidden to play this sort of counter-revolutionary music at school.

"Why so?"

Their leader was the bass player, an intense, diminutive man called Andrius who looked even shorter beside his double bass. The other three smoked and looked away from me. But Andrius had a commanding presence for all his lack of height. He said, "*Segodnia on igrajet dzaza, a zsvitra rodinu prodast.*"

It turned out it was a popular Russian saying: "Today he plays jazz, tomorrow he betrays the fatherland."

"Who told you that?" I asked.

"The university rector."

People were suspicious of one another in the Soviet Union. People were trained to believe anyone could be a spy, or worse, a turncoat lured away by the hollow glitter of the West. To show enthusiasm for a piece of foreign culture showed someone already starting to slide away. And if you were sliding away, you had to hide your slither.

They didn't trust me, a potential provocateur, so I needed to offer them something. A gentle approach did not always work in the Soviet Union.

"Why don't you know who Oscar Peterson is?" I asked.

They looked at one another.

"Why should we know of this man?" asked Andrius.

"Because you are playing jazz. You should know the great jazz musicians, and if you don't know him, your education is incomplete."

"So educate us."

It took a while for them to warm up. In the long run, they were hungry to know more, so they let me talk for a bit about the Black Canadian virtuoso jazz pianist. They didn't even know there were Blacks in Canada. I promised I would try to get them an album from somewhere.

"Where did you ever find out about jazz in the first place?" I asked.

"There is a Polish jazz magazine," said Andrius. "Nobody bothers to keep the Polish magazines out of the country because not that many people bother to read the language."

"But to read is one thing. You have to hear it to play it."

They hemmed and they hawed and they never answered the question, but further down the line I learned they had been listening to the *Voice of America Jazz Hour*.

So I made them an offer. They were skeptical, not really believing I was who I said I was and could actually offer them money to play in a public venue.

"All I hear in restaurants is schmaltz," said the accordion player, which was quite something to hear from an accordion player, who I had imagined played nothing but schmaltz by virtue of the instrument on his lap. But accordions were taken a lot more seriously in Eastern Europe, so I learned never to insult them. And anyway, who was I to insult someone who spent hours and hours on any instrument?

"There's classical music in some restaurants too," Andrius conceded.

"Light classics," spat the accordion player.

But nothing was as convincing as the offer of income to these young and hungry men, and they agreed to come around to check out my place. I booked them to open up for me on October Revolution Day, the day upon which Zorin had said we could not open. Now I needed to find a way to make it happen.

"HOW DID YOU get these?" asked Zorin. He was looking down at a dozen small microphones not much bigger than large coins, with a sister box of receivers, though not as many, and not nearly as small.

"Half a sheep and a case of sweet Caucasian wine that gives you a headache as soon as you pop the cork."

"And they work properly?"

"Of course they do. You can test them if you want. But look, I've made pencil marks on the sides of them. Some are better than others, so I have ranked them from one to twelve, from best to worst."

"I'm not a fool. We have experts. We can test them ourselves."

"I understand that. But I am cooperating with you, trying to help out. The number one is the best microphone, so you should install that in the most important spot, and the number twelve is the worst, so you should save it to use as a backup."

"You are irritating me."

"Surprising, given that I'm helping you."

"I wonder why you would bother."

"Because I want to open the café on November 7. You will also find I have a hundred metres of excellent copper wire coming in tomorrow. Happy, darling?"

He scowled at me, and I admired his paisley tie, the same tie he always wore. He seemed to treasure it.

OCTOBER REVOLUTION DAY was as big an event as Vilnius ever saw during the year. It was like the Santa Claus Parade in Toronto, but without the reindeer and the man in the red suit. But Santa Claus was for kids. October Revolution Day was for adults, and my mother adored it.

There was no question of opening the Seaside Café Metropolis during the day when the whole city closed down, but by special dispensation we were going to be allowed to open at six for dinner, three hours after the festivities ended. I should have been at the café from early morning, and I was, but my mother needed an escort for her favourite midday events and I needed to play the role of faithful son.

My mother wore a black beret and a red scarf that was a bit too long. She looked like an aging Young Pioneer, the Soviet equivalent of the Boy Scouts and Girl Guides. As if everything she needed to know she had learned as a communist child, and she was still obeying her troop leader long after he had died. Too bad she didn't have any cookies to sell.

It was drizzling, but that didn't seem to dampen her mood.

Red banners saying "Hail to Lenin" were strung up all around the cathedral square. There were massive panels up there with photos of the heroes of the revolution, and not just your famous Marx, Engels, and Lenin. Stalin, obviously, was not there, but Khrushchev was, along with some Lithuanian lesser lights on smaller panels set out on the square. It was like Hollywood, and only the top stars got top billing.

"Ah, the local heroes," my mother said. She was looking at a pair of panels of dead Lithuanian communist heroes. The first was Zigmas Angarietis, whom Stalin had shot during the purges, and the second was Vincas Mickevičius-Kapsukas, who was lucky enough to die of natural causes in 1935, although his wife lived long enough to be shot as a Trotskyist in the same Stalinist purge.

My mother, my mother. I could not reveal these historical truths to her. She would not have lost any of her admiration for the revolutionaries and would only have been disappointed in me for bringing up the dark sides of their stories. Each of us lived in our fantasies, I suppose. The facts would do nothing to change her fantasy, but I'd had the good fortune to find a way to inhabit mine. Neither of us could make the other see our point, so we expressed our love by saying nothing.

We stood on the damp sidewalk of Lenin Prospect to watch the parade that worked its way up to Lenin Square, where bouquets of flowers would be laid at the feet of the statue of this Bolshevik hero. Marching bands in uniform, folk dancers in soggy ethnic costumes, open cars of Communist Party functionaries — all these rolled up the street past my café. There was even a tableau of revolutionaries with drawn pistols on a flatbed hauled up the road by a tractor. You had to admire the actors, who held their threatening postures frozen like villains in a silent film while top-hatted bourgeoisie held their hands up in fear.

On our way up to Lenin Square, we had to walk by the front of the Seaside Café Metropolis, which had no sign announcing its imminent opening. None was necessary. Word was already out. There were some young people loitering on the sidewalk, clearly pretending to watch the parade but waiting for the doors to open in case they got a chance to slip in.

"Look, Mom," I said. "This is my new café."

"So it is," she said, after glancing at the place.

"Maybe you'll want to join me later for opening day in there."

"I'll be too tired by then. Besides, it's wet outside. I'll need to get home to get dry and warm."

And it did get more miserable as the day wore on, with a constant drizzle just one degree or so above turning into snow or ice. My mother was shuffling her wet feet as we stood in the audience toward the end of the wreath-laying ceremonies. I wasn't sure if she was cold or getting desperate for a cigarette. The people who crowded the square had been driven there by their workplaces. You'd think thousands of people packed together would have brought some body heat with them, but the damp came down from the sky above and up from the concrete below.

When the interminable speeches finally did terminate, I walked my mother over to a stop and waited with her until a bus arrived.

"Do you ever miss Toronto?" I asked her quietly. It didn't do to speak English too loudly because the language was rare in town and caught the suspicious attention of people nearby.

"All the time."

"What do you miss most?"

"The easiness of life. I mean, it was hard in its own way, making the rent and all that, but getting food and clothes wasn't hard at all if you had the money. Money was the hard part."

I was amazed that she said these things to me. She had never admitted as much in the past.

"And then there's the food," she said.

"You never cared much for food."

"No, but the Tel Aviv and Switzer's delis were nearby, and I developed a weakness for corned beef sandwiches on light rye. The pickles are good here, but there is nothing like the memory of Silverstein's rye or corned beef when you're living in a country that prefers pork."

"So you'd go back for a decent corned beef sandwich?"

She looked at me as if I had broken wind.

"Who said anything about going back? If I wanted comfort, I would have chosen another life altogether and another husband. I signed up for social justice, and discomfort is just part of the price I pay."

She didn't quite realize that by *I* she meant *you*. I was paying part of the price too, but I didn't mention that, and she wouldn't have thought of it.

"But you have to believe social justice is right around the

corner to make it worthwhile living with the shortcomings here, don't you?" I asked.

"The future is not that far off. Mr. Khrushchev says we will surpass the United States within a couple of decades. I hope I'm still alive to see that. You'll be here, and that's what makes me glad. Your role is to bear witness after I am gone. Remember that. It will be a vindication of your father's death."

There had been a moment of weakness in her while she was talking about food, a moment when I'd thought I might be able to press her, but we were at a bus stop, after all, and I had my café opening within a few hours.

When the bus arrived, it was full of exhausted men and women who had been forced to spend an afternoon in the rain or risk censure back at work. Women in head scarves, condensation on the interior windows, rainwater dripping down on the outside. My mother pressed in among the damp passengers without looking back.

As for me, I had to leave it at that and get to my baby.

I LOOKED AROUND the sidewalk out front, and although it was only four thirty, there were a couple dozen young people lingering nearby, mostly standing in doorways to keep dry. Among them were a few beautiful women and handsome men I would let in if the situation permitted it. Then I walked around to the back door and went into my office to change out of my wet clothes and into a decent suit.

Soviet suits were not usually cut well, but if you had a little knowledge and a little cash, you could find a pre-war tailor who'd sew a custom suit for you. Lithuania had been independent before the war, so there were still some talented specialists about, but you needed to search them out. A third of the pre-war tailors may have been Jews, slaughtered in the Holocaust. Many of the other tailors had fled the advance of the Red Army, and some ended up in the gulag, but a smattering of decent tailors could be found, so it was possible to get a good suit.

That is, if you could get decent fabric. And how did I manage that in the wasteland I inhabited? It was true I had not been in the Soviet Union very long, but even in the West, even in a grand place like the Royal York Hotel, so much depended on who you knew and what they could get their hands on. From a very young age, I'd practised sourcing rare goods with the help of foragers, some more disreputable than others. Both Żubrówka and absinthe were illegal in Canada, for example, but I had supplied us through a network of Polish émigrés.

I was therefore equipped in some ways for my life in Soviet Lithuania, where finding rare goods was not only desirable but essential because anything from butter to beef could disappear from the shelves without warning or arrive in amounts so vast you wouldn't be able to find a place to store them. Sourcing goods was a kind of game that I played for my amusement. And I was very good at it.

My office was big, with blond wood panelling and a heavy desk with a long boardroom table protruding from the far side so I could hold meetings while seated in an imposing position. I had bookshelves on the wall behind my desk with a couple of excellent titles I had found in an antiquarian bookshop, including my greatest prize of all, a copy of *Larousse Gastronomique*, the 1938 edition. I turned on my radio and went to my closet to get the suit, and while there I pushed aside the hangers and removed the wooden panel at the back to look at the switches numbered one through three.

My electrical engineer kitchen helper, Genius Nagle, was very skillful indeed. The hard part was finding time for him to do his work because Zorin and his crew were almost always in the café.

The Seaside Café Metropolis

The switches had small speakers beside them, giving me access to conversations at various strategic tables. I closed the panel.

The kitchen was buzzing with a disciplined and composed Niko standing on a low stool where everyone could see him. Neither of us could source a thermometer for the deep fryer, so he had one of the assistants keep dropping small pieces of potato in the oil to make sure it was sizzling properly, browning evenly but not too fast, then pulling out the potato so it wouldn't burn. Beside the deep fryer were a dozen chicken Kievs ready to go, with the rest of them stored in a very cold refrigerator so the knob of butter in the heart of the chicken would not lose its chill.

I walked down the basement hall and knocked on Zorin's door and then stepped in without waiting for a response. He scowled at me from his desk. There were six men seated at various stations, headsets nearby, but they were not doing anything. Just troops getting ready for battle, I figured.

"What are you doing here?" he asked sourly. "I didn't invite you."

"No, but I am inviting you. I appreciate your letting us open on Revolution Day, so I'd like to offer you dinner over in booth number one after the place closes."

"Isn't that the spot beside the band?"

"Yes."

"I can't stand the sound of their screeching American music."

"The band will not screech, I promise you, and anyway, American music, as you call it, or more properly jazz, has a whole range of moods."

He looked down at some sort of document on his desk, but he didn't say no, which was as good as saying yes as far as I was concerned.

Thuggish John and Joe were both on the front door because it was opening night and I needed full staffing. Having been well trained by the KGB, they were suitably intimidating to most people but toadying to anyone who looked like a superior. Some of the more artistic Communist Party members had been invited and said they would come, but none from the upper reaches of the politburo because they were a serious and puritanical lot, just my mother's kind of people. There was one exception, a certain minister who loved food, but I wasn't sure he would show. Two opera singers and a theatre director, one poet and two composers were coming, so we'd have an artistic contingent. I had a few spare places but told John and Joe to let in no uninvited guests without my permission.

I was the director, but Bob was to manage the house most of the time. He was a tall, dark Finn of Polish origin whose real name was Boguslaw, but I insisted on his using "Bob" just to add a little British zing. If I was the Argentinian, he would be my Englishman — restrained, almost silent, proper to the point of absurdity, giving the impression of being some sort of lord down on his luck but with a keen sense of gentlemanly propriety.

Together we checked the front of the café, the more relaxed part, which was neat and ready to go. The bartender was shaking a cocktail mixer in the middle room between the two parts of the café. The fountain there bubbled merrily into the small pool below. A cocktail mixer! No one in Lithuania drank cocktails, but they had seen cocktail mixers in movies. Perfect. If someone did ask for a cocktail, the bartender could always shake a lemon peel with vodka and ice and Georgian white fortified wine, and who would be able to tell if the martini was wet or dry? No one in this part of the world would have any idea about a Singapore sling, a Manhattan, or a G and T.

The boys in the band were noodling onstage at the back of the main dining room, and I went over to Andrius for a few last words.

"A lot of officials might be here tonight," I said, "so let's not scare them away at first. Don't play 'The A Train.' Just for tonight, go easy, say 'My Blue Heaven,' a slow 'Blue Moon,' maybe 'Pennies from Heaven.'"

He bristled.

"I know, I know. Jazz is freedom, and here I am putting restrictions on you already. But they are temporary. We're going to swing and jive eventually, but we need to start off easy so as not to frighten the censors."

"Is that a promise?" Andrius was ready to fight. I needed to both placate him and show him who was boss.

"You will get your freedom, but in the meantime, just be happy to get paid or you can kiss goodbye to a new drum kit for your impoverished percussionist."

Julia, my head waitress in the back, had her daughter, Ona, set up in my office, where the cute little girl was drawing pictures of father Lenin. Her grandparents were indisposed that day, and the kitchen was too busy that evening for her to play down there. Julia at the back, Angela at the front, and all the other wait staff wore white blouses buttoned to the neck and black skirts with pleats, suitably severe. The one dish that was sure to be a sensation was the chicken Kiev. But the patrons needed to have it explained to them that there was hot butter at the centre of the chicken, so they had to be careful not to get sprayed as sometimes happened when they cut into it. Julia and Angela knew exactly what to say and how to say it.

Luminaries did not like to wait, so I took Bob with me to the front door because he knew everyone who was anyone in this town, and we brought in our important people in stages. The minister of agriculture was my personal guest, and he appeared with seven of his closest friends, no wives, but luckily the booths were very large and could seat them all together. We had the head of the linguistics department from the University of Vilnius, the director of the National Theatre and the director of the opera, two pop singers, a television news reader who was well-known on the five hundred televisions in the country, and a couple of serious guests I did not recognize but Bob assured me were not to be turned away. KGB, I guessed, but if he knew who they were, how could they be secret agents? There was much I did not understand. We also had a movie star visiting from Moscow. Once the important guests were seated, part of the front of the café was still available, and I looked out upon the hopeful people on the sidewalk. One handsome couple, three young women, two fresh-faced young men, and so on until the place was full.

Certain places and times have an attractive vibe to them. The rooms must be full, more or less, and people outside on the sidewalk must want to get in. The place must be gay, say in the manner after two glasses of champagne, but not riotous, as after three martinis. Holding this line was difficult in Soviet Lithuania because it was a drinking culture, and it was not unheard of for a man to down six or seven shots of vodka over a meal. But Bob and I, the waitresses, and the band all exerted a kind of pressure of style. It would not do to be sullen in the Seaside Café Metropolis, and it would not do to sing off-key or shout, or to drink to the point where one's head rested on the table.

I needed to establish the tone of the place on that first night, and the machine was working very well indeed. But there were crises. There are always crises in a restaurant. We ran out of bread. Who could have imagined such a thing? We were short of glasses and therefore had to wash and dry very quickly as the second and third waves of guests came in. We needed to gently usher out people who wanted to stay too long. We needed to calm down the disappointed patrons who came in late for the third serving and whose dinner would be cut short at eleven. And we needed to hold firm on the closing time in order to demonstrate that we were the ones in command of this place, not some collective farm director who had rolled into town and wanted to show his superiority to his lackeys.

Dominic, the architect who had hired me, came in unexpectedly in the second wave. Luckily, Bob and I had held back a table and a booth, and Dominic was pleased to be offered the choice between the two. He came with his brother, a near twin, and he didn't say much. He opted for the table because it gave a better view of the interior, and he ordered beer while his brother ordered white wine. They tasted the chicken Kiev and caviar crepes, ordered coffee and cognac, and smoked one cigarette after dinner. On his way out, Dominic nodded at me, and that was the highlight of my evening.

Or almost the highlight. The best part came after all of the guests and most of the staff were gone. I had previously invited Piotr Zorin to join me in the booth closest to the stage in order to try out our new dish. I asked the pianist to stay behind and play "Moscow Nights" right next to the booth where Zorin would be seated. My KGB man was originally from Moscow, and I had sent down a few trays of vodka to his room, so I believed we might find a vein of sentimentality in him if he had any emotions at all.

"This is exactly the kind of pop shit we were told we'd never have to play," hissed the pianist.

"Just this once. And you are to begin as soon as I sit down with him. I need you to play it through at least three times on my signal."

Julia had made good money in tips, so she was not unhappy to stay behind and do me a favour. I told her to bring a bottle of champagne to the table and set it down very heavily at a precise moment.

I went down to get Zorin. Everyone else in the room was gone, and he made a great show of being busy when I arrived, but he grudgingly came along. No one had picked up the empties from

Zorin's room, and I saw two dozen shot glasses about. But Soviet men knew how to drink, and he did not act drunk.

We came up to the front booth beside the pianist, who was playing another pop tune by Edita Piekha, "Red Bus." It was a boppy knock-off tune of the worst kind, like something out of French music hall, with some casually anti-Semitic lyrics that nobody seemed to pay much attention to.

Sure enough, Zorin noticed the tune, and I heard him hum a little of it. I sat him facing the piano and called for shots of vodka for each of us followed by a bottle of champagne and the chicken Kiev.

"My Argentinian friend," he said, "you have managed to pull off a remarkable project here. I am impressed."

"Let's drink to this," I said when the vodka arrived. We threw back a shot each, and then I called for another.

"I am grateful to you," I said, "for letting us open on Revolution Day. It makes for an auspicious beginning, an inspiring debut."

"Building socialism is hard," said Zorin. "But when we cooperate, nothing is impossible."

"Now I want you to try our new dish, the chicken Kiev, and nothing goes with it like champagne."

Julia was awaiting my signal, and she went to the kitchen to bring the food and the bottle. I nodded to the pianist, who started "Moscow Nights," and right on cue, Bob appeared at our table.

"I'm sorry, Mr. Argentine, but there is an important phone call for you in your office."

"A phone call? It's late. Tell the caller I'll call him back. Can't you see I'm entertaining my friend?"

"It's a secretary from the politburo."

Zorin and I looked at one another. A shadow passed across his face because if I was going to be in trouble, he might catch some of it too.

"Please go ahead," he said.

I stood up and walked over to my office and shut the door behind me. Little Ona's pencil drawing of Lenin lay on my desk and another one was propped up against a book on my shelf. Ona was very talented. One day she might find work in agitprop.

I had no doubt there was a listening device in there somewhere, but I had not had a chance to search it out. I turned on the radio to a scratchy late station that played music out of Poland, opened my closet, stepped inside, and shut the door behind me. I turned on the light, which Genius had installed for me. It was unusual for closets to have lights in them, but odds were no one would notice.

Then I pushed the hangers aside, opened the secret panel, and flipped switch number one.

Sure enough, the sound of "Moscow Nights" playing on the piano came through clearly. I waited. Julia arrived with the champagne. I heard the cork pop, and then came the thump of the bottle on the table, followed by silence. Hmm, as we'd thought, the connection was imperfect. But if bumps caused the microphone to misfunction, that might still be all right. The KGB and I could both listen to the conversations at that table, but if ever I wanted to silence their reception, perhaps I had a method. I flipped the switch back, replaced the panel, and returned to the table where Zorin sat.

In civilized society, one does not eat until everyone is at the table and has been served, but Zorin did not come from civilized society. The food had already arrived, and he cut right into the chicken Kiev while I was still some distance from him. A tiny stream of melted butter, as if following instructions from me, shot out precisely at his paisley tie. The damage was all the more gratifying for the fact that Zorin, although he did not show it, was quite drunk and unaware of the stain.

"I adore this dish!" he said to me now in full good humour and with his mouth full. Some of his gold teeth twinkled in the light. "The melted butter on the plate is a nice touch. I can drag my mashed potatoes through it."

And so we sat there, drinking champagne and talking, he with the terrible stain on his tie, I vindicated and happy. After we finished the bottle, I was tempted to call for a second one, but enough was enough. As it was, I had to hold him up and lead him out to the street, where we had a taxi waiting, and he drove off into the darkness. In the morning, he might not even remember who to blame for the stain on his precious tie.

It was very late, but I asked my electrical engineer, Genius, to have a few words with me. He was a worried man, as well he should be, having spent years in the gulag, and he wore an anxious expression although he should have known he had nothing to fear from me. The opposite. I gave the pianist and Julia each a bottle of champagne and sent them home.

"Thank you very much for your help, Genius. Things worked precisely as you said they would. Can you explain the principle to me again?"

"It's not complicated," he said, standing there and twisting a cloth napkin in his hands as if he were being blamed for something.

"You can sit down."

"I would rather stand."

"Go on."

"A microphone is a simple device. It has an electromagnet inside and a coil. If the coil is loose, the sound will not function properly. It is like a solenoid switch that sticks."

"All beyond me, really. But when we banged the table, the sound indeed disappeared. Will that work every time?"

"Hard to say. It's unpredictable; you might need to bang the table a couple of times to get it to work again."

The Seaside Café Metropolis

"It's important to me to be able to reliably turn the microphone on and off. Banging the table might work and it might not?"

"Yes, that's right. But there's no way to turn it on and off systematically unless you install a switch somewhere along the line."

"Too obvious?" I asked.

He nodded.

I let him go home.

Sometimes things really do work out, I thought as I surveyed the room, all cleaned up and set up for the morning service.

Zorin had suspected me, as I'd known he would, and indeed he had installed what I had described as the worst microphone close to the band because he'd assumed I was a liar and it was the best microphone, and indeed, he was right in a way. With any luck, I'd be able to turn the sound on and off at that particular table.

A café is a kind of restaurant and a kind of theatre. We all play our roles, some more outlandish than others. This particular evening had been a comedy with a happy ending. If only I could manage the tragedy of the rest of my life with my mother in this country, I might end up with a happy ending as well.

I decided to walk home that night. The drizzle had let up, and the air was brisk with the promise of winter. It was all very fresh after the hustle and bustle of the Café Metropolis, the cigarette smoke and the music, the smell of food and the sound of conversation. I heard nothing but the click of my heels on the pavement beneath my feet, and I tipped my hat at the policeman (called the militia here) who watched me as I walked up Lenin Prospect. There were no police in Soviet Lithuania because a socialist society did not need police. However, there was a militia that took care of traffic, misdemeanours, and crimes. In other words, a rose by any other name.

Chicken Kiev

4 half chicken breasts
100 grams softened butter
2 minced cloves of garlic (optional)
2 teaspoons minced parsley (optional)
2 eggs, beaten with a little water
Flour
Breadcrumbs
Salt
Pepper
Oil for frying

Combine butter with minced garlic and parsley (if using) and roll into a log and refrigerate or freeze until firm. Then cut into four knobs. Beat each chicken breast until very thin, being careful not to tear the flesh. Apply salt and pepper to taste. Place a knob of very cold butter on each flattened breast and roll the breast tightly, folding over the edges as you go. Roll the chicken in flour, followed by beaten egg, followed by breadcrumbs. This process can be repeated to make a second, thick outer layer.

Chill chicken Kiev for a time. Fry in oil that is not too hot so the outside does not burn before the centre has had time to cook. Warn diners about the hot butter inside.

It should be obvious how many persons this recipe serves.

-3-

Mushroom Trumpets

"ABOVE ALL, YOU have to keep out the riff-raff," Anthony had said more than once when he was training me to work the Imperial Room at the Royal York Hotel.

By that point, I knew the operation of the kitchen very well, and I had moved on to other duties. I loved food, but I wanted to get out of the kitchen to where the guests were. I had covered the so-called Library Bar whenever the regular man was away, and I'd handled banquets and the lunchroom since I was a teenager. But the Imperial Room was something else, the apogee of sophisticated dining and dancing, and Anthony was its doyen.

I'd admired him without reservation when I was starting out and listened to his stories uncritically, but eventually one begins to see the shortcomings of one's heroes. That came much later.

He was so discreet, his shoes made no noise no matter what hard surface he was walking upon. Others walked, but he floated.

Anthony pronounced on worldly matters as if he were writing an advice column for *Vogue*. He believed that taste could be taught, and he wanted me to learn it.

"If the tone ever slips anywhere in this hotel, but in particular in the Imperial Room, watch out! The reputation of the Royal

York will fall faster than the market in October of 1929. And the next thing you know, the patrons of the Ford Hotel could be moving in here, and we'll be serving meat loaf, mashed potatoes, and rice pudding."

It was said of Anthony that he'd once refused entry to the room to Frank Sinatra because he wasn't wearing a tie, but then he'd pulled his own tie off his neck and handed it over. Sinatra was not known as a forgiving man, but Anthony had qualities of his own. Sinatra chose to be amused.

Anthony was of a certain age, and he carried himself with the dignity of someone from a higher station — as if he'd lost a fortune in that 1929 crash but managed to retain his breeding and poise in reduced circumstances. He was solicitous but in no way obsequious. Thin and dapper, he modelled himself on the Duke of Windsor by wearing a ready half smile, implying you and he had some secret joke in common.

I didn't believe any of it after I'd worked with him for a while, but I didn't blame him for putting on airs. The front of the house is where people create themselves. Back in the kitchen, there is only reality — you prove your competence among clouds of steam while being spattered by oil and working your hands raw until they build up calluses in the right places. You need creativity, of course. Put baldly, your food must not only look exquisite but also taste sublime.

At the front of the house, on the other hand, you must look a certain way, dress a certain way, and act a certain way. Your job is to create the ambience in which the taste of the food is exalted by its setting and atmosphere. Why does the wine you serve at home never taste as good as the wine served to you in the restaurant? Why does the beef stroganoff taste less special at your home's dining room table? Because in the finest of restaurants, a spell has been cast. You and your guests inhabit the illusion.

The Seaside Café Metropolis

What you really are outside that artifice is of no consequence until you step out the door.

The Imperial Room was a place of consequence all right. Moxie Whitney led the band in his signature bow tie and closed every night with "I'll See You in My Dreams." And now in Lithuania, my dreams were the only place I ever saw the Royal York Hotel.

I did occasionally have nightmares too. In them, the bland brick walls of the three-towered Ford Hotel featured as three faces of banality writ large. In that place, if you asked for a room with a view, you got to see the bus station on Bay Street. If the place ever had a motto, it would have been, "We're good enough for someone like you."

I forgave Anthony for his pretensions and lies, explicit or implied. He managed to create and maintain a certain tone, or at least the air of a certain tone. Of course we had celebrities who helped to keep the spell alive: Marlene Dietrich, Cary Grant, and even the queen when she was still only a princess — we were the *Royal* York, after all. Anthony was not the one who brought them in, but he knew how to serve them and how to help them cast their magic on the room. I'll admit he did a good job of discouraging fawning fans and loud-mouthed drunks, but he had a blind spot.

You could be as raw and crude as you wanted if you had the ability to keep your talk below a roar and you had enough money and were willing to spread it around. We had convention ballrooms gushing with Stetson-wearing Albertan accountants, the twitchy Telegraph Operators' Unionists, and even numbers of Odd Fellows, with and without their wives. Some of them would drift into the Imperial Room if there was any space for them. As long as they were not too loud and tipped Anthony well, in his eyes they did not seem to diminish the tone of the room at all.

The Royal York was never going to fall so far as to become the Ford Hotel. That mediocre brown brick hostel was the kind of place that you told your current wife was tolerable for a visit to Toronto. Better to save a few dollars and put the money toward a dinner at a steakhouse and ignore the frayed collars and shifty eyes down in the Ford Hotel lobby.

The Ford Hotel, across from the nameless bus terminal, served the Greyhound company — in other words, shifty canines trying to make an escape. On the other hand, we at the Royal York were across the street from the train station, and trains have first class whereas buses do not. Union Station was the place that brought together people from across Canada and the United States.

Anthony's principle about riff-raff was suitable for the Imperial Room, but it would have been completely wrong for our Seaside Café Metropolis. We *did* need riff-raff, but of a certain kind.

The deep end of the Metropolis, beyond the fountain and the stand-up bar — the more imposing part of the restaurant with its live music and massive booths — was for people of a certain social level (professors, directors, opera singers, generals, mid- to high-level party members) but not the very top rung — they almost never appeared in public, with the exception of the minister of agriculture and his deputy, both of whom loved food and sometimes came by. This restaurant portion was also frequented by artists with achievements of a Lithuanian- or even Soviet-wide reputation.

They were all very fine in that room, the top rung of a certain class, very gifted and even witty, but generally not very young. Some were accomplished indeed but just a bit too content, verging on smug. We needed to have a little fun, a little life, a little naive and youthful zest to act as both an audience for the lions in the back room and an antidote to them. I didn't exactly want the riff-raff for the front of my café. I wanted the riff-*raffish*.

The Seaside Café Metropolis

As the months rolled by, four irregular regulars installed themselves at the less expensive front of the café. These were young men who fit the bill for us, and for whom we tried to have a table if at all possible. There were various circles of aspiring young men and women of one kind or another, but the ones who brightened the place the most for a time were Rudy the writer, Kalistas the philosopher, and our two artists, Marcel and Sarunas. However, their initial impression had not been promising.

They had first come to my attention when they'd disappeared.

A pretentious aspiring Soviet realist writer had asked them to listen to his verses, and they brought this hack to my café. The man was a little too old to be hanging around with youths, but he had worn down the nerves of his own generation and was now trying to impress a younger crew. My four youths ordered veal cutlets and beer as well as cakes and coffee to feast upon as the neo-Stalinist poet read through a thick sheaf of his work.

This versifying went on for some time. My young men finished their cutlets, drank their beer, reduced their cake to crumbs, and saw the poet still had many pages to go.

"You look a little nervous," said Sarunas.

"Not at all," said the poet, glancing up from his pages.

"A bit pale, actually," said Marcel.

"You should go to the bathroom and splash cold water over your face," said Kalistas.

"I don't think I need to do that."

"You are flushed. Your blood pressure must be too high for a man of your age. We insist," said Rudy.

Our poet was a drudge, the sort of propagandist my mother might have liked, and as a result he almost never had an audience. He agreed to do what these talented young men wanted him to do, so he set down his sheaf of papers and went to the bathroom as instructed.

As soon as he was gone, the four young men left the restaurant, telling Angela that the poet would foot the bill. When he returned and Angela delivered the news, he didn't protest. On some level, he knew the game that had been played, and luckily enough, he had enough to cover the bill. He hung his head, gathered up his papers, and began to leave. He dropped a sheet, looked at it on the floor, shrugged, and did not bother to pick it up. Angela threw it in the trash.

These four young men were exactly the kind of scoundrels Anthony would have barred from the Royal York. But I had just a little of the scoundrel in me too, in order to offset my deference to my mother.

Angela was laughing as she told the story, and while I didn't want my café to be the scene of theft, I put the incident down to hijinks. Besides, they had scored some kind of revenge in the same way I had had my fun with Zorin. I imagined the four bohemians would never come back, but it turned out the poet was the one who kept away. The brazen foursome returned, and I let them do it.

Why? Because they had some charm, some humour, some liveliness. They were all *aspiring*, the kind of bohemians who kept waiting for Chance to knock on their doors to make them famous, but Chance didn't even know their address. What they lacked in success they made up for in high spirits and ardour. I got to know them better.

Rudy the writer always wore a leather bomber jacket, unusual enough at the time for suspicious police on the street to notice him as a potential troublemaker, and attractive enough to young women who liked a whiff of rebellion. He also carried a Zippo lighter, rare indeed, and the envy of his friends even if proper flints were almost impossible to find.

He looked like an American World War II pilot who had

wandered into the wrong movie. He actually did write a great deal. He kept notes and wasn't fussy about his pencils, often worn right down to stubs he held between his thumb and index finger. He would record phrases that leaped out of the mouths of witty drinkers and then bank them for a forthcoming masterpiece. He had a manuscript of some size somewhere, hidden away from the terrible Soviet censors, and it might have been a masterpiece or it might have been unreadable, but nobody knew because nobody had seen it.

Kalistas talked. I'm not sure he was a real philosopher as he claimed so much as he had wide-ranging interests and enthusiasms and access to books. He had read not only Hemingway, of whom the authorities approved, but also Orwell, of whom the authorities did not. He wore a long coat with many pockets, and his words were not so much conversation as a long stream of interconnected observations about the many books he had read. And as in a real stream, you never stepped into the same thoughts twice. His knowledge may not have been deep, but it was broad. And he had some kind of charisma that made him engaging — it's a short step from raconteur to blowhard, but it was a step he never took. If some young women liked to look at Rudy, others liked to listen to Kalistas. Some women fall in love through their eyes, and others fall in love through their ears.

The two artists, Marcel and Sarunas, had finished art school but had not been granted entry yet to the Soviet art system; they made occasional sales to individuals who wanted portraits or funeral monuments. Sarunas could never afford to buy bronze, let alone find someone to cast it for him. Therefore, though he sometimes carved stone, he usually worked in clay, and he was always a rather dusty fellow with dirty fingernails and smeared eyeglasses. He wanted to be Auguste Rodin, he wanted to be Mark Antokolsky, and he wanted to be greater than either of them because he had heard that there were nonfigurative sculptures but could find no images of them to emulate.

Marcel of the magnificently rich and flowing dark hair had been working on a painting called *The Parting of the Red Sea* for three years, but since the colour red was so close to the communists, how could he dare to do a biblical scene? Actually, no one knew what the scene was because no one had ever seen the painting. His work of art, like Rudy's novel, achieved mythical status by virtue of its invisibility.

These men had serious aspirations in their own way, but they were young, and they drank and laughed and talked and had the kind of charm that attracted other young people. But it was hard to break into their circle. Like the hack poet, if someone was flush and bought my four bohemians an evening of food and drink, they permitted him the honour of having his pockets emptied, but no more than once if the rich youth was a dullard. Maybe twice if the dupe still had enough money to spend. Although this sounds cruel, the abused youth who had treated them could imagine he was part of a select circle.

They were too poor to sit at the front of the café daily, and Angela and the other waitresses barely tolerated them because they usually ordered only coffee and then sat there too long and had no extra money with which to tip. They were young and good-looking in their own ways, so that helped the image of my café. But even I couldn't let freeloaders hang around all the time because I was expected to move around fifteen rubles a day from each table. Still, at certain times when the room was not full, late morning and midafternoon, they also served to fill my chairs.

These young men were not above making forays into the more imposing back restaurant, hoping to impress someone who might do them some good or to meet an associate of their parents or some distant relative they could borrow money from. They were always hungry, but they couldn't pay for anything much and couldn't bear to be away from the atmosphere of our café where they might meet someone important or make an impression.

If it came to a choice between being present at the Metropolis but able to afford nothing but coffee without any food at all or being away from it and seated at the kitchen table of a senescent spinster aunt out in the growing concrete block suburbs, it was better to be hungry.

These men were not that much younger than me, only about a decade, but they were on the other side of a divide in more ways than one. I had never been artistic, and my mother's asceticism had cured me of the romance of poverty. I wanted to live well, to lead a good life while not doing too much harm to anyone, without telling any more lies than usual, and perhaps even helping out others a little whenever I could. Still, I admired these bohemians, their need for expression, their artistic sensibilities, their lack of care for practicalities. I felt protective of them, so one day I went downstairs to discuss targeted menu development with Niko.

At the bottom of the steps, I looked down the corridor first and saw little Ona and another child sitting at a small table where they were drawing pictures. These were part of an evolving miniature classroom of future restaurateurs — kids with no other place to go. I was filled with wonder at the quiet absorption of children in this town. Unless they were the damaged offspring of alcoholics, unfortunates with no sense of self-control, the children here were like model miniature citizens, already subdued. I loved the ease of having kids like this around, but I worried sometimes that they could have used a bit more spark.

Niko was sitting on a stool curled over a small notepad, the very picture of concentration as a heavy metal pan clanged on the burner on one side of the kitchen and newly washed dishes clattered onto the dryer on the other side to await a wipe from a cloth. Fair-haired Lucy, the technical school graduate, was tapping along as she chopped carrots at speed, and pork cracklings popped in their oil as Genius kept the bits swirling to prevent scorching.

Niko looked up at me as if slowly awakening from a culinary dream and listened to my idea with increasing misgiving.

"You want something cheap on the menu?" he asked.

"Economical."

"I thought we were trying to establish certain standards here."

"We are."

"And then you come to me with this odd proposal."

"I'm trying to be kind."

"That's the wrong word. You're becoming sentimental. Those young men upstairs will take advantage of you."

"Sometimes you don't mind being taken advantage of. You act out of charity."

"You haven't suffered enough, my friend. If you had seen some of the things I saw during the war, you would be more concerned for your own survival."

"I haven't suffered enough? You know the story of my mother?"

"You told it to me yourself."

"If I were more concerned about my own survival, would I even be here in the first place? Do you know about the Royal York Hotel and its magnificent restaurant?"

"You've only told me this story ten or twelve times, enough to make me suspicious. And why do you always contrast your magnificent Royal York with the drab Ford Hotel? Never mind. All right. I get the picture. What did you have in mind to put on the menu?"

"Something a little cheap, but not common. Stylish, in its own way."

"You want a silk purse out of a sow's ear."

"Pork is too expensive. I was thinking of a potato dish."

"Gratin dauphinois in cute ramekins?"

"Too naked. The potatoes look too much like potatoes."

"Pommes boulangères?"

"Practically the same thing."

"Rösti?"

"It presents like a giant potato pancake. We want something that looks different."

"Looks different," he muttered bitterly.

"Could you do something with a croquette in mind?"

"A croquette? Do you know how hard it is to manipulate a croquette? It is a lowly food, a way of using up leftovers. It is not dignified to make something new out of a croquette."

He stood up and continued to mutter as he walked away, opening the door to the cold room and closing it behind him. I waited in case he was going to get something to show to me, but he did not come out after a couple of minutes, and I realized he had gone in there to cool down.

"He's a genius," said Lucy, all without ceasing to chop her carrots.

"What do you mean?"

She looked up for a moment while continuing to work.

"Stop!" I said. "You'll nick your fingers."

"I was taught to tuck my fingertips when I chop, and I've never had an accident yet."

She had startling green eyes that made me catch my breath. Lucy ignored the awkward moment and went on.

"You've planted a seed in him, and a difficult assignment brings out the best in a creative mind like his."

"I'm sure you're right," I said, and I walked out, not entirely sure what I planned to do next.

Lucy was right. Three days later, Niko called me back to the kitchen.

Half a dozen assistants were standing around in their aprons, not because he had commanded them but because they sensed something was up and they wanted to see what it was. Lucy even stood on a low stool to look over the shoulders of the people in front. She was sweet and earnest and serious, and just looking at her made me feel the Seaside Café Metropolis was succeeding in attracting the best and the brightest.

Niko sensed my distraction and cleared his throat.

"Behold," Niko said, and he set before me on the counter a plate with two golden trumpet-like croquettes. They were long and curved a little and opened up at the end to reveal mushrooms in the manner of food spilling out of a horn of plenty. He offered me a fork.

I cut from the broad end to include a bit of the mushroom sauce. The mashed potatoes had been seasoned and formed into shape and rolled in flour and then fried in oil, so the outside was crunchy but the mashed potato inside was soft. The filling added at the wide end of the trumpet was made of a blend of fresh and reconstituted dried mushrooms, which had a taste much stronger than fresh mushrooms alone and therefore flavoured the mild potatoes in an impressive way. The filling was the simplified Lithuanian version of what the French called duxelles, a component of beef Wellington, but there was to be no expensive beef in this dish.

One look at Niko and he understood my admiration.

"How did you brown the slight hollow of the trumpet?"

"Blowtorch."

"Unconventional."

"Not practical either, not really. I'd prefer to make cups rather than trumpets — much easier. I'll keep working on the problem.

The Seaside Café Metropolis

But new problems call for new solutions. This dish is cheap. Very cheap. And dried mushrooms and onions are available all year round, so we never have to worry about supply."

There were nods all around in the kitchen. These were my people. They understood what we had achieved. I even caught Lucy smiling at me. Niko had come upon an elegant solution, and there was enough glory in it for all of us.

THE SMALLEST OF actions can lead to a series of unexpected events in life, and so it was that Niko's mushroom trumpets led to one of the most romantic yet tragic stories I would witness at the Seaside Café Metropolis.

Thanks to the availability of a dish that cost not much more than two cups of coffee, my bohemians could afford to sit in comfort for longer periods of time, telling their jokes and exhaling the heady breath of young people on the hustle for their careers.

I had let them stay into the evening one day when Marcel saw the editor of the *Lithuanian Soviet Socialist Art Weekly Magazine* go into the back room with his latest mistress. Her name, I later learned, was Mona, a young woman who made an impression — even without a name — of the sort a man did not forget. She had a high forehead made all the taller by the sable turban she wore on arrival that night at the restaurant. She bore the kind of radiance on her face that I have seen very rarely. It was as if some kind of grace, more powerful than beauty alone, had alighted on a human being. I felt as if I were looking at a movie star, but Mona had never been in any movie I'd ever seen.

Beauty is a fickle creature, and natural poise can't be learned. The combination descends wherever it wants without caring at all for the class, education, or character of the person upon whom it lands. Mona looked like she had just come from a night out at the

Bolshoi Ballet, like she was a member of the high artistic class. She would not have been out of place in London or Paris.

What was her beauty made up of? It's so hard to talk about the word we use so freely. Regular features? Long, rich brown hair with natural highlights that tumbled down after she removed her sable turban? A radiant smile? Yes, all of those things as well as an elegant bearing that she must have been born with. One part of beauty is charisma, and she had that, but the rest is hard to pinpoint. It is like radiation. You only know it is there by the effect it has on those around it.

What made all these qualities more surprising was that Mona had once been a country girl from a provincial village so deep in the bogs that you needed a high wind to clear the mosquitoes before you could actually see across the muddy street.

At least, that was part of the story that I later learned. There were various passages in her life, both horrific and lucky, between that forgotten village and the night she walked into my Seaside Café Metropolis.

She had suffered in her life and needed to rise above her tragic background to prevail. She had made it to the Lithuanian capital somehow, the way aspiring people do, and now she was under the protection of a powerful man who might himself make minister of culture one day. She was said to sing, but no one knew exactly where. At the time, it seemed to me unlikely a woman of such beauty could have another gift as well.

The man she was with, the editor of the *Lithuanian Soviet Socialist Art Weekly Magazine*, was a Khrushchev-era man. A party member, yes, of course. But no longer just a political hack — in his late forties, perhaps separated from his wife and perhaps not, greying elegantly around the temples. He really was interested in art, had once been a graphic artist in his youth before choosing a more public career. He wanted to expand the realm of the politically permissible while not frightening the old guard of Stalinists who still held a lot of the local party posts in the cultural sector.

He had to maintain a tough political balancing act while trying to be a man of style, no easy task in a country that was supposed to be a working-class paradise. Lithuanian food was heavy and beer was popular and many men became chunky in their forties, but not him. It would not have been stylish. Men's hair tended to be short at the time, but his was slightly long, both to be different in style from the rest and to hide a line that was receding.

He liked to have a beautiful woman on his arm.

The pressures of being on art's cutting edge without alarming the authorities, of keeping one woman in public while another stewed in private, all made him irritable, but young people don't notice that sort of thing.

My ambitious bohemian artist, Marcel, he of the flowing mane of gorgeous hair, sensed an opportunity. In his threadbare grey suit and stained cuffs, he crossed from the front of the café, through the bar with its fountain in the middle, all the way to the back to the editor's table. An opportunity like this might not present itself again.

After a cursory self-introduction to the editor of the *Lithuanian Soviet Socialist Art Weekly Magazine*, Marcel proposed an article on the subject of the colour red in Soviet art and then went into some detail while standing at the edge of their table. The editor stared out across the restaurant as if searching for a ship on the horizon. He barely responded to Marcel's feverish and enthusiastic pitch for a chance to write for the most prestigious arts magazine in the country.

Poor Marcel, in his shiny suit and his father's tie, was beginning to garner the attention of the other diners for his zestful speech. The editor was about to dismiss him, but Marcel was young and fresh and lean, with thick, wavy hair that was all the more impressive for not receding. These attributes meant very little to the editor, but Mona liked well-shaped young men almost as much as she liked older, powerful ones. Marcel had his own sort of appeal, and she asked him to sit down.

The editor didn't frown, but he did look away, still searching for that distant ship.

All of the bohemians could talk, and Marcel was animated with nervous energy that only exaggerated his chattiness, so he talked about aesthetics for quite a while. The editor was not listening to him, but Mona was.

A prominent man who is unnoticed feels the sting. Mona was paying attention elsewhere, and Marcel was blinded by her. He finally needed to pause to catch his breath before resuming his thesis on aesthetics.

"And what do you think of my ideas about art?" Marcel asked Mona after unsuccessfully battering his conversational ram against the barrier of the editor.

"She doesn't think about art at all," snapped the editor.

A more clear-headed young careerist would have stopped talking to Mona directly and focused on the editor, but Marcel's young heart was already beating faster for his being looked at by Mona, and all his thoughts about his canvases evaporated. He was genuinely curious about her.

"What do you think about if you don't think about art?" asked Marcel.

"I usually don't think of things in particular because I love my life and I think about everyday impressions. The taste of an orange or the song of a skylark in spring," said Mona.

Marcel nodded and reflected on what she had said while the editor stewed.

"So if you are sensitive to sound, you must be musical," said Marcel.

"I do sing and I was trained for a while, it's true."

The editor brooded as he listened to the two of them talk about popular and classical music. Mona called for a glass of wine for Marcel, which was a bit unusual because ordering drinks was ordinarily the man's job, and here she was, so caught up with Marcel, she was acting as if the editor was not there at all. He could not put up with all this anymore.

"All this talk of music, music, music. What about art? Tell me, Mona, is it true as you said, that you don't care for art at all?"

Mona was deaf to the bristling words. She was barely aware she'd offended the editor. "I don't mind art."

"Then what is it you find appealing about me if it's not in what I do?"

"I find you interesting in yourself. I admire you for who you are and not for what you do."

A more mature man might have been gratified to hear this and let his mistress have her mild flirtation with a young man. But the editor had been drinking, so his judgment was not at its best. He had counted on Mona to soothe his irritable mood, but now that she kept talking to someone else, ignoring her date, he felt as if a bandage was slowly being torn off a particularly tender wound.

Looking deep into the eyes of Mona, Marcel had no idea he was in danger of inflicting great damage on his career, one that hadn't even taken off yet, but even if he had noticed it, he wouldn't have cared. He was hardly aware of anything else at all, and Mona, deep in her fascination with Marcel, couldn't imagine the impression she was making on the room. Anyone who cared to pay attention would have said that this was the behaviour of two young people in love, and the editor was beginning to graduate in his emotions from irritation to humiliation.

"Come on. We're going home."

Mona turned to him in surprise. "But I haven't even had dessert yet."

"Dessert is making you fat. You should thank me."

Of course there was not a bit of fat on Mona, and he said this only to wound her. If anything, she was more than a little wan and pale, but this look suited her, somehow. A lesser woman might have wept or shouted at him, but Mona had been through a great deal in her life, and the simmering rage of the editor didn't bother her at all. She turned to Marcel.

"I have to go. But we often have parties on Saturdays. I want you to come to one of them. Next time, I'll send you a note here, at the café."

Marcel, oblivious, stood up and reached out to shake hands with the editor but was surprised to find his outstretched hand ignored. He was so enamoured, though, that he barely thought anything of it, and when Mona stretched out her hand, he imagined himself in a movie and kissed the back of it before returning it to her.

YOU MIGHT WONDER how a man like me would know all these details of what went on. Well, the café was a complete world, and everything that happened in it, everything that was said, all came back to me, more successfully than to the KGB men down in the basement, listening through their headsets. They could not see the stunned, even funny look in Marcel's eyes. But I could. Anyway, whatever I did not hear from the principals of the story themselves I had reported to me by the employees, because we were like a small town that knew the business of every inhabitant. To a certain extent, Vilnius was like that too, a small city with a medieval heart where you always saw the world unfolding

The Seaside Café Metropolis

before you, but what you did not see yourself was reported on and discussed thoroughly at the Seaside Café Metropolis.

ON MY WAY home that night, I stopped by my mother's apartment. She was the most bohemian person of all, of course, because she kept no schedule, day or night. If I opened her door and found her asleep, she would get up to smoke and talk with me. I know it sounds curious for a full-grown man to go looking for his mother in the middle of the night, but there was something I wanted to find out. Mothers know us better than we know ourselves, but they also have secrets of their own. Well, not exactly secrets, but things they never bothered to tell us, or answers to questions we never bothered to ask. And we need to know the answers at unexpected times.

"Do you want some coffee?" The smoke, the ashtray, the unmade bed were all the same, but I appreciated the slightly unusual hospitable act. Maybe she sensed something.

"What was it like when you met Dad?" I asked as I sat on her bed and she began to fill a small pot with water.

Her hackles went up immediately. Why did she save her warmth and passion for her politics and act so aggressive when asked to speak of her feelings? She went on reluctantly.

"It was normal. We fell in love. We got married, and then you came along. What more is there to say?"

"Come on."

"What?"

"You don't need to be tough all the time. There must have been tender moments."

She turned on me in the most unexpected way. "And what good are those tender moments in the long run, eh? If you want to be soft and tender, someone is going to hurt you."

"Did Dad hurt you?"

"Of course he did. He went off and died. How much more painful do you think it could possibly get?"

I held my silence for a while as she fussed around the pot and searched for matches to ignite the burner. She finally calmed down, and I went over to sit across the table from her.

"But what was it like at the beginning?" I asked.

She had told me about his heroism in Spain so often I could hardly imagine any other side of him. He was more like Ivanhoe in my mind than an ordinary man. My mother was deeply political, so much so that she found personal details embarrassing, but she did have a heart there somewhere under that flinty exterior.

She'd cooled down a bit, enough to talk.

"I heard him before I saw him. I was eating a sandwich at the Bedford Park lunch bar with a girlfriend; the back room was just around the corner, and there was a meeting going on. This was years before the financial crash in '29, and there was a man there talking about how the rich were taking us all to hell. The exploitation that was going on couldn't last, and it was time to change things before the working man suffered in an economic disaster."

"So he was a prophet, eh?"

"Yes, he was. He saw the Depression coming before the smarty economists did. But that's not what I'm getting at. I heard his voice from around the corner of a room, and after a while I wasn't following what my girlfriend was saying to me anymore. I could only hear two out of every three words your dad spoke, but I knew I had to meet the man who could talk like that. So I waited until the meeting was over and went in to see him."

"Just like that?"

"Just like that."

"What about the girlfriend you were with?"

My mother looked at me dully for a moment and then broke into laughter. "I don't know. I think I just stood up and walked away. I know I didn't go back to see her."

"You mean you ditched your friend because of love at first sight?"

"Not even first sight! Remember, I heard him before I saw him. The sound of him was enough at first. And then I saw him on a low stage with a worn suit and eyeglasses and a cowlick on the crown of his head that made him look younger than he was. No microphone, but a strong and steady voice filled with passionate intensity. I stood with him as the room started to clear, and there were others who wanted to talk to him, but he spoke only to me. And then finally there were just the two of us, and we went back to the lunch counter, and we sat and talked there until the place closed, and then we talked some more on the street as he walked me home."

"What did you talk about?"

"Everything. It was like we were discovering the world together. I told him about the farm near Whitby where I grew up, and he talked about his Scottish grandparents."

"His what?"

"This is news to you? I must have mentioned it at some point."

"There are plenty of things you've never mentioned. I didn't know about Scottish grandparents. So where did the name *Argentine* come from?"

"Oh, his grandparents had lived there for a while all right, but the name was just an alias, and we hung on to it."

"Why an alias?"

"Your father was an activist. Everybody makes up stories about themselves, even people with no reason for it. He was covering his tracks."

"So what was the name before that?"

"I'm not sure. Something Scottish. One of the many Mac-Somethings."

So nothing was as it seemed. I was startled because I'd built up various Argentinian fantasies in my mind when I was a boy. Why had my mother never alerted me before? Had she never paid attention to me even when I was a kid? I had planned to learn Spanish. I even thought we might have family there. I wasn't all that interested in my father's politics, though. I had heard too much about politics in my life.

"I was drunk on his words," she said. "And I wanted to keep on drinking them in until the end of time."

I was a little tired. Maybe that's what made me say it. "And look where it got you."

"It's not about the destination, Emmet, it's about the ride. And I had the most wonderful ride with him. I wish it could have gone on, but even though it didn't, every moment was worth it."

I wished I could say I had found the ride with him worth it. I remembered him as kind enough but always busy. And slightly incompetent in everyday matters. He once tried to take me fishing but could barely bait a hook and ended up slipping and falling into shallow water. Not only did he not play sports, he didn't understand what they were for. He didn't drive, and he couldn't follow a map if his life depended on it. What business did a man like that have volunteering to go to war?

It was hard to square up what I knew of him with his reputation as a brilliant orator, an excellent organizer. A brave man who sacrificed himself. If he was so forward-looking, why did he give me that speech as he was leaving, the one about being the man of the house? Why would someone tell a kid still in short pants that he was supposed to look after his mother? And why would the kid believe it and keep on believing it long after he should have known better?

The Seaside Café Metropolis

Mushroom Trumpets

For the croquettes:
1 kilogram potatoes, peeled, boiled, mashed, and refrigerated
Salt
1 or 2 eggs, you decide
Sufficient flour
Breadcrumbs
Oil for frying

For the filling:
1 glass dried wild mushrooms, soaked
Fresh mushrooms if any are available
1 onion the size of a fist, diced
Salt and pepper
Butter for frying
Sour cream

Mix beaten egg(s) with the cold mashed potatoes and add a quantity of flour so the croquettes hold their shape. Two eggs may make this impossible. Salt to taste. Form them into trumpets, and roll in breadcrumbs and then fry. It takes an experienced hand to keep the trumpet shape from falling apart. This may be beyond your capabilities. If so, you may make a simple short sausage-like croquette and indent one end with your finger.

Wash the dried mushrooms to remove as much sand as you can. They must be soaked for two hours or more (or overnight) in warm water and then rinsed again, but save the soaking water, making sure to discard any of the grit. Boil the mushrooms in their cleaned soaking water for half an hour until the liquid is mostly reduced. Fry the diced onion in butter. Add the cooked dried mushrooms and add any fresh ones you may have on hand.

Simmer, reducing any liquid until the mixture is almost dry. Salt and pepper to taste. Add sour cream and heat briefly.

Spoon the mushrooms and their sauce onto the horns of the potato trumpets, if you have actually managed to make them successfully. If not, use the traditional croquette. If you fail at even that, use the mushrooms as a topping for mashed potatoes.

–4–

Blancmange

FIRST WE WERE a fresh sensation, and then we became an institution. The Seaside Café Metropolis was *the* place to be seen, *the* place to secure a birthday party dinner (if you could get a reservation), and *the* place to meet not only interesting people but boring ones as well. However, the boring ones had to be beautiful or accomplished. We had mysterious guests too, and a few of them didn't hurt the mix, like a bit of garlic in a sauce.

We settled in, some for better and some for worse.

Piotr Zorin's necktie had long since disappeared after the adventure with the chicken Kiev, and he fell back on a rotation of three frayed ties in shades of patriotic red. He was usually in the basement office from which he directed the shadowy and irregular listeners who came and went. I was still Canadian enough to find it troubling to have an alternate police universe in the basement, a world within my world. Could I imagine red-jacketed Royal Canadian Mounted Police in an office by the kitchen in the Royal York Hotel? Of course I could, because the imagination knows no bounds, but the picture in my mind was ludicrous, not least because it led to images of those men in Mountie hats moving among waiters with tureens of soup.

Zorin concerned himself not only with the sound system of the café but also conveying instructions of various kinds to me from various ministries. It might be the ministry of communications, public safety, social welfare, education (under the category of apprentices), or some others I had never heard of, but they were all simply covers for the KGB. At his direction, I was forced to take on a too-eager and friendly apprentice, a fresh-faced country boy named Linas, broad of smile, bright of eyes, dull of intellect. He had a socialist realist shock of light brown hair that fell across his forehead. He kept chatting up the kitchen staff and making them nervous, in particular my former electrical engineer, Genius.

The kitchen noises with their banging of pots and clattering of dishes were too loud, we presumed, for a microphone, so Zorin had installed a human microphone there. Not only that, but a primitive form of quality control as well. Linas frequently took food to the listeners in the basement, so we could no longer give them inferior items. All we could serve them was food merely on the verge of spoiling. Linas spent long periods with the listeners. Everyone knew what he was.

I had placed a bas-relief plaque of Marx and Lenin on the wall behind my office desk above my chair, both to please my mother if she ever came in and to act as some sort of talisman or guardian angel in case anyone got the wrong idea about me. I was not political at all, of course, but you must not offend the reigning ideology, whatever it might be. And there always is one, wherever and whenever you may be, and it will always present itself as virtuous. It was a bit heavy-handed of me to have such a plaque at that moment in history, but probably the only one who thought it was ironic was me.

We like to think of ourselves as individuals, but most of us are just fish swimming in a current of dominant ideology. Heroes, contrarians, and cranks swim against the current, but I was none of those. When I was a child, I was told to recite the Lord's Prayer before class in school each day, and in the cinema we stood to sing "God Save the King" (later the Queen) before each show. Every era has its pieties, its desire to make the masses adhere to whatever current virtues it professes. I didn't mind. I played along, but I didn't take them seriously. I just tried to take care of myself and other decent people in ways that were within my means.

Zorin always chose to sit across my desk to my far right when he came to visit, and I became suspicious of this position. When alone, I searched very carefully with my fingertips until I found a minute hole by the front right corner of my desk. There was no need to look any further. I placed a paperweight near that corner to remind myself the microphone was there, and I kept a bit of window putty in my drawer in order to fill the hole temporarily whenever I found it convenient.

I was sitting at my desk one morning when my two doormen, the brothers John and Joe, came in together to speak to me. If they'd been in tights, they'd have looked like a pair of tag-team wrestlers with their stocky bodies and crewcut hair, but as it was, they wore the standard-issue shapeless Soviet grey suits.

"We're sorry to disturb you, Mr. Director ..."

"... but we've come on a sensitive matter."

"Just a minute. One of you speaks at a time. If you split up each sentence, it'll be as if I'm watching a Ping-Pong game."

"It's a little embarrassing," said Joe. I could distinguish him from his brother because he had a nick out of his right ear, a little scar from an old wound like something sported by an alley cat.

"There's nothing to be embarrassed about in our place. We are a family. Just a moment."

I reached into my drawer and took out my small piece of putty and then came around the desk and placed the putty over the microphone hole on my desk. Likely, no one was listening at that hour, but I felt protective of my doormen. Did my actions arouse their curiosity? Not at all. I was the director doing something, and what I was doing was none of their business. Besides, they had something they wanted to tell me.

"Very well," I said. "Go on."

"It has to do with the time when the war was ending."

Silence. For some reason, they needed to be prodded, so I said, "Yes?"

"In 1944, after the Soviets liberated us here, we were called upon to volunteer for the Red Army marching toward Berlin."

"Ah, yes," I said. "Very heroic."

"But we didn't go. We had a sick mother who could not be left alone."

That may have been true, but I happened to know that Lithuanian youths of the time, first occupied and then press-ganged into the war, were called the Barefoot Army for obvious reasons. Anyone who could avoid service in the Red Army did so because the Red Army had occupied Lithuania before and had been a harsh tool of the Soviet regime. As for the story of their mother, it seemed everyone knew about my own mother and took every opportunity to draw parallels.

"So what did you do?"

"There was an option to join the home guard instead, so that's what we did."

"Both of you?"

"Our mother was very unwell."

"What did the home guard do?"

"Just as the name says, we were supposed to deal with bandits and German commandos left behind the lines. There were not many Germans but quite a lot of men hiding illegally in the forests. They called us *stribai*, based on the Russian word for destroyers, *istrebitel*, but the name was a joke. We were in danger of

The Seaside Café Metropolis

being destroyed ourselves. We received no pay, hardly any weapons, and the nationalists hated us and always tried to kill us first before they turned their weapons on Russian soldiers."

"And were there a lot of nationalist resisters against Red liberation?"

"Thousands! Mostly local boys who didn't want to collaborate with the Soviets or walk to Berlin with hardly any weapons. But they were too foolish to take our alternative. My brother and I were fine with joining the home guard. Really, what other choice was there? The nationalists lived in some kind of dream of bourgeois democracy and independence. Fanatics, really. They fought us viciously. We managed to get most of them, but the operation to destroy them dragged on for years."

"The government started paying us eventually," said John.

"But not well," said Joe.

"So where are we going with all this?" I asked.

Joe leaned forward, rested his elbow on my desk, and then caught himself and jerked back from this potentially insolent gesture of familiarity. In this country, no one ever confused a superior with a friend.

"We served right up to 1952. But the important date is 1949. Some of the nationalists had managed to slip away to the West, but then they came back that year to go underground here."

"How is that possible?"

"The British brought them in close to the coast on fast boats, and then the nationalist bandits paddled in by rubber raft. My brother and I were on a team that hunted them down. There were a lot of us in that operation, but I have to admit the two of us played distinguished roles."

"What did you do?"

They looked at one another. They had probably been sworn to silence, but they were obedient types. They must have thought

I was an organ of the state as well, and it was their job to follow orders.

"We caught one just after he landed and then handed him off to the authorities, and we thought that was that."

"But it wasn't?"

"No. The man's name is Tomas Klimas, and he is both alive and free and comes here now."

"Into this café?"

"Once or twice might have been a coincidence," said John. "But *regularly* is a provocation. We arrested this man more than ten years ago, yet he comes here in a suit better than mine and sits in the corner drinking cognac and giving us insolent looks. I thought he should be in prison, or worse, yet he swans around here."

For some people, the past kept coming back up like acid reflux from their guts, and the burn it left in their throats lingered for some time.

"What would you like me to do?" I asked.

"Denounce him to the authorities. We have no connections. We've been out of the service for so long that nobody knows us anymore."

"I'm not sure what I can do about this," I said.

They nodded, resigned. So little could be done about anything in the Soviet Union. And then they offered me a pair of tickets to their retired National Guard male choir concert the following Saturday. They acted as if they were doing me a favour.

"Let me know the next time he comes in so I can look him over."

After they left, I removed the bit of putty from the hole in my desk and reflected that there had not been much in that conversation that needed to be hidden anyway. No former British spy could come around unless he was working with Zorin in some way. I had to admire the thoroughness of the KGB, though. A man in the kitchen, men in the basement, a man on the floor, and microphones throughout. We were being carpet-bombed with informers, which made it all the more challenging to keep up our style and maintain our relative freedom.

It didn't take long for Tomas Klimas to appear. He was a man in his fifties who carried himself with a slightly superior if wounded air, and his face had once been handsome but showed some hard living. James Bond fallen on difficult times, living on bread and potatoes and drinking too much liquor.

Klimas worked in a publishing house doing something or other in translation and was beginning to come in after work on some weekdays to sit at a corner table in the front part of the café (in other words, the lesser part) and drink two small carafes of cognac and sometimes more, depending on who he was treating. He never ate much. I call it cognac, but it was Armenian brandy, very good in its own right. We named it cognac because you can elevate the price if you elevate the name. And this was the interesting part. Publishers' proofreaders, and even editors, didn't make a lot of money. They were paid like teachers, yet from time to time this heavy-set man bought liquor for people he happened to fall into conversations with in the café.

Once, when Kalistas, the long-coated philosopher of my young bohemians, was in the Metropolis alone, I proposed to him that he make the acquaintance of Klimas, and Kalistas agreed because the man's propensity for buying drinks for strangers was beginning to become known.

That night, Klimas bought two extra carafes of cognac for his young interlocutor, and when I later asked my bohemian what they had talked about, Kalistas was enthusiastic. He sat across from me at my desk in the office and was filled with so much enthusiasm he shifted frequently in his chair and waved his arms twice to make his point. The cognac helped fire his high spirits.

"Klimas talked about Paris and Sweden. He knew about the existentialists! He's been in the cafés where Jean-Paul Sartre drank coffee. He's been around, this man. But he was interested in me too. He asked a lot of questions about me and my friends."

I wasn't sure at the time who Jean-Paul Sartre was, but I'd find out soon enough. I looked at Kalistas severely. The young man was a local. His father had once been the minister of education. Kalistas should have known better than to say too much to strangers, let alone in public.

My expression explained itself.

"He was just fishing for incriminating information," said Kalistas. "And let him fish in my ocean as much as he wants as long as he is paying for the cognac and I offer him no fish to catch."

Cocky young man. Paid informers, and Tomas Klimas had to be one of those, were not as stupid as all that. They were after tone as well as facts or signs of sedition. I thought it must be time to get involved. The next time Klimas came in, I, as director, introduced myself and sat down beside him without invitation. He did not protest, just rested his chin on the upturned palm of his hand, raised his brows a bit, and held the cigarette slightly away so the smoke did not go into his eyes.

"My Argentinian. I was wondering when you'd notice me."

"I'm a Canadian, and I'm not yours. And I'm here to say that you are making my doormen uneasy."

"Uneasy? I'm the one who should be uneasy. They are brutes. They are the ones who arrested me all those years ago. Did they tell you they beat me as well? I suppose not. A few of the blows came after they had me pinned down and I was no longer a threat. They did it for fun. Are you going to buy me a drink?"

"You seem to be the one who buys drinks for everyone else. Maybe you should buy me a drink."

And he did, although what I asked for was a cup of tea.

The Seaside Café Metropolis

"We are a very popular café, and we can afford to be selective," I said to him once the pot of tea was brought to me. I let the tea sit for a while to steep. Even the Metropolis could not always get good coffee, so I drank strong tea instead. Klimas seemed neither intimidated nor intimidating. He smiled faintly as though world-weary. "You make my doormen feel uneasy. I could fill your chair two or three times over, so let me know why I should permit you to keep coming here and buying my cognac," I said.

"This piss you call cognac may be the best in this town, but I've tasted the real thing. And you're being a little aggressive. Not democratic at all for a man originally from the West."

"I have an establishment to run. I serve the interests of my house."

"So do I, really."

"What house do you serve?"

"Why, yours."

"What do you mean?"

"I am an object lesson to your patrons, especially the younger ones, that group of quasi-bohemian youths. Really, what kind of bohemians are they? Their parents are all up high in the regime, so they can play at being artists and bad boys and not suffer the consequences. This is not even a real bohemian café. It is a fashionable café. If you want to see real bohemia, you should go to the part of town they call the Bermuda Triangle over on Gorky Street."

"The Bermuda Triangle?"

"People disappear there."

"Very interesting. And what is the lesson that you teach?"

"Not to dream too foolishly the way I did. Or they will end up like me."

"And I imagine you have some secret life that intrigues the young."

"There is no secret to my life. My confession was published all over the newspapers."

"I must have missed those issues."

"Do you want to hear it?"

"Do I have any choice?"

"And do you maybe want to go for a walk, in case anything I say upsets the authorities and gets you in trouble?"

"Mr. Klimas, as far as I'm concerned, you are the authorities."

I sat back and waited for him to begin. His autobiography was his repertoire, the stories he told in cafés and bars, and he wanted the Metropolis to be his latest stage. I was willing to audition him. A moody regular, a heavy drinker who brought down others, was the last thing I wanted in my place. Let those kinds of sad men find perches in a beer bar somewhere. But an amusing or shadowy regular was an asset, like having Mack the Knife as a habitual guest.

Klimas was unwilling to start without a little prodding, but I had all the time in the world, and I simply waited without speaking. I poured my tea and sweetened it, sipped a bit, and sat back. Eventually, he could not bear my silence and began to speak.

"First, I want you to know I worked against the Nazis when they were here," he finally began.

"I understand that everyone here resisted the Nazis in one way or another, and those few who didn't had ailing mothers to care for. Remarkable, really. Close to one hundred per cent resistance against the Nazis and no collaborators at all; at least, I've never heard anyone who didn't claim it to be true for them. Collaborators are always *other* people, aren't they?"

Everyone I'd ever met here had declared himself to be a hero of some kind during the Nazi occupation. In the future, if ever the Soviet Union fell, everyone would say how much they'd fought against the Soviet regime as well, or at least hated it, and those who collaborated only did so because it was better to save the nation from within the structures of the occupying power.

Klimas ignored me.

"I went into the underground the moment the Soviets came back in the summer of 1944. There were thousands of us hidden out in the forests. We were so dense on the ground, the mosquitoes had a bumper year feasting on us. We were young and foolish and didn't see that socialism was the future and the Soviet Union was the vehicle to deliver it. Never mind. There is no excuse, really. Like so many others, I was hypnotized by romantic nationalism."

The re-education people had done a good job with Klimas. He almost sounded sincere in his remorse.

"But I wasn't a fool, even within my erroneous system of belief. I knew that this little country wasn't going to get out of the Soviet Union on its own, so I decided to head west."

"When was this?"

"At the end of 1945. Berlin had fallen back in May, and the heat was rising here because the Soviets could now focus on us."

I sipped at my tea and considered if this could be true.

"You just walked out of the country?"

"In a way, yes. The borders weren't all that tightly controlled yet in those days, and my friends had relatives in Poland, and those relatives had friends that helped me get to Gdańsk."

"And you just walked out of Poland too?"

"Not exactly. I stowed away on a Swedish ship in the port, and then I asked for political asylum once I got there. The Swedes hated me! They were trying to play nice with the Russians and would have given me back, but an émigré organization sponsored my visa to Paris."

"Émigrés?"

"Tens of thousands of them. But they had no money, just high ideals, with which they infected me. The British were on the lookout for fools like me, and they sent me back here with a radio in 1949."

"And you chose to do this why?"

"I thought of myself as a hero. I could do anything. I was like your four young fellows who talk so well at the front of the café. But I think I was both braver and more stupid than they are. I can't imagine one of your philosophers or artists rowing a rubber raft onto the beach at night."

"Very impressive. How long did you last?"

"Barely two days! The beaches were being raked by night in those times, so my footprints across the lines, let alone the track left by the boat we dragged up, all gave us away."

"You weren't alone?"

"No. There were three of us. One was supposed to go up to Latvia, and two of us were supposed to stay in Lithuania, but my partner was a double agent. He would have got me even without all those footprints we left on the beach. One morning over breakfast I found my jacket suddenly pulled up over my head and my hands pinned. As I said, I was incapacitated, but they beat me anyway. And now you see me here."

The story seemed implausible, or rather his presence was. He should have been dead.

"Stalin was still alive in 1949," I said.

"Yes, but he died in 1953."

"So what happened during those first years of captivity?"

"I served the Soviet Union. The British had given me a radio, and I dutifully sent messages back to them. They started to doubt me after a few years, but luckily, by the time they ditched me, the authorities here were gentler and grateful for the services I'd rendered. Stalin was dead. They gave me a job and set me free."

I looked at him. We both understood that one was never free

of the authorities in the Soviet Union. We both knew he was lucky not to have been shot.

"I have no regrets but one," he added after a while.

This was turning out to be a conversation unlike any I had ever had in Soviet Socialist Lithuania. To describe one's regrets was possible, but only if one was terribly drunk and in some very safe place. To talk about regrets in the Metropolis was to shout them from the rooftops.

But I was not going to give him the pleasure of having me ask exactly what his sorrows consisted of. I waited, and as before, he eventually spoke.

"Part of my reason for coming to your café is that you have the most sophisticated menu in Vilnius, and I was hoping you might serve me one of the dishes I miss so much from Paris."

"So you do miss those carefree cafés of your past?"

"They were never carefree. I had no money. I didn't know how to make my life go forward. I was lost to everything but the moment, but there were two dishes that were cheap and that I adored and that I have not eaten since."

Talk of food always piqued my interest.

"What were they?"

"First was oeuf en gelée."

"I am unfamiliar with this dish. We did not serve it at the Royal York Hotel."

"It's a cold poached egg wrapped in ham and placed in a ramekin and then covered in aspic. When you cut into the unmoulded dish, served cold, the yolk runs out onto the plate and you dip your bread into it."

I thought about it for a moment. "We have many aspic dishes here, but a cold yolk is out of the question. Lithuanians abhor undercooked foods, and cold egg yolk sounds like a mistake. What is the other dish?"

"It's not really French, in spite of the name. The English serve it. It's called blancmange. Do you know it?"

"Remind me."

"It is milk flavoured with almonds and sugar and made into jelly. A sweet aspic in this case. It is served either alone or with a sauce of pureed fruit. You can melt raspberry jam, if you like, and it makes a pretty dish of red over white."

I looked at the mess of a man sitting across the table from me. Once a spy, once a hero of sorts, and now a tired old alcoholic. Could I believe his story? The tales people tell about themselves usually consist of a mixture of truth and lies. Very few people lie about everything, so there was likely some truth, anyway, to what he was saying.

And the truth lay, I believed, in the dishes he'd named. The first proved he had been to Paris because it was too unlikely to have been made up, and the same was true of the second, which meant he must have been to England for training. The oeuf en gelée was too exotic for me to attempt in the Metropolis, but the blancmange was simplicity itself, similar to Lithuanian and Russian dessert puddings but different enough to be novel. I could have the dish made, but I still had a problem.

"What about my doormen? They are part of my family, and you make them uneasy."

"Maybe they should apologize to me."

"That will never happen."

"No, I didn't think it would. You know the one with the nick in his ear? I caused that back in 1949. I used my teeth when I couldn't use my hands to fight back."

We were at an impasse. Should I let him stay or should I make him go?

"It occurs to me," I said, "that those who suffered in this country and those who caused their suffering are all living in the

The Seaside Café Metropolis

same place now. Except for the dead. The Jews here were mostly killed, so they don't need to reconcile themselves with anyone here. But maybe the rest of you do."

"Oh, I've been getting used to my lot for quite a number of years now."

"I can't give you the right to come to my café unless my doormen agree. I'll tell you what. Offer to buy them drinks. If they agree, and you can talk quietly here for a while without causing a scene, and if they permit it, I will let you be an occasional guest here. But if you continue to make them uncomfortable, you'll have to go."

With that, I went downstairs to talk about the blancmange with Niko.

"I've never made that before," he said. "And to tell you the truth, I've never even heard of it."

We looked it up in my *Larousse Gastronomique*. It turned out to be a very old dish, a medieval dish that had once contained shredded chicken. But we were not going to get carried away with replicating the distant past. Niko gave it a try and found the right sweetness and the right amount of almond flavouring to the mix so the piece looked like sculpted snow when it was turned out of a mould. It sliced cleanly and well, and as Klimas had said, a streak of bright red runny jam made it very attractive to look at.

We had a hit. Desserts before then had consisted of cakes and compotes, and this blancmange added a fresh, new texture. Aspics were already going out of fashion when I worked at the Royal York, at least those terrible Canadian versions made of jellied tomato soup with tiny marshmallows inside. But a true aspic, like one made from chicken boiled down to its essence, is a miracle of flavour and lightness. We had them on the savoury menu of the café, but blancmange was something new and delightful on the dessert side.

As for my doormen, I saw the pair of them come in on a night off and sit for a long time with Klimas. They stared at one another for a while, murmured reluctantly at first, and then finally talked seriously. After the second carafe of cognac, they spoke gaily, and when they finally got too loud, I made them break up the party and go home. They shook hands warmly and then staggered merrily on their way.

I wasn't sure if I was seeing the triumph of humanity over the tragedy of war or merely an allegiance of alcoholics who could bear anything as long as they had someone to drink with. Alcohol has much to answer for in society, but it does have its virtues.

Klimas was obviously yet another informer for the regime, trolling for dissidents in my café, and I suppose I should have despised him. Informers came in all stripes, though. He was on the same side as Zorin, but he wasn't the same as Zorin. I pitied Klimas, though I guess I shouldn't have because once you pity informers and collaborators, you become complicit. And yet how is it possible to think all your enemies are the same?

Once the doormen had permitted him entry, he became one of my guests and deserved a little hospitality of his own.

Blancmange

1/2 litre milk
20 bitter almonds (poisonous unless cooked — optional)
1/2 glass sweet almonds
2/3 glass sugar
2 grams gelatin

Soak the almonds in hot water for a few minutes in order to loosen the skins and then remove them by rubbing them with a cloth. Work the

The Seaside Café Metropolis

almonds (double the sweet ones if bitter ones are unavailable or if you are a coward) with a mortar and pestle, crushing them into a paste while adding a little water from time to time. Once this is done, bring the milk to a boil and add the almond mass along with the sugar and the gelatin, which has been melted in a little water. Heat for a few minutes while stirring constantly, and then pour into a mould and chill. To remove the blancmange from the mould, immerse it in hot water for a few moments and then turn it out. Forget to chill the blancmange long enough, and you will spoil the creation. If you haven't spoiled it, you can celebrate by decorating this white dessert by adding berries in season or melting jam and pouring it over in a pattern pleasing to the eye.

In French recipes, the ground almonds are removed from the flavoured liquid by pouring it through a cloth or fine sieve. This is wasteful. The French are a wasteful people.

-5-

Napoleon Cake and Champagne

IN SOME PEOPLE, love is incendiary — it flares out hot, burns up a victim or two, and then the heat goes off just as fast as it started. But Marcel's infatuation and then love for Mona smouldered for weeks and months before it gave him the courage to go to one of the soirées that she and her editor lover held in their charming apartment in the old part of the city. Did her editor friend have a name? Of course, but he played only a secondary role in Mona's story at first, so I'll leave him as "the editor" for now — and the fact of the matter is, that was how he mostly saw himself, not as a person but as a function of what he did. He will become a person later on.

I'll say this much for the man. He was far ahead of the curve in sensing what would be fashionable. In the 1960s, Khrushchev's initiatives started a building boom of concrete low-rises all over the outskirts of Soviet towns and cities, including Vilnius. Decades later, they would come to look dowdy, but back then, they seemed fresh, and everyone wanted one. For the regular folk, the waiting list was ten years and more, but people with connections could get one of these modern apartments faster.

The editor was different from the common throng. He had managed to get himself a very large space in the medieval heart of Vilnius on a top floor with windows overlooking a pleasant small courtyard below. If you looked up through those same windows, you saw the domes and steeples of the many baroque churches of Vilnius. You paid for the view with the effort of climbing the staircase, but it was worth it.

In good socialist egalitarian form, at that time you were not permitted too much room to live in. Each person was allowed only so many square metres of living space. The editor had laid claim to the magnificent apartment by including his wife, their two children, her parents, and his own mother and father in the calculation required by the state to apportion living quarters in those days. Then the editor moved them all out to country houses where he claimed the air was healthier. This left him with an apartment grand enough to hold what he liked to call "salons" for the artistic class, by which he meant the arts administration class.

"And how did it go?" I asked Marcel when he came to me to tell me the story of his visit to one of the parties thrown there. He seemed shaken, poor man, so I took him into my office, and his friend the sculptor, Sarunas, tagged along.

Everyone wore suits and ties in those days, even the artists, and careful ones took off their jackets or put smocks on top when they were working. But Marcel and Sarunas shared youthful indifference to caring for their clothes. Marcel had spatters of paint on his suit here and there, and Sarunas had small bits of clay on his sleeves.

Marcel was the more flamboyant of the two. The attention he refused to give to his suit he gave to his flowing dark hair, which dipped and curled up like a sea swell on a windy day. Sarunas, on the other hand, leaned toward a working-class coiffure, a kind of

The Seaside Café Metropolis

buzz cut that made him look as if he had recently left the army or joined the criminal class.

As Klimas had rightly pointed out, both young men had powerful parents, and their messy clothes and distinct hairstyles would have been affronts to those parents, a kind of youthful rebellion. I, on the other hand, had never really rebelled against my mother, but from her perspective, I'd still failed her because I hadn't properly joined the class struggle. I had sold out to the fashionable tribe, which was another word in my mother's vocabulary for the ruling class. The fact that I had followed her to Soviet Lithuania did not really register with her one way or another. It never occurred to her that I might be looking after her.

"Are you so upset that you need Sarunas's support?" I asked Marcel when the two of them had sat down.

"He was there with me that night too."

Ah, the frightened lover. Marcel had brought along a friend to give him courage.

"So what happened?"

"The food was very good," said Sarunas as Marcel paused to brood, hunched over and rubbing his hands together on his lap. Sarunas, by contrast, beamed at the memory of a good spread. "I managed to get a couple of sandwiches into my pockets, but most of the rest were open-faced, so I had to eat my fill without getting any more to take away. In retrospect, I could have put two open-faced sandwiches on top of one another, but it didn't occur to me at the time."

"I'm sure that made quite a bad impression in high society."

"Not really. Nobody was looking at me. They were all looking at him. You should have seen the editor. He was furious," said Sarunas.

Marcel snapped to life. "'Who invited you?' the editor asked me at the door," he said, "but Mona wasn't far behind him, and she came up and said she did."

"You should have seen the place," said Sarunas. "Maybe thirty or forty people and red and white wine set out along with spirits and brandy in these fancy bubble glasses I'd never seen before. One man had his nose stuck in the glass as if he were going to inhale the brandy instead of drinking it. And the women! I could have done a room of bronzes because their looks all deserved it. You know, in the style of Aristide Maillol, nude bronze women, but tall ones."

I didn't know who Sarunas was talking about. Marcel, my bold and cocky Marcel, was sitting in my office with a stunned look on his face. It might not have occurred to him at first that someone like the editor might not like him, and if it had occurred to him, he wouldn't usually have cared.

"And then the editor asked me what I'd brought, and of course I hadn't brought anything because I don't have anything. How was I supposed to know guests always come bearing gifts?"

"How long have you lived here, Marcel?" I asked.

"My whole life."

"Well, welcome to the adult world, my clueless young man. In this country, a guest never arrives empty-handed unless he is a child."

I'm not sure my observation even registered with him. He was at an age when his needs were at the forefront of his mind and his obligations didn't occur to him.

"It got worse. I was just talking to people, but the editor kept stomping around me and saying rude things."

"Marcel was not talking to *people*," said Sarunas. "He spent an hour sitting beside Mona, and the two of them were talking like there was no one else in the room. It was obvious! Even I noticed it from the other side of the buffet table. The editor finally exploded and said he had seen Marcel's art and it was useless and he should take up another trade, like sign painting."

The party, it seemed, had contained many smart people who immediately caught on that Mona liked Marcel very much, the two were flirting without even being aware of it, and the editor disliked Marcel intensely because of it. If the editor had had any friends there, they might have sympathized with him, but he didn't have any friends anywhere as far as I could tell. He was a careerist, and he just had colleagues. So the room was full of fashionable associates who were willing to be amused by his discomfort.

"Marcel," I said. "You have fallen in love with another man's wife. How did you expect the other man to act?"

"She's not married to him."

"They live together. It's practically the same thing."

"It was all so strange there. I'll admit I was out of my depth. I dropped a wine glass, and he called me a clumsy drunk and told me to go. I couldn't even comprehend what he was saying because I was so deep in conversation with Mona. The whole room was looking at us. He said to leave and never come back."

"And how did Mona react to this?"

"She was as shocked as I was at first, and then furious. She said I should come back the following week to the next party."

"So you've cast your sorry charm over her. I just hope you don't ruin her life as well as your own. Are you going to go to that party?"

"Yes. But this time I am bringing something."

"And you expect the editor will let you in?"

"I don't care about him. Mona asked me to come, so I will."

"And if he does go," Sarunas added, "and Mona lets him in, the editor said he was kicking Mona out of the house. He said she'd been a collaborator with the Nazis and she'd only get what she deserved."

"A collaborator?" I asked. "She couldn't have been more than a teenager then. And anyway, why are you telling me all this?"

"Because I *am* going to her party next week," said Marcel. "But I want to take along something special, and I'm hoping you can help me out."

"What do you want?"

"A napoleon cake and a bottle of champagne."

"I think you should worry about other things besides dessert."

"I'll worry about my problems in order, and I'll deal with the small ones first. Can you help me?"

"Why don't you just buy one?"

"Because I can never be sure there will be one in the bakery."

I knew what he meant. We lived in the land of deficits. Lemons, girls' shoes, napoleon cakes. Any one of them might disappear for weeks or months and then reappear in excess. Once there was even a shortage of flour, and people stood in line to buy bread. Thankfully, my contacts at the Ministry of Agriculture stood me in good stead, and the café rarely had to worry about shortages of basics. Mind you, the supply of meat and fish was unpredictable.

"And anyway, even if napoleon cakes appeared in the bakeries by some miracle, I wouldn't have the money to buy one."

"You want me to spend my resources to help you impress a married woman?"

"I'll pay you back when I have money."

I looked at him skeptically. I wasn't sure he ever had money. "You didn't answer my question. You want me to help you impress another man's woman?"

"The answer is yes."

I was exasperated, but in the manner of a parent who indulges

The Seaside Café Metropolis

his child even when he knows he shouldn't. After all, the deepest love, the most foolish love of all, is the love for our children. Just why I was acting *in loco parentis* was bewildering to me, but I was unable to restrain my need to help out. Marcel aroused not only my sympathy but my curiosity as well, so I agreed to provide the cake and champagne and said I would go along with him on the night of the party as far as the courtyard, just to get an idea of the lay of the place.

We had served napoleon cakes at the Royal York Hotel, simple pieces of puff pastry with pastry cream between the layers. But every rich dessert could be improved by Lithuanians, who modified it to make it richer. The Lithuanian version contained nine layers of modified pâte brisée, and the pastry cream had a generous amount of butter blended into it. One or two of the layers might have an apricot glaze to vary the flavour and give a bit of acidic contrast to the sweet cream, or a plum jam glaze might be used if apricots were not available. It was a special cake, a celebratory cake.

As for champagne, well, what was sold in the stores was really terrible sweet white wine fizzed up like soda water. Just as the Soviet Union pretended to be a socialist paradise, so the wine pretended to be champagne. But it served its purpose of getting one tipsy very quickly, and quite queasy after three or four glasses. Everyone had read in books about how champagne was very good and appropriate for celebrations, so they adhered to the *idea* of champagne when the real thing was not available.

Discussing the menu with Niko was unnecessary aside from putting in the order. He already knew all there was to know about napoleon pastry. The emperor after whom the cake had been named had slept in Vilnius not three days after Czar Alexander had been there during the War of 1812. Napoleon arrived in Vilnius at the head of a grand army and returned the leader of a defeated band of cold and starving men. How would Marcel fare while bearing the cake with Napoleon's name?

Vilnius was not well-lit by night, and it had many alleys and courtyards that were still a mystery to me after over half a dozen years in the city. You couldn't just get an address from someone and go to that place by following street signs and numbers. The streets had various offshoots, like the branches of a tree, and each of the branches might have the same name as the main street. You could follow numbers ten, twelve, and fourteen and suddenly find the next building was number twenty-two because there was another street that led through closed gates that you had to have the confidence to push open. Some of the courtyards still had sad Hebrew lettering above windows that had once contained Jewish shops before the genocidal slaughter of the war.

These urban curiosities and mysteries particular to Vilnius were not valued much at the time. Old Vilnius was still derelict after the war, with brutal concrete infill popping up here and there but not much restoration going on. The editor seemed eccentric to most people in those days in his choice of an old-town neighbourhood, some kind of romantic who was trying to live in an echo of *Belle Époque* Paris while keeping a mistress in the manner of that time. And to be a mistress seemed anachronistic as well. In short, he was playing a role, and I couldn't really blame him for that. Who wasn't?

Marcel led me onward, the bottle of champagne getting a thorough shaking as he kept it in his pocket, the heavy napoleon cake, a good sixteen inches wide and four inches high, held with both hands in a box in front of him.

We stumbled our way through passageways and over broken cobblestones until we came into a small, fresh new courtyard. Lit by the windows of the apartments on high and a single lamp burning above the entrance to the passageway through which we had come, the courtyard had no cars in it — rare at that time — but instead an odd assortment of furniture. There were three wooden chairs, a kitchen table, a couple of stools, and two trunks laid there on their sides.

On one of the chairs sat Mona, wearing a green party dress and smoking a cigarette. A few other people were there (no one I recognized), standing around in party clothes of their own. One of the men looked impatient, his partner embarrassed, and the others amused. It was all very strange, as if part of an elegant party had been lifted out of a room and laid gently upon the cobblestones outside.

"Oh, Marcel," said Mona, standing up and leaving the cigarette burning in an ashtray. "I'm glad you've come or all of this would have been for nothing."

Marcel went to her, awkwardly stood for a moment with the cake in his hands, and then set it down on the table and reached out to take Mona's hands.

"What's happened?" he asked.

It was a warm night, and many of the windows overlooking us were open. Soon another window swung creakily open from far above.

"I've thrown the whore out!" came the call from the editor four storeys above.

"I'm not a whore, and I left because you're a terrible man," she shouted in return.

"And you're going to do what? Live in the courtyard? I'll call the police."

"If I don't call them first."

He slammed the window shut.

"I told him he had to give me back everything I came with. I made him carry these things down here. I won't stay with him anymore."

"Does it have anything to do with me?" asked Marcel.

"Not you. Or anyway, not *just* you. He wanted to own me. Nobody owns me. Now listen. I hate that man. We are going to irritate him as much as possible. We are going to have a party down here. I see you have cake. Good. Everyone will eat cake."

I had never been in a situation like this one, and nobody else had either, but what were we to do? Marcel opened the box. He carried a folding pocket knife, and he cut pieces of cake for those of us in the courtyard, and we took our slices on bare hands. I introduced myself to a few of the people, a theatre director here and a television announcer there. Marcel opened the bottle of champagne, half of which he lost to foam, although the sound of the popping cork was festive. Someone found a glass that we all shared from which to take a sip each.

"It's not a party without music," said Mona. And she stood, composed herself, and then opened her mouth, and the rest of us listened as she sang a lively version of a song called "Kam gi liūdėti," which translates as "Why Be Sad?" It only took me a moment to understand it was the bouncy old classic "Cielito Lindo" with Lithuanian words, intended to mock the editor upstairs. And what a voice! Untrained, I thought at first, but clear and pure and moving, and very, very contemptuous. And if that was not enough, she followed with a rendition of "Quando me'n vo'," from *La Bohème*, and I realized this opera aria could only have come from someone who had indeed been trained and had the talent to make it worthwhile.

I did not know much opera at the time, but the Puccini classic struck me then and has continued to haunt me across the countries I have gone on to live in since that time. Mona must have had more than a little training because she hit the high notes and held them, and the entire courtyard was filled with the kind of magic that hardly ever descends on a place, and never twice. I use the hackneyed word *magic* because I can't think of a better one. There wasn't a heart in that courtyard that wasn't moved in some way by the song.

I looked up to the window the editor had slammed shut and saw he was watching through the glass. He put his hand to his eyes, although the purpose was unclear. Was he shielding his eyes or wiping away tears? I couldn't tell. I hoped it was the latter because it would have meant that he had more than a stone for his heart, and at the same time I hoped that heart of his was breaking.

After the moment passed, silence hung on the courtyard to punctuate the remarkable event. Then Mona sat down and lit a fresh cigarette.

"What happens now?" asked Marcel.

"I have no idea," she said. "Something will turn up. It always does."

"I'll take care of you!" said Marcel, overcome with youthful passion beyond his actual means. And I could see he meant it while at the same time knowing he had no idea what to do.

"Thank you."

He looked at me as if I were the concierge of his life. It seemed to be my lot that people threw their problems on my shoulders, and while I can't say I was eager for their burdens, some part of me could never shake them off.

"Can she stay with you?" I asked him.

"I have a small room, but I do live alone."

"Go find your friends and have them carry these things to the café. I'll find a way to store them. And hurry up. It's a warm night, but it might rain. I'll wait here."

As the show seemed to be over, some of the party people who had stood about now cleared away, and the two of us were left waiting for Marcel to return.

Mona and I knew one another slightly from the times she had come to the Metropolis in the past, but we had never really had a conversation before. Now there were just the two of us in an unlikely place in an unlikely situation.

"What a strange night," I said to her.

"I've been through worse. I'll get through this."

"You're not worried? Marcel seems struck by you, but he doesn't really have anything of his own beyond his room."

"That's all right. He's handsome and kind. I like him very much. Maybe more than that. It's too soon to tell. But he lit me up, and it made me realize what a dull man I was living with."

"A dull man with resources. He is powerful and knows people. He could do things for you."

"I'm still too young to worry about that."

"You have a lovely voice. Do you know a lot of songs?"

"Some. I've been singing since I was a little girl, and in the past certain men took an interest in me and my voice."

"Maybe you could sing at the Metropolis. I have musicians, but I don't have a vocalist."

"I could do that."

"They play jazz, not opera. It wouldn't be beneath you?"

She laughed. "I've seen more than a few things. Nothing is beneath me, and anyway, I believe all music is equal."

"You seem so unconcerned. And you have a bit of an accent. Where are you from?"

In those decades after the war, there were many sad stories. Most people did not want to tell them, and more people did not want to hear them. But I was curious about the lives of others, especially in this place, so vastly different from the Toronto where I had grown up. The life stories in Toronto were dull, not because the place was uninteresting but because there seemed to be some

The Seaside Café Metropolis

kind of dour cloud over it that forbade people from talking about the dramas in their lives.

She sighed. She had been through this before.

"I'll give you the short version. My father was Lithuanian, but I grew up in Poland. My father was called up for service at the start of the war in '39, and he left me with my stepmother. But she was a Jew, and they took her away. So I spent the war in Poland, here and there, and after it all ended, my father came looking for me and brought me to Vilnius."

"How old were you then?"

"Twelve."

"So how did you survive the war when you were still a child?"

"Neighbours helped out for a while. When I got a little older, I sang in the street for coins."

"Your stepmother never came back?"

"A Jew come back from a German camp? What do you think?"

"And your birth mother?"

"Died when I was little."

"What about your training?"

"Not very long. Men saw me in the street and came to me with offers, and one of them was from a man involved with the opera in Białystok."

"Yet here you are, on the street again."

"It's better than being owned, being treated as a piece of property or a trophy."

"But you have to live."

"I've found my way so far. I'll land on my feet this time."

I had never run across anyone so unconcerned about her day-to-day life, unless maybe my own mother. But my mother chose her life, whereas Mona had had hers thrust upon her. And she seemed so calm. The only thing that betrayed any nervousness was her habit of chain-smoking despite a nasty smoker's cough.

"That can't be good for your voice," I said as she lit yet another off the end of the one before.

"In the long run, maybe, but I'm not concerned about the long run. For now, it's a beautiful night, and my young lover will be coming for me soon."

Napoleon Cake

This is not French napoleon cake made with puff pastry and pastry cream. That is a diet dish. Lithuanian napoleon cake is a richer alternative that takes only two half days to produce if done at home. Professional chefs are faster.

For the layers:
4 glasses white flour
500 grams cold butter
2 glasses sour cream
1 beaten whole egg
Pinch of salt
1 glass of wine or a bottle of beer

For the pastry cream filling:
8 egg yolks
2 glasses milk
1 1/2 cups sugar
2 soup spoons white flour
1 vanilla bean
300 grams butter at room temperature
Apricot jam, or preserves, or dried apricots

The Seaside Café Metropolis

For the layers: Using two large knives, chop all the flour and cold butter on a board for a long period of time until the mass forms into grains about the size of a shelled hazelnut or a little smaller. (An alternative method is to grate the very cold butter into the flour and then add the sour cream and beaten egg and mix lightly without any chopping at all.) Add the other ingredients and mix well, working quickly to keep the dough cool.

Divide the mass into eight to ten mounds. Press the mounds lightly into disks and wrap in paper and then refrigerate at least four hours or overnight. If using white wine or beer, refrigerate it as well. Red wine need not be refrigerated.

Preheat the oven to baking temperature and roll out one ball at a time into a very thin sheet at least thirty centimetres across. Do not worry if the edges are ragged. Place the pastry on a baking pan and bake for around five minutes, more or less, until the pasty is crisp and lightly browned but not burned around the edges. Do not look away for a moment! You must keep careful watch to prevent the pastry from overcooking. The unbaked pastry is difficult to transfer cleanly onto a sheet while kept thin and unbroken. When baked five minutes later, it is fragile as well. Set the baked sheet aside and do the same with the remaining layers.

Once all the layers are done, sit down and drink the wine or the beer in order to give your heart a chance to calm down after the stress of baking. Generally, do not go directly to making the pastry cream next. Take a nap or wait until the next day to make the pastry cream (unless you did it ahead of time). Do not spread pastry cream on warm layers. Let them cool first.

For the pastry cream: Heat the split vanilla bean in the milk for a while. Beat the egg yolks with sugar until the mixture is smooth. Gradually add in the flour and continue mixing. Then remove the vanilla bean from the milk and slowly pour the hot milk into the egg, sugar, and flour mixture, stirring all the while. Heat this pastry cream carefully until it thickens (add more flour a little at a time if it does not thicken enough), and once that has happened, set it aside and let it cool. Once it has cooled, beat in the softened butter a little at a time (but be sure the pastry cream is cool or the butter will melt and lose its fresh flavour and the warmth of the pastry cream will soften the cake layer, which should remain crisp.)

Put a teaspoon of pastry cream on a plate and set the first baked layer upon it (in order to prevent the cake from sliding later on). Spread some pastry cream on top of this first layer, and then continue to build the cake. About halfway up, spread a layer of apricot jam instead of pastry cream. If you are a little short of pastry cream, you can spread two layers of apricot jam, or apricot preserves, or softened dried apricots. Spread pastry cream on the very top layer as well. Now take a knife and chop the ragged edges of the cake to make a symmetrical shape. Further chop the offcuts into crumbs and sprinkle them on the top to complete the cake.

This cake is best served cool. It is not recommended for picnics or hot summer days. Because it is crumbly, when serving, first cut a small circle in the centre so that the pieces cut from the outside have a blunt rather than pointed tip, which would fall apart too easily. Once the outer layer has been served, a small inner cake can be cut normally.

Champagne

There is no French champagne in the Soviet Union. Only sweet Sovetskoye Shampanskoye. It tastes fine by the end of the second glass and is memorable the morning after.

-6-

Riga Sprats

I WENT DOWN the stairs to the kitchen to speak to Niko and came upon the staff huddled together. When they heard my steps, they turned as one, and their faces showed expressions that ran the whole range from stoic impassiveness to concern and even fear. The men and women slowly parted to reveal Genius standing in the back, still dressed in his suit and with a little girl around four years old in his arms.

"I'm sorry, Mr. Director," he said haltingly, "but I had nowhere else I could take her."

Niko was generally the spokesman for kitchen staff downstairs, but he was out somewhere.

"What's this all about?" I asked. I didn't mean to sound officious, but I was in a bit of a hurry, and I didn't understand what was happening. Genius tried to respond, but he couldn't speak and began to weep, and the girl threw her arms around his neck and sobbed as well.

Julia of the powerful legs, chief of the restaurant waitresses, stepped forward and put her hands on her hips as if to defend him.

"His wife died suddenly yesterday, and he has nowhere to put the girl."

"What's wrong with nursery school?" asked Linas.

"Don't be a fool," Julia shot at him.

"Did I say something wrong?"

"Close your mouth," said Julia, and she turned back to me. "Nursery school is not an option. Almost none exist, and they are always full. She is a quiet girl. As you know, I have a daughter close to her age as well, and she usually stays with my parents while I'm working. I could bring her in here, and the two would amuse themselves with the other children who are around sometimes. The corridor is very broad down here. They can play in a corner."

"Mr. Zorin won't like that," said Linas.

"I thought I told you to keep your mouth shut."

"Mr. Director, do you see the way she's speaking to me?"

"Listen to her," I said, finally beginning to absorb what was going on.

I told Genius to stay home until the funeral the day after next, and I agreed with Julia's solution to his problem with where to put his daughter, but I had to wait until Niko came up to my office later on to get the backstory. He watched me as I first put the piece of putty over the microphone at the edge of my desk. He didn't seem surprised at all.

"Spare whoever you can to go to the funeral visitation," I said, "and let me know what all the panic was about down in the kitchen."

"Genius and his wife were former residents in the north, where their daughter was born. When the mother became ill, they returned here with their daughter in the hope she would get better. But as you have heard, she didn't."

"That's very sad."

"It gets worse. He doesn't have any relatives here, so he has nowhere to put the girl, and our mischievous Linas knows she can't go into a nursery school not only because there is no space but also because Genius doesn't have all the proper registration papers."

"So he fled the prison camp illegally?"

"Oh, yes."

"How is that even possible?"

"No prison is ever perfect. Sometimes people find methods to slip away."

"All that hope and it comes to this."

"It gets worse. If he is caught and shipped off again, you can be sure they won't send the girl with him. She'll end up in an orphanage."

"We have to protect them."

"That's what Julia was all about."

"Good woman."

"She has a few problems of her own. She has a daughter, as you know. Ona, who you've seen around here sometimes. There is no husband, and I believe her parents are drinkers."

"Oh, no. I was wondering why she didn't offer to take Genius's daughter there. Are the parents dangerous?"

"More incompetent than dangerous, the kind that might forget about a pot of boiling water on the stove. Julia takes all the shifts she can because she needs the money, but her daughter isn't in school yet and is growing up a bit too fast in the company of her useless grandparents."

"The world intrudes upon us, Niko. But at least we can do this. We can make a safe haven here, as much as we can. The corridor downstairs is ridiculously big anyway. It's amazing to me that in a country where half the people have no decent place to live, the corridors in these buildings are big enough to be apartments. We'll put a little play table down there outside your door."

"Zorin won't like it."

"Well, maybe a little further down, under the staircase. We'll put in a lamp. But Zorin, feh! He doesn't like anything. And what about that mischievous envoy of his, Linas? Are you sure there's no way of getting rid of him?"

"You know as well as I do that we must do as the ministry directs us. Within reason."

"All right then. We'll put up with Linas, within reason, until we find a pretext to get rid of him."

Niko stood up to go and then gestured without a word to the putty on my desk. It didn't do to be silent for too long because it raised the suspicions of the listeners. Once I removed the putty, we chatted a bit about the weather and the shortages of men's shoes. It didn't do to sound too sunny to the listeners. Better to sound mildly disgruntled but not mutinous. That tone would pass for normal.

EARLY ONE EVENING, I walked into the front of the café to find that my four bohemians — the artists Marcel and Sarunas, the writer Rudy, and the philosopher Kalistas — had a friend sitting with them. Rudy had brought in this literary lion, and, unusually, he'd kept his bomber jacket on. This was against the rules, as he should have left it in the cloakroom, and I was surprised Bob had permitted it. The jacket was part of the image Rudy was trying to affect, and to me it smelled like a whiff of insouciance. To exaggerate the effect, he was flicking his Zippo lighter open and shut, another way to make himself stand out.

Rudy had managed to snag a prize for their group. The man was a good two decades older than the young men, with wild, matted, long black hair and beard, his eyeglasses slightly askew, and a sheepskin coat such as I had never seen outside of Russian movies. Two men with coats in the café!

The Seaside Café Metropolis

"How did you let that man in?" I asked Bob. He was an excellent manager, so much so that I hardly ever needed to confer with him.

"He was with your young protegés," said Bob, "so I thought you would approve."

"And what about their coats? Rudy's bomber jacket is bad enough, but in a civilized café, no man sits among others while wearing a coat, let alone a sheepskin. Leave this to me."

I took myself to their table and found the four young men were ever so slightly less enthusiastic than usual in their greetings to me. Something had transformed them into teenagers and me into their rather dull father. Rudy introduced their friend, a poet of local renown who had just come back from a year of self-imposed exile in Moscow.

The table was not exactly covered in glasses because Angela was fast to clear them, but I could tell they had been drinking quite a bit. Their friend's eyes betrayed his drunkenness, but of a special kind, habitual. He was a lush surrounded by admirers. They told me his name was Paul Sakas, but I had never heard of him. I pulled up a chair.

"So you are the famous Argentine," he said. "I know some Spanish." He began to speak.

"He speaks ten languages," Rudy the writer enthused, "three of them dead languages."

I wondered how many people could confirm his knowledge of the dead languages. Now, while it is true I am a Canadian, my last name had motivated me from time to time in my youth to learn some Spanish, although I was never good at it. Even with my limited knowledge, I could tell he was not speaking Spanish, and I told him so.

Sakas looked at me as if I had insulted his manhood.

"I am speaking Latin, the precursor of Spanish."

I didn't like his tone.

"By that measure, you could claim to be speaking Italian and French too, both of which have Latin as a precursor. Maybe Romanian as well, eh? For all I care, you could be grunting Neanderthal, speaking the precursor of all languages. What I want to know is, why are you wearing that coat?"

He was a great man in a small city in a small country, and great men were not used to being challenged. He looked at me in surprise, struck silent for a moment.

"It's his signature," said Rudy; as the group's writer, he was the one who admired Sakas the most. "He and his famous white sheepskin appear in stories and poems by other Lithuanian writers. He even wrote a children's book about this coat."

The young men looked at me a bit self-righteously, as if the fame of their idol was his shield and theirs. This from the four youths I had cared for.

"People don't wear coats in this café. They leave them at the coat check."

Expressions of panic shot among my young men, but not the poet. Sakas looked around the room. "I see what you mean," he said. "This is a room for the intelligentsia, the polite, the fashionable. Not real bohemians. I am from the working class, and I have stumbled into a café for the ruling class."

"And you can tell by virtue of their clean clothes?"

John from the door had wandered in and stood nearby. Bob must have let him know about rising tension in the room. I shook my head at John. I could handle this alone.

"By virtue of their false propriety," said Sakas.

I thought back to Anthony at the Royal York Hotel. Sakas was exactly the kind of riff-raff he would have kept out of his dining room. I could get rid of him easily enough, but I was mildly interested in him and further didn't want him to serve as a poor model for the four young men I liked and who were admiring him a bit too much for their own good. What was it about this man that excited the admiration of my bohemians? His extremism, his literary renown? Or was he the equivalent of a man on a motorcycle — more than a little frightening, but powerfully attractive in some manner too?

"Propriety, eh?" I said. "So what do you mean?"

"Would you permit a lion in here?"

"Don't be a fool."

"I am completely serious. I know a café in the Gorky Bermuda Triangle where a photographer comes regularly with his lion on a leash. Maybe he's there right now. Would you care to see him?"

Drunkards and idiots existed in every culture. Sakas was both, but unlike most marginal types, he also had some talent, which gave him a kind of free pass in some circles for his bad behaviour. Ordinarily, I would have put an end to the conversation there and then, but that evening I was a little restless, and I told him that indeed, I would like to see the truly bohemian café where one of the patrons came regularly with his lion.

It was early evening when we stepped out onto the sidewalk, six of us in all, when John called me back for a word at the door.

"That coat of his stinks of sheep, comrade," he said.

"I know. Never let him in with his coat again. If he gives you trouble, call the police."

"No need. I can take care of his kind alone."

Lenin Prospect was one of the main streets of Vilnius, with the cathedral down at the bottom. Toward the end of the last century and up to the war, it had been a grand, modern street, with majestic four-storey buildings lining both sides and plaster ornamentation of all sorts near the top floors, none of which you would notice unless you looked up.

"Behold this street," said Sakas.

My four young men did as he asked, but I knew the street well enough that I didn't need to. He looked at me for a while as if waiting for me to follow instructions and then gave up and went on. "What you see is in no way the real world. This is the road of those who adapt, those who rule, and those who kneel before them, as well as those who chase after frivolous things."

"I see what you mean," I said. "Store clerks. Restaurant workers. The lower class."

"That is precisely *not* what I mean. Those people are authentic. The ones who go to your Metropolis are not."

Authenticity is overrated, or maybe just misunderstood. We don't want to meet authentically angry women, authentically violent men, or children authentically having temper tantrums. Maybe what we really mean when we use the word is sincerity. But, of course, fools and idiots are sincere too. I wasn't sure what Sakas really meant, but I didn't feel like standing around searching for a definition.

"Well, then, take us to the place where the people are authentic. I'm all ready for the experience. And show me the café with the lion."

Rudy kept looking at me as if I were a parent coming along on an excursion with his best friend and I was in danger of ruining the fun at any moment. We walked down to a cross street into the medieval part of the city, and there Sakas stepped into an alley and asked us to wait. He knocked on a door, money changed hands, and he came out with two bottles of homemade vodka and two more of 777, a local port, basically vodka mixed with boiled grape juice and sugar.

"Quite a party," I said.

"It's going to be a long night."

He didn't ask for money, so he must have had some of his

own, and this too surely appealed to the young men. A generous companion is always welcome.

Sakas drank a mouthful of vodka from one of the bottles as if it were pop, then passed it around to the others. Rudy and Kalistas both coughed because they were less adept at drinking hard liquor in that manner. A mouthful of 777 served as a chaser. I declined. Sakas put what remained of the first bottle of vodka into one pocket, the other one into another pocket, and told the others to hold the two remaining bottles before leading us into the labyrinth of the old city.

My mother lived in the old city, and I lived not far away, and I had been through it so many times I thought I knew it well, but there was something about that part of town, a kind of defensive look to buildings that seemed to turn their backs on people, or sometimes to let them in only to ensnare them in some fashion, as if a city could be a Venus flytrap.

I was certainly caught in the Lithuanian Soviet Socialist Republic with no escape that I could navigate, but the old city of Vilnius had traps of its own. Legend said there was a basilisk that lurked there, one whose gaze would knock you dead. But the modern basilisk was probably no more than one of the hooch sellers of the kind Sakas had bought his bottles from. There was no need to kill drunkards who would kill themselves eventually.

In the poor light of the old city, as I followed the lead of Sakas, I was constantly tripping on broken cobbles. The ground-floor windows that we passed had protective bars on them, designed to look as if they were just decorative sprays leaning diagonally but giving the impression of drunks getting ready to pitch over. Most of the windows were dark, but some were illuminated, with the interiors masked by thin curtains. Occasionally, through a parting of the curtains, I could see fragments of life — a man alone at a table with a bottle and a glass in front of him; a family playing cards without speaking. As always in the evening, there was at least one shouting man somewhere too far away to make out the words or imagine the cause of his rage, likely an unlucky woman or child.

We finally made our way through this maze to Gorky Street, one of the main streets in medieval times, a street that widened dramatically at the top before the old neoclassic city hall and thus was shaped like a triangle, or a funnel. This was the notorious Bermuda Triangle, where there were cafés without standards and where a drunkard could disappear never to be found again.

The café we went into was called an ice cream bar, but it never had much ice cream to begin with. It had long tables along which mostly young people sat, with two older vagabond types in one corner. The place served cheap coffee from second-hand grounds that coloured the water without flavouring it. Some genius had figured out he could sell used grounds, and the café that bought them cheaply could pocket the difference in cost between fresh coffee grounds and old ones.

So how did the place stay open? The wieners perpetually floating in a pot of water whose steam scented the place were not exactly tasty but were bearable, anyway, and very cheap. Sandwiches were reasonably good: Riga sprats on black bread no more than a day or two old. I had never tasted Riga sprats before I'd ended up in this part of the world. They were very much like sardines, but better for being smaller fish, more delicate, and smoked and therefore more savoury. I lunched on them myself occasionally, but only in my office so as not to offend the kitchen, which considered them to be working man's food, the kind of thing you brought along on the way to your construction job. Even when you are aiming for the stars, culinary or otherwise, it's good to let your feet touch the ground from time to time.

The Seaside Café Metropolis

The place smelled of mould and hot dogs and cigarette butts under our shoes, and of the toilet if you sat too close to that door. Riga sprats themselves are pungent. This was what all cafés were like before the Metropolis opened up. It was as if dirt, stink, and grit were worn like some kind of working-class badge of honour in Stalinist times. My mother would have felt right at home here.

The real reason for the café's popularity with a certain class was that it had no assigned sales targets and could serve as much or as little as it wanted. More importantly, Danute and Maryte, the two women who ran the place, permitted people to bring in their own bottles of wine or liquor as long as they kept them in bags under the tables. You might need to order the coffee in order to have something in front of you at the table, but there was no law that said you needed to drink it. If you had a little more cash, you could have a sprat sandwich to accompany your drink.

We settled ourselves along one table with our backs to the wall and our eyes facing the entranceway, and in a burst of sentimentality, I ordered Riga sprat sandwiches for all and tea for myself because I knew the reputation of the coffee.

Sakas kept on his signature sheepskin coat. He did not eat his sandwich. Instead, he poured some vodka into his own teacup and passed the bottle along. Serious drinkers did not eat. They just drank, but they also tended to die not all that long after they stopped eating. Korsakoff syndrome is a nasty way for an alcoholic to end up, a form of amnesia and dementia, and serious but not reckless drinkers ate something to prevent the condition from developing, or at least to delay its onset. So since he was not eating, Sakas was some distance along a certain trajectory that would cause not only dementia but also unusual and unpredictable behaviours. Russians loved holy fools, and Lithuanians in their turn indulged eccentric drinkers.

How did I know all this? Alcohol was a major attraction at the Royal York Hotel. We had not only restaurants and cafés but bars as well, and some of the mature hard drinkers who had enough money to be our patrons would find their way into the Library Bar. We had an old bartender there named Henry, and from long experience, he could read how far down a terrible path some of his customers had gone. Henry was also a talker who liked to tell stories about his customers whenever he wandered on down to the kitchen during a quiet moment in order to have a sandwich. Like some bartenders, he never drank himself because he had seen too well just how things went wrong on the slippery slope of alcohol.

"If you drink, it's good to take some food with it," I said to Sakas. What was it in me — some kind of paternal instinct to offer advice to those who didn't want it, didn't deserve it, and wouldn't take it?

"Food just feeds the body," said Sakas.

The place had become quite full. There was no such thing as a private conversation there. A young man leaned in toward us, all pale and filled with certitude.

"It is impossible to live in this system without alcohol," he said. "And besides, if there's one thing we've learned, it's that you need to drink if you want to write or paint. It brings on the inspiration. Look to the past. The great writers and artists were drinkers — Paul Verlaine, Émile Zola, Charles Baudelaire … Paul Gauguin and Toulouse-Lautrec."

"All French," I remarked. "Maybe only the French need to be drinkers to succeed."

The young man was impervious to irony.

"Look at the man you have come with, the poet Paul Sakas," he said. "Without alcohol, where would he be?"

"Shut up," said Sakas. And because he was a local hero,

prominent in his way, the young man did. It was kind of an honour to have been told off by a famous man.

"Talent doesn't lie in the alcohol," said Sakas. "That's just the lubrication of the machinery of genius. Otherwise, every drunk would be a poet."

Halfway across the room, I saw a young woman writing down Sakas's words. Café wisdom. I'd never really believed in that. I believed in café amusement, storytelling, and maybe an occasional insight, but probably not wisdom. Thoughts that come to your lips too quickly over too much wine evaporate just as fast. Yesterday's wit is like the dregs of a highball in a glass from the night before.

"So you need alcohol to survive under this system?" I probed.

A bit of a chill fell on the room. Everyone knew you didn't criticize the system too insistently. At least one person and maybe more in the room were reporting to the KGB.

"The young man means the weight of everyday life. He doesn't mean any kind of system."

That seemed to settle the matter, and I didn't want to provoke anyone anymore. We all knew that Big Brother's hand was on our shoulders, but none of us wanted to have his hand creep up toward our necks.

"We are all wounded," said Sakas. "There is a poet I know, he isn't here now, who was born in an orphanage and works in construction and calls this place home. But he is authentic. Over on Lenin Prospect, where you have your café, you have plastic people."

Sakas was a local celebrity, a kind of small star, and the room appreciated the light he gave off. There was so much more glitter at the Seaside Café Metropolis, where you needed to shine like the sun to be noticed, but here in the darkness, the smallest sliver of light was appreciated, and Sakas had that. As I looked around, I measured the tastes of the patrons. I was sure that almost everyone in the place had read Dostoevsky — Tolstoy was just for high school kids, not serious enough — but I wondered how many of them would turn out to be artists and writers. My four young men! I had hopes for them, but there were dangers everywhere, alcohol not the least of them.

After a while of listening to the young people talk about various writers while Sakas stared off into the middle distance, I began to get restless.

"I see no lions being led on leashes. Isn't that what we came here for?" I asked.

"The lion is a kind of metaphor," said Sakas, "if you know what I mean by the word." He waited a bit, and I did not respond. "Everyone in this café is potentially a lion, whereas over in your café, every customer is potentially a hare."

"So you are saying there is no lion."

"There is a lion, but this is not a zoo. The lion lives in the wild. You'll be lucky to catch a glimpse of it."

"Well, I'm sick of sitting around here. If you can't produce a lion, you shouldn't talk about one as if you can."

"So you want to see a lion?"

"Am I giving that impression?"

"I'll show you a lion. I know exactly where the lion is, but I can't take all of you. Pick one of these kids to come along, and we'll go to see the lion."

None of them wanted to be left out, of course, but I chose Rudy to come with us because he was the one who wanted to be a writer, after all, and Sakas was an esteemed poet. One in a bomber jacket, the other in sheepskin. Each tried to draw attention to himself by his unusual clothing. Having attracted attention, each would need to show some kind of talent. Sakas was already esteemed, but Rudy had not made his mark yet. He was game, though. Waiting for an opportunity.

The Seaside Café Metropolis

The bohemian class includes all sorts who are not romantic at all. There are bricklayers and bachelor labourers who spend their evenings drinking, hanging around the streets, smoking cigarettes, and measuring you up and down as you walk by. Then there are the criminals, the petty young ones anyway, who will beat you up for fun as much as for pocket change; the prostitutes or the good-time girls who are not exactly prostitutes but who will take a month's rent from you if they happen to be short of cash. Dancers on their nights off, waiters too wired to go home after their shifts, young women of strong constitutions who can work in a shop all day and drink all night.

These were the types of people on the street by the time we went out. It wasn't even that late yet, just nearing eleven o'clock when Sakas led us in his dirty white coat through yet another incomprehensible and unreproducible route to the courtyard of a yellow brick apartment block five storeys high. I could hear noise from above, and as I looked up, I could see what seemed to be the silhouette of a female lion's head staring down at us from an open window.

I looked over at Sakas. He said nothing but turned up his palms to demonstrate that he had delivered as promised, and I had to admit it was true.

The door to the apartment building had once had a lock, but the jamb was broken where someone had kicked it out, so we had no trouble getting in. The ground floor smelled of concrete, cigarette butts, and piss, and the odour did not improve much as we walked up the steps past landings with doors shut tight. I would have locked my doors tightly too if I had an apartment with a lion above me. The noise grew louder as we climbed, with people standing and sitting on the steps by the fourth floor, and then the landing outside the apartment on the fifth was packed with smoking drinkers in intense conversations.

Vilnius is a small city, but there was no one I knew on the steps, the landing, or even inside the apartment once we got in. There were worlds within worlds in that compact space, social circles that did not overlap at all. We walked in, and Sakas put the unopened bottle of vodka on a bookcase as well as a bottle of 777 — our contribution to the party — then saluted the host from across the room.

His name was Lokys, a tall, hungry-looking sort with a beard along his chin but no moustache, making him look faintly like a prophet. He had his arm over the shoulder of a beautiful, calm-looking woman, his partner, Alina. Her features were very fine, her cheekbones high and eyes deep-set — she would be beloved by the camera. Her dark brown hair, parted in the middle, was tied back as if she were about to do the laundry. In other words, this was not a party I was seeing. It was everyday life.

They were standing by the big open window where the lion had its paws over the sill as it surveyed the courtyard outside.

The walls were covered with pinned-up photographs of various sizes. They were arresting pieces, including a big one of Lokys running across the rooftop of a church, looking like some kind of criminal in Paris. There were many, many photographs of the woman at his side, Alina, most of them nudes, sometimes of her alone and sometimes of them both. There were studies of the faces of country people whose skin was deeply lined by age and the elements: farmers and their wives sitting on stools in their fields and facing the viewer, men with no ties but their shirts buttoned at the neck.

Talent, like beauty, needs no introduction, no explanation. And it makes no apology, for better or worse. Secure in itself, it pleads its own case. I could tell there was something to these photographs, something that made me want to keep on looking at

The Seaside Café Metropolis

them without quite knowing why or what I might be looking for.

Sakas had seen me staring at the photographs and again he turned up his palms, and again I had to admit he had delivered. I certainly would not have permitted Lokys to come to the Metropolis with his lion, but I had to admit the man with the lion was worthy of note. Sakas poured himself a glass of vodka and took Rudy under his wing in a circle of poets. I received a glass of Starka, a strong local spirit that reminded me a bit of Canadian Club. I sipped it and enjoyed the familiar-seeming taste that carried me back to my younger Canadian days, watching football's Grey Cup parade while drinking rye and ginger from a paper cup on the sidewalk. But I was far, far from my hometown in that room that night.

Sakas had shown me that maybe there was something to what he'd said, although he'd said it disagreeably. The room was an ongoing celebration, a lively one with talented people, and some kind of energy flowed through the place. Had I considered myself discerning and merely turned the Seaside Café Metropolis into a centre for snobs? I wasn't sure for the moment.

I floated through some of the conversations in the room and, uplifted by the talk, had a second glass of Starka. In one circle they were discussing the poet Yevgeny Yevtushenko, who was newly popular at the time; one of the women could recite long passages of his work. In another they were talking about the best way to cook a carp, and in a third there was an argument about whether the Baltic Sea looked more beautiful from the Lithuanian coast or from the Latvian one.

I was just at the point of introducing myself to Alina and Lokys when the lamp in the ceiling above them went off, flickered, and then went off again.

"Your bulb has burned out," I said to the couple before I could introduce myself.

"The wiring here is awful," said Alina. "The lamps flicker, and sometimes I smell smoke at the outlets."

"That's very dangerous. You could have a fire. I know an electrical engineer who might be able to fix it for you. Would you like that?"

Why was I offering help to people I did not know from a man who worked in my kitchen and might not be entirely willing to do it? I was under a kind of spell. The atmosphere in the place was electrifying, and Alina herself was very beautiful. Her slightly almond eyes might have had a bit of Tatar in them from some generations past. Her hair was rich and dark, and she exuded a kind of stillness that was contrary to the electric mood of the room. If the room was a hurricane, she was the eye of the storm. Lokys had caught this quality of hers in the photographs on the walls.

Lokys did not say anything, but he smiled at me in a kind of distracted way. His mind seemed to be somewhere else. Beside them, the lion turned around to glance at me from its perch at the window.

"How do you know when your lion is hungry?" I asked.

"She licks her chops."

The lion did so while looking at me. Alina laughed. "Don't worry. She is very well-fed."

"How did you get her?"

"Lokys was offered a cub by the Kaunas Zoo. They already had more lions than they knew what to do with, and no other zoo needed one at the time."

"Isn't she dangerous?"

"Not usually." She smiled again.

"I think your work is outstanding," I said to Lokys, but he didn't say anything at all. He just ran his hand over Alina's hair and smiled. The lion looked back out the window.

"Are you an artist too?" I asked her.

The Seaside Café Metropolis

"No. Two artists in a couple would be one too many. I'm training to be a nurse. Are you an artist?"

"No. I run a café. The Seaside Café Metropolis over on Lenin Prospect. Have you heard of it?"

She shook her head, and I was stung a bit. I wanted her to admire me, but I wasn't sure how to go about it, and now I felt awkward.

"Are you serious about the offer of an electrician?" she asked.

"I am. When could he come over?"

"Oh, the door here is never locked. Half the time the place is like this. Do you think he'd be afraid of the lion?"

"That would be a reasonable attitude. But I could come with him, and we'd be sure to knock first."

Through all of this, Lokys said not a word. He wasn't being standoffish. He was just living in some kind of private world. I would have to get to know him a bit, I hoped, as the author of the photographs on the walls. If he had genius, where did that genius come from? Nobody had ever figured that out, but I was interested in probing.

We talked some more, and I stepped out onto the landing. I talked a bit about the parks of Vilnius with one man, and a little about jazz in another circle. Time passed. I drank a third glass of Starka for the first time in my life, and it made me slightly less clear about what happened next.

Sakas was talking intensely to Lokys, who seemed irritated by what he was hearing. The lion was nearby, and Sakas did two things at once, stepping very close to Lokys and stepping on the tail of the lion as he did so. The lion turned abruptly, grasped Sakas between its paws, and then lost its balance as Sakas reeled toward the window.

I had never seen a cat lose its balance. Maybe a cat raised in a fifth-floor apartment is less agile, but as the lion released him to rebalance itself, Sakas reached forward and pushed with all his might, and the lion fell out the window.

After a sickening moment, I heard the thump from below. This was no cat landing on its feet. Sakas and Lokys both leaned out the window and looked down, and Lokys turned on Sakas, filled with rage, and pushed him out the window too before anyone could do anything to stop him. The room was frozen for an instant, but Alina came out of nowhere and put her hands on Lokys's shoulders.

"My love, why did you do that?"

He did not answer.

"My love, my love. Now everything will be over. Why did you do that?"

He shook his head. "I don't know. Did you say everything is over?"

"Not everything, no. Not everything. We will come out of this somehow. But now a hard time will come."

The rooms were emptying fast. I could hear shoes banging frantically down the steps. Some would want to get away before the police arrived. Some would want to see what lay on the cobblestones below.

Lokys looked at Alina. "No. I've made a mistake. Everything really is over."

And he stepped out the window where the other two had gone.

I grasped Rudy by the shoulder, and we joined the cascade of people going down the stairs. Rudy stopped with the others to look at the confusing mass of bodies below — two men and a lion, the white coat streaked with blood and some kind of liquid seeping out of Lokys's cracked head. Soon the police would be there. Blame would descend in its unpredictable way on some, and it was important not to be there when that happened.

The Seaside Café Metropolis

I DIDN'T SEE Rudy for three weeks, and I waited uneasily, expecting some kind of inquisitive policeman straight out of a detective novel, or perhaps a KGB inquiry. Rudy's friends did show up, but they knew as little as I did. As the time passed, I began to think that I should be the one going to the police to make inquiries, if only for his sake.

And then suddenly Rudy in his bomber jacket was there with his friends when I came in late one day at lunch. My poor young aspiring artists were eating beefsteak and drinking cognac and it wasn't even one o'clock in the afternoon. They regarded me with satisfaction.

"What's this all about?" I asked.

"Rudy's rich," said Kalistas.

"For a couple of days anyway," said Rudy. "I was paid my commission, and we're celebrating."

"Celebrating what?"

Rudy paused to light a cigarette with his Zippo lighter, which was working for the first time I'd ever seen. What magic had found him the right flints and fuel? He took a puff and then reached into an ancient leather briefcase and handed me a copy of a newspaper. He must have had twenty more copies inside, and I took mine to my office.

The headline read: "A Tragic Lesson and the Loss of a Great Man."

The so-called great man in the article was Sakas, and the one to blame for his death was Lokys and his ridiculous lion. It was a very long piece, easily over five thousand words, larded with extensive passages from the works of Sakas, barely mentioning the work of Lokys and showing none of his arresting photographs.

Rudy had written a morality tale, and I could see it was the kind of thing ordered by the authorities. He depicted himself as an innocent and credulous traveller, which wasn't far off the mark, but painted a picture of Paul Sakas that bore no resemblance to the man I had seen that night. He depicted Sakas as the genius in that pair, someone come to talk reason to Lokys, to moderate his eccentric ways. Sakas became an unfortunate sacrifice by appearing at the wrong place at the wrong time. I wasn't mentioned in the article, which managed to both relieve me because I'd suffer no consequences and irritate me a little for being left out of the story.

How quickly Rudy had found his way. He was the moralizer the authorities wanted, the shocked and appalled innocent, yet he had been there with me, eager to be part of a scene so bohemian it practically shone with glory. He had seen the deaths of two men and a lion, and he had been among those crazy bohemians that everyone wanted to read about. He was at the heart of a successful scandal. Everyone would know who Rudy was now. All he needed to do was write something else and he would be sure to get published, because the easiest way to get published is to get famous first. Rudy had arrived. His literary career was launched in the glow of communist government approval. He now had more to himself than his bomber jacket and his Zippo.

When I came out of my office and went into the café a little later, I could see that two other young men and a woman had pulled their chairs up to his table, and Rudy was retelling the story, one that he would be able to use for the rest of his life. Even my chief waitress at the front, Angela, was spending more time at that table than at others. She too was attracted by his success.

Rudy was no fool. I had underestimated him. He understood perfectly well what he had just achieved, and when he looked over at me and met my eyes, he seemed like a satisfied cat being petted by its admirers.

Indeed, Angela was one of his admirers too. She doted on Rudy then, and again the few more times he came in before disappearing from the regular crew at the front. Angela gave notice

The Seaside Café Metropolis

soon after. I had always imagined that the Seaside Café Metropolis was a destination, but of course I was mistaken. It was a conveyance to the future, and therefore more of a ship than a port, and the passengers got off whenever it was convenient.

NOT LONG AFTER that, I was sitting in my office doing accounts when Bob knocked at my door to say there was a woman who wanted to see me.

For some reason he had not asked her name, and I thought it was someone looking for a job, so I barely looked up and then saw it was Alina, Lokys's widow. But had they ever married? I didn't know for sure.

Her hair was pulled back, and she was wearing a cardigan over a blouse and a grey wool skirt. Even in this modest outfit and without makeup, she was striking, but you'd never imagine she would be the subject of many nude photos and the hostess of a never-ending party — or rather, a long party that had ended tragically. I asked her to sit down and had Bob get a waitress to bring us coffee.

"I hope you don't mind that I'm disturbing you," she said.

"You're not disturbing me. I'm so sorry for what happened. You must be having a hellish time."

"Oh yes, that's exactly what it's been. The police kept calling me in. They wanted to get the series of events down clearly, and eventually all the stories lined up with the other witnesses."

"I was never called. Should I have volunteered?"

"There was no need. We had old friends in the room that night. You were there for the first time."

"Did you read Rudy's article in the newspaper?"

"Oh, those writers. So keen to be recognized, so keen for fame. They write anything at all, and the kernel of truth they started out with gets buried in exaggerations and lies." She said this without bitterness, like someone commenting on the unfortunate climate she lived in. She paused for a moment and looked me in the eyes. "You must have been shocked."

"I was. Why do you think Lokys did what he did?"

"It was an impulse. He never thought about things too deeply — he just acted. That's why his photographs were so good. He could feel and sense what others might feel, and he could barely hold those emotions in."

"It couldn't have been easy living with him."

"No. There were other women. He had at least one child and maybe a second one. Life was a whirlwind with Lokys. The flat was always full of people. He'd disappear for weeks at a time to take pictures in Georgia or Kazakhstan. Now it is all very quiet. Very silent."

"Your life must feel empty now. I'm sorry for that too."

"Yes and no. Silent, yes. Empty, no. I loved Lokys, but he was exhausting. I was always out of breath with him, running to keep up. Sooner or later, I wouldn't have been able to maintain the pace."

"Those photographs."

"Yes. He had something, didn't he?"

"He did."

"But it burned him up. It would have burned me up too. I'm wondering if he knew that. I'm wondering if that's why he stepped out the window."

"He was still young," I said.

"He was forty-seven years old, not quite ready to move on but exhausted by our way of life, still burning but on the verge of burning out." She had answered, but she wasn't really interested in pursuing my banal consolation. She had something on her mind.

"You made me an offer that night before everything happened."

"Yes, I remember. To fix the electricity. Is that what you mean?"

"That would be good. Thank you. But there's something else."

"I'll do whatever I can."

"I'm concerned for the photographs. What you saw up on the walls wasn't all that much. He had a darkroom too, and there are hundreds of good photographs there. Maybe thousands. Negatives, mostly. I need a safe place to keep them."

"Do you think they're in danger?"

"Maybe. The authorities were losing patience with him. But the photos are in danger mostly of neglect. Someone will take over the darkroom. Somebody might come to my apartment. It's been a party room for so long everyone feels they have a right to it and anything in there. They'll pick the photographs right off the walls for souvenirs. I need to keep the negatives safe, and I was hoping you could help me."

I asked how much space they would take up, and it sounded like not much more than a couple of large boxes, and I had plenty of room at the café, so I agreed to do what she wanted.

"Why did you think of me?" I asked. "We barely know one another. I mean, I'm flattered, but aren't you taking a risk?"

"I sense something in you," she said. "Our friends are very fine. A lot of them are talented. But you are stable. I need someone stable."

I agreed to her request, but my heart sank. I wasn't even middle-aged yet, but I was already *stable*. I was doing her a favour, but it made me feel as if she was admiring me for what to me were the unfortunate failings of my character.

"I'll take the photos. I have a safe place. Our storerooms are big enough. Do you think you'll organize them into a show of some kind? The photos are exceptional. Someone will publish a book of his pictures."

"It's too soon to think of that. I need to find a way to live my life, to get out of my old life and get into a new one. I just need to put the photos someplace where they will be safe until the time is right."

"Maybe you could come here and visit them from time to time."

"I don't understand."

"I mean, maybe you could come to the café sometimes."

"I wouldn't want to impose. I'm still a student, and this place is too expensive for me."

"No. You'd come as my guest."

"Thank you. I'll think about it."

I was slightly ashamed by my offer. I wanted to see her again, but I didn't want to come across like some sort of man looking for a mistress, some version of the editor who had kept Mona. But all I could offer was the café, practically all I had.

I HADN'T SEEN my mother for a while, so I went out to visit her later that day, to take her for a walk in the Youth Park with its gardens and miniature elephant fountains. Vilnius has its charms. My mother loved ideas and principles more than she admired physical things, so she always seemed uninterested in the blooms I pointed out to her, or the quality of the sparkling light as it fell across the surface of the stream that ran alongside the gardens.

"Have you heard the latest tragedy about the photographer and the lion?" I asked.

"I don't really know what you're talking about."

So I told her the story, which she followed with only mild interest until I came to the end and mentioned that Alina had come to see me to help her protect the photographs. This last bit seemed to interest her more than anything I'd said before.

"Tell me about this Alina."
"She's training to be a nurse, but she has just suffered a tragedy."
"And you want to help her?"
"Of course."
"That's just like you. Verging on a martyr. Is she beautiful?"
"Stunning, but in a quiet way."

The news seemed to bother my mother. She didn't say anything more, but I could see she sensed I might be interested in Alina beyond doing her a favour. My mother's most common emotion was disinterest in my affairs. I wasn't sure if I should be hurt or pleased that she was jealous there might be another woman in my life. Alina herself gave no evidence of wanting to be that woman.

Riga Sprats (small fish, smoked and tinned) three ways

1. Alone: Open the tin, drain the oil, put the sprats on dark rye bread.

2. With guests: First cut the crusts off the slices of rye bread and quarter each one to make it dainty. Apply mayonnaise if you have any. Slice hard-boiled eggs and place one or two slices of egg on each quarter of bread. Lay one or two sprats across the egg and serve off a fine plate.

3. In times of war, famine, or poverty: Do not drain the oil. After you have eaten the sprats, dip the bread into the leftover oil. If you have no more bread, you may use any other starchy food on hand, such as leftover rice, mashed potatoes, or buckwheat. If you have none of the above, drink the oil in small sips with pauses between each sip in order to achieve nourishment without turning the stomach by pouring in too much rich food too quickly.

–7–

Cold Borscht and Hot Zeppelins

I DIDN'T REALLY know who Jean-Paul Sartre and Simone de Beauvoir were beyond having heard their names on the lips of various café philosophers. When I found out we were going to have this pair of famous French philosopher-writers for dinner at the Seaside Café Metropolis, my first reflex was to serve them French food.

Niko down in the kitchen wanted to discuss this idea.

The kitchen staff gathered around, as well as our two little girls, now a little older, who stood holding hands in the doorway to the corridor. The children of Genius and Julia, little Monika and Ona. They'd adapted well to life by the kitchen and were spoiled by everyone who worked there. They were not the only children. We had an occasional boy of ten in miniature whites his mother had sewn, and he showed sparks of interest in food preparation. The children's parents had taught them not to interfere, but they were children and they made mistakes, and the staff loved them anyway.

The employees all assembled for major discussions. Each of us owned a part of the reputation of the Seaside Café Metropolis, and each of us was invested in its success. So little else was under our control in our lives, from the flats we lived in to the foreign destinations we dreamed of visiting but would never be permitted to see. For us there was *No Exit*, which was apparently the title of one of Jean-Paul Sartre's plays. At least in the kitchen we could determine a small part of our lives.

Back at the Royal York, we had all felt ourselves part of a team. We'd do anything to uphold the reputation of the hotel and its restaurants. The management, to its credit, paid some attention to our suggestions. By contrast, I understood that the Ford Hotel was hierarchical. One simply did what one was told over at that lesser establishment.

So the kitchen staff stood about as Niko sat on a high stool with his chin in his hand, considering our options. I stood across from him with a notebook in my hand. Once Niko had reflected enough, the hand dropped from his chin to his lap.

"They are from Paris, so why should we try to replicate what they already know? We will seem like provincials trying to ape the customs of the capital. I am sure we could cook just as well as the French, but even if we do, the guests' context is different here. Let's serve them real local food."

"Lithuanian food is very heavy," I cautioned.

"So is Alsatian food, but the French like that well enough. Serve the guests cold beet borscht and I can guarantee you will astonish them and please them. It exists nowhere else in the world from what I can determine from my research, and the shocking pink colour will alert them that they aren't in Paris anymore."

I hadn't eaten any sort of borscht, let alone cold beet borscht, before coming to Lithuania, but it had become the first food I longed for when the weather warmed in June. It was a mixture of cooked grated beets, raw cucumbers, green onions, and dill in a kefir base. You could garnish it with chopped hard-boiled eggs

The Seaside Café Metropolis

and serve it with steamed potatoes on the side. I'd never heard of kefir either in my days at the Royal York Hotel, but it turned out to be a lot like buttermilk. Had I read about this dish before tasting it, I probably would not have eaten it, but the soup was light and refreshing, especially in warm weather, and the bright pink colour was set off nicely with traces of crumbled hard yellow egg yolk and egg white as well as sprigs of green dill.

The second dish, the signature dish of Lithuania, was a potato dumpling stuffed with pork, veal, and beef. When assembled, this meat and potato dumpling was about the size of your fist and shaped like the Zeppelin of its name. The sauce consisted of fried onions, bacon lardons, and sour cream. If the first dish was light and made me think of summer breezes, Zeppelins, for all their high-flying aircraft name, made me think of earth and work that brought on sweat and hunger that needed to be appeased with serious nutrition.

"I wonder what kind of wine you should serve with those dishes," mused Lucy.

I had been looking at her more and more whenever I went down to the kitchen. I had found out a bit about her life from Niko, who said she was a young woman from the provinces, one who had been trained in the elements of cuisine in a technical school. But technical schools usually trained cafeteria and buffet chefs. She betrayed more knowledge than she could have picked up in a regular Soviet training school. And she was a little older than what you'd expect for a graduate from a technical school.

"How do you come to wonder about wine? Few people in this country are knowledgeable about it," I said.

"I've been reading."

This turned more than a few heads because our kitchen staff were not noted for their love of books. They generally liked to have a smoke and maybe a drink on the back stoop during a break if the sun was shining in that spot, and they went for some other form of comforting pursuit once they got home. They did love food and they did want to be educated, but not through books, if at all possible.

"What do you suggest?" I asked.

"Côtes du Rhône."

"Why Côtes du Rhône?"

"Simple. A cut above house wines. Earthy, but reliable."

"Have you ever tasted Côtes du Rhône?"

"No. My knowledge is theoretical."

"I'm afraid it's going to stay that way. The odd bottle of French wine does float through the Ministry of Agriculture sometimes, but there is none that I know of now."

"What about Khvanchkara? It was Stalin's favourite wine, Georgian."

I was amazed this woman could know so much. I would have to keep an eye on her to make sure her intelligence wasn't overlooked.

"Khvanchkara is semi-sweet," I said, "and the French drink only dry wines with their meals. So we have a problem, Lucy. You seem to have a head for these sorts of questions. How do you suggest we solve our problem?"

"In that case, serve no wine at all," she said. "The beer is good here. We could stick to beer and shots of vodka with a local liqueur such as Malūnininkų for dessert."

The woman was brilliant. Niko had the makings of an educator in him, so he too was proud of his young minion. He did not need to dominate, and she, for her part, was unselfconsciously bold enough to speak while many of the other beginners were terrified to open their mouths.

"No wine, eh?" he asked. "Not even the excellent black currant wine?"

"It would be an abomination to them," I said. "They imagine only the grape can make wine, and their minds are closed against other options. We can save that for people who appreciate it."

"We could also serve a little caviar. That always impresses foreigners."

"Yes, but it's too Russian," I added.

We stopped at that moment. We loved most things Russian, the people above all, and as for food, the delicious solyanka soup, for example, we loved that too. But we were in Lithuania, occupied territory, and somehow the food of the occupier might send the wrong message to the diners.

Just then I heard a bit of childish laughter, and I looked over to see Monika and Ona, our hallway children, had been joined by a small boy, and they were kibitzing with a great deal of enthusiasm.

"Whose is the boy?" I asked.

Nobody knew. I was about to have Bob ask around, but just then a mother came down the steps and took the boy by the hand, shot us a poisonous look, and led him away.

"What was that look for?" I asked.

"She's a customer. The child got away from her upstairs," said Bob. "The boy must have been attracted by their laughter. His mother was just being protective."

"One of those kids is going to get underfoot and get scalded here one day. It's just a question of time."

It was Linas, the KGB man in our kitchen.

"Are you the safety inspector?" I asked, challenging him, and then I regretted my words because a safety inspector was exactly the kind of interfering bureaucrat Linas might call down upon us.

"I grew up in a hotel kitchen," I added, "and I suffered no ill effects. Many families ran restaurants in my town, and the children were always around."

Linas shrugged and muttered something about bourgeois exploitation of children, but before I could challenge him, Bob cleared his throat. It was as forward as Bob ever got.

"Actually," he said, "I was hoping my grandson might occasionally join the children out there. He's a quiet boy named Auri, and I don't think he'd cause any trouble. My daughter's husband has become an invalid, and she finds it hard to place the boy."

"You're not the only one," said a voice I did not recognize from among the staff.

I threw up my hands. "Am I to be responsible for not only you but all of your children too?"

A stony silence followed, and I felt bad.

"All right," I said. "We will take the problem of children under consideration. But for the time being, can we just focus on our famous French philosophers?"

THE NEWS OF the philosophers' visit shot like a meteor through the Lithuanian Soviet Socialist Republic. Nobody from the West ever visited Lithuania for all kinds of different reasons. The first was that hardly anybody knew Lithuania existed, and even many of those who did would have been hard-pressed to find it on a map. The second was Moscow did not like foreigners snooping around a country it had annexed during the war. And third, many foreign governments, including the French, never recognized the annexation and so discouraged their nationals from going there and legitimizing the occupation by their presence.

One afternoon, Kalistas, my young bohemian philosopher, burst into my office all aglow with the sweat of his enthusiasm for the coming visit.

"They're from the West," he blurted, stating the obvious.

The Seaside Café Metropolis

"Nobody from the West comes here," he added, restating the obvious. He looked at me, pushed his eyeglasses up his nose, and corrected himself. "At least, no one with intellectual credentials."

Was I insulted? I was from the West, but it was true I was merely a restaurateur. Still, I sighed. The West was practically a myth for the local intelligentsia. They read about it in some of the books that were permitted to be published, heard bits of information that seeped in from the freer Polish airwaves and the crackly *Voice of America*, and remembered old movies their parents had seen before the war. The West was practically like the Emerald City to them, a fabled place where people were rich and free. Some of the intellectuals even thought the West lived by exalted liberal values, unlike the more barbaric eastern tyranny. They could never understand why someone like me had chosen to leave the place. I wasn't sure either.

"I need to be in that luncheon party," Kalistas said, sitting across from me at the desk in my office. He had wild hair, this young philosopher, to match his wild and passionate thoughts, but the eyeglasses in their metal frames added a bit of bookishness. And indeed, he could always be found with a book on his person. He wore a long coat in cooler weather, one with many pockets in which he could put his books. He hated summer for the reduction it brought about in his pockets and therefore the reduction in the number of books he could keep at hand.

"Are you out of your mind? This is a meeting arranged by the highest authorities," I said. "By Moscow itself. What makes you think you could be permitted to enter a circle like that?"

"By virtue of my need to know things," Kalistas said. "By virtue of my admiration for the French philosophers in general and Jean-Paul Sartre in particular. And Simone de Beauvoir as well. I am a philosopher myself!"

"A student."

"A postgraduate student! I am surrounded by Marxist-Leninist hacks!"

He put his hand over his mouth. He had let himself go too far. He didn't have to worry around me, but I wondered what Zorin and crew downstairs thought about what he had to say.

"You'll never succeed in getting an invitation."

"There is no one in this country who knows the man's work better," Kalistas said when he overcame his hesitation and spoke again.

"So what is the core of this Frenchman's philosophy?" I asked.

"Authenticity."

"I'm not sure what that means."

"Being true to yourself. Not giving in to pressure. And Simone de Beauvoir is important too."

"What for?"

"She speaks of the condition of women."

"What about their condition?"

"How they are constrained in the West."

"What about here?"

"Well, here, of course, they can do whatever they want."

"What an admirable place *here* is. I keep forgetting that. Ah. Well, you seem to know the heart of the matter, but I'm not the gatekeeper. I don't know who can get you into that lunch."

He was chewing on his lip and looking up at the ceiling.

"I suppose I'll have to ask my father," he said.

His father had once been the minister of education. The old man was one of the great supporters of the incoming Soviet regime during the war and after it. A fervid communist activist and intellectual, perhaps retired now. I wasn't sure. Kalistas never spoke of him, implying he wanted to break free of his father's influence.

The Seaside Café Metropolis

For all his youthfulness, Kalistas had a sharp eye, and he must have caught traces of my ironic thoughts on my face.

"I will not judge my father," he said, somewhat defensively.

No, I thought, but Kalistas had no trouble judging everyone else.

I AND THE entire staff, including the kitchen workers from downstairs, stood in a line to greet the visiting philosophers as they came to lunch. Even Piotr Zorin joined us from his listening post. We had never assembled anything like this, and I felt like I was part of the staff at a great English manor house meeting a lord and his lady. Even Dominic, my architect patron, appeared, looking nonchalant but pleased in his own way to have his café be the place where the distinguished guests were being welcomed.

No one would mistake Jean-Paul Sartre for a handsome man. He was short with round spectacles and the pale, lined face of a desk-bound chain-smoker. At the time, we thought Simone de Beauvoir was his wife, and she towered above him. Both looked underdressed to us, wearing serviceable clothes but well-worn. They seemed shocked to have us all lined up like this, and would likely have preferred a low-key lunch, but we were supposed to honour them, and everyone wanted to get a look at them, the first Western visitors some had ever seen in their lives. To their credit, the pair shook hands with each of us, a good twenty in a row.

They were accompanied by a party of four — Zina, their young Russian translator; a middle-aged member of the writers' union named Almantas; an older poet; and last of all came Kalistas. Since the French guests had shaken hands with everyone, the rest of their party chose to do the same thing, and it was beginning to feel like a wedding party receiving congratulations, minus the envelopes full of money.

When Kalistas reached me, he gave me a knowing nod, and I smiled and shook his hand in wonderment and admiration at what he had succeeded in doing. There were a hundred or more who would have liked to be in his place. He had been estranged from his communist father, but not so estranged as to miss the opportunity of a lifetime.

In good Potemkin village fashion, the café was rather full, although with guests I had never seen before. There were families with remarkably docile children in the back, as well as serious, professorial types in good suits. We had regular professorial types of our own all the time, but not these ones. At the front, we had a more casual crowd, and yet again, few I had seen before. It was amazing to me how many extras could be called in for a show. I did notice they didn't order all that much. Mostly coffee and cakes at the front, and only a few main meals in the back. The KGB was thorough but frugal.

The band was playing American jazz, and Mona was sitting on a chair by the stage, ready to go up and do a few vocals. Her lover, Marcel, would have liked to be there, but he did not have the pull of his friend Kalistas. I handed over the house to my floor manager, Bob, and returned to my office, where I went immediately to my closet, removed the panel, and flipped the switch that permitted me to listen in to the conversation at the table punctuated by the sounds of bottles being set down and cutlery moved about.

"Mr. Sartre," said Almantas, the writer who seemed to be the host of the event, "perhaps you could tell us a little of how people live in France today."

Everything was slowed by the necessity of translation, which made the conversation protracted the way a heavy snowfall impedes a walk across a meadow.

"The people of France live largely as they lived before, but some are struggling to change for the better."

The Seaside Café Metropolis

"And do they read the works of Guy de Maupassant? He is a great favourite here."

"My friend, Maupassant is read in France by the bourgeois. No one takes him seriously there anymore."

A silence fell on the group, which might have been awkward if the first course of cold borscht had not arrived.

"Pink soup!" said Simone de Beauvoir. "Is it a strawberry soup?"

"Beets," said the translator.

"Alas!" said Sartre.

In the background I could hear Mona begin to sing "A Foggy Day in London Town" with Lithuanian lyrics. This was what it meant to be cosmopolitan: a car crash of an American song about a British capital sung in Lithuanian for the pleasure of a French couple.

A knock came at my office. I stepped out of my closet and opened the door. Bob was standing on the other side.

"Do you know the French philosopher is holding hands with his translator?" he asked.

"I don't know it because I can't see through walls. You came to tell me that?"

"I thought you'd want to know. Do you think it's French to hold hands with your lover in the presence of your wife and foreign dignitaries?"

"I don't know. I've hardly ever seen dignitaries appear with their wives here."

"We're trying to keep up a certain style in this café, and now the foreigners come in and show they don't give a damn."

"Damned foreigners," I echoed.

"Right," he answered without reflecting on who he was talking to. "Mona's voice is sounding a little ragged," he added, "and the woman friend of yours is at the service door with a box she said she's brought for you."

Alina with the late Lokys's negatives. This was not a good time. But I had to go out to see her, and I walked past the table of guests to go to the back entrance. Sartre was eating his soup with one hand and holding his translator's hand with the other. It seemed awkward. Everyone could see this, but Simone de Beauvoir was the only one who seemed not to be put out by it. How French, everyone would say later. Nothing bothered them but bad food. As for Mona onstage, she paused between verses, put her hand over the microphone, and cleared her throat. The poor woman must have had a cold. Foggy London Town had got down her voice box.

I stepped downstairs to the kitchen, which was humming with controlled intensity, and asked Niko if he could spare Lucy for a moment. He waved okay, and I asked her to come with me to the back where Alina was waiting. She had two boxes with her on the stoop.

"I know you're busy today," she said, "but some curious men have been hanging around the apartment, and I wanted to get these things to safety."

"It's all right," I said. "I'll keep them in my office for now."

"Do you mind if I come with you? I just need to see where the boxes end up."

"Sure. Lucy, can you give us a hand?"

Due to all the commotion happening at the back and in the kitchen, I chose for us to go around to the front and come in through the café with Lucy carrying one box and I another, Alina in tow. Bob looked at me with pursed lips. One did not make deliveries through the front door. Luckily, we did not need to pass by the French guests to make it to my office, but we could see the band and Mona on the stage. We placed the two boxes well behind my desk so they would not be visible to anyone walking into my office. I was not sure why I bothered, but some instinct in me veered toward secrecy. Alina took my hands in hers.

"I'm a little bit afraid," she said, and then she looked over my shoulder at Lucy, who was still in the room.

"Lucy," I said.

"Yes?"

"Could you leave us alone for a minute?"

"I could, but I wanted to tell you something."

"Is it important?"

"Maybe."

"Well?"

"Your singer has a trickle of blood running down the side of her mouth. She hasn't noticed and the band is behind her and the diners aren't looking at her. I thought you should know."

"Thank you. Go to her at the end of the song and take her downstairs. Bring along a napkin, and try to keep out of sight of the guests."

"How will I do that?"

"Imagine you're invisible." I turned to Alina. "I need to do some pressing things just now. Wait for me at a table in the front. I'll come for you."

She did as I asked, and I had Bob watch over her and have the waitresses bring her tea and cake. I returned to my office, shut the door, and stepped into my closet. Simone de Beauvoir was speaking.

"It is fascinating how the mind works. You see pink soup, and you are told it is pink because of the beets in it. But the eyes see pink, and the mind turns this colour association to strawberries, and each spoonful of the soup is a shock to the palate. It disturbs one's expectations, and I believe that is a good thing."

Almantas the writer ignored what she had said, not knowing that the French cared for food as much as they cared for philosophy, perhaps more. Almantas had been assigned a propaganda task by his masters, and he was going to fulfill it.

"There are those in the West who claim Lithuania is an occupied country," he said. "What do you think of this notion?"

I could almost hear the shrug. "I see a café full of people listening to good music and eating good food. I remember the sullenness of Paris restaurants during the occupation, and there is none of that here."

"And your French government, which claims to agree the country is occupied?"

"My government consists of fools who do not recognize that Lithuania joyfully joined the Soviet Union. I thumb my nose at my government. I believe the people in the East are involved in a grand socialist project, and those within it can criticize, but those in the capitalist world have no right."

I heard a thump on the table as the next dishes were served, and my microphone cut out. I would need to get the waitress to set down something heavy so the microphone worked again.

There was a knock at the door. I opened it to see Marcel had arrived.

"What do you want?" I asked, a little short-tempered because my mind was on other matters.

"I hear Mona is unwell."

"That's right. Lucy took her downstairs by the kitchen."

"I need to go to her."

"So go to her. The stairs are on your left."

I closed the door and returned to my closet to find the microphone was working again. Sartre was speaking.

"The world is meaningless. People need to create their meaning by being authentic." He went on to describe a scene with a waiter in a restaurant. Apparently, the man played at being a waiter, using

The Seaside Café Metropolis

all the flourishes of a waiter. These were a form of acting, not true to his essence as a man.

"How do we achieve that?" asked Kalistas. He was the perfect apostle, eager and willing and a little too enthusiastic.

"You express yourself, your true self. You don't play roles."

His words irritated me a bit. If all the world was a stage, how could we avoid playing roles? As far as I was concerned, authenticity was overrated.

"You don't live a lie. These Zeppelins are enormous. Why are there three on my plate?"

"Three are a normal portion."

"Very well. I'll do my best. Very generous with the bacon lardons, I see. There must be a quarter of a pig on this plate. I am liking Lithuania better and better with every morsel."

There was much clinking of forks on plates and slurping of beer as they dug in.

"I am sure you eat better than this when you are sitting around with your friends at the Flore."

I had to hand it to Kalistas. He had somehow done his research. No other Soviet at the table knew what the Café de Flore was, but I did. It was a café for Paris intellectuals, or had been.

"No one goes to the Flore any longer," said Sartre. "The place is full of tourists. Is that crème fraîche you have there? It goes on the food as well? An outstanding idea."

There was a knock at my door. I opened it to find Piotr Zorin standing there. He walked right past me and looked around.

"I understand a certain Alina has come to the café. What is she doing here?"

"How do I know, and what business is it of yours?"

"Her dead boyfriend was an anarchist. She is not suitable to be in the café while an important guest is here."

"I'll decide who gets to stay."

"You know that's not true."

"I am not going to take orders from you."

"These are not orders. They are friendly suggestions. If you don't heed them, I can bring along people who will give you orders, but you won't like them much, and you won't like how they behave."

"Go ahead. Get some toughs in here while the guests are dining. I dare you."

"Listen …"

But I pushed him gently out the door and returned to my closet.

"Freedom is a terrible burden," Sartre was saying.

"It's not a very heavy burden in this part of the world," said Kalistas.

Silence ensued. I could only imagine the uproar that would follow his suggestion that we were unfree in Lithuania.

"How do you mean?" asked de Beauvoir.

"I am sure he means that the people of the east are freer than the people of the west and thus their burdens are lighter," said Sartre.

No one disagreed with him.

"And do you think revolution is necessary to change society?" asked Kalistas.

"Look around yourself and see the advantages you enjoy," said Sartre. "You only achieved these freedoms through the violence of the Russian revolution, so if violence is what it takes, then that is what it takes."

There was a knock at the door. I answered it to find Bob.

"Did you want that young woman to wait for you?"

"Do you mean the one at the front of the café? Alina?"

The Seaside Café Metropolis

"Yes. Because a rather serious-looking man came, and she left without finishing her cake."

"What did the man look like?"

"Security type."

There was nothing I could do. I thanked him and closed the door and returned to my closet.

Sartre was just finishing talking about how there was no truth and how this was part of the existential condition. Well, anyone who had lived in the USSR knew that the whole system was a lie. And if it was a lie, there had to be truth somewhere. Again, Kalistas came up with a question of the kind no one else in the country could have. He must have had excellent sources of information thanks to his father's books and connections.

"There was a certain Polish intellectual who grew up in this town," he said, "named Czesław Miłosz. We heard he went to Paris. Did you ever meet?"

Did Sartre wrinkle his nose as if something was smelling bad? I wasn't there, so I cannot say for certain, but I could hear the disdain in his voice.

"An indecisive man," said Sartre. "He found Paris not to his liking. He disliked communism but then claimed he disliked capitalism just as much. I told him he must choose, and when he said it was impossible, I told him he was a Galapagan."

De Beauvoir laughed, but no one else seemed to get the joke.

"I'm not sure I understand."

"My meaning, young man, is that one must choose, and if you cannot choose between the two, you are doomed to be a throwback, or irrelevant to the modern world. You belong on the Galapagos Islands. Nothing will come of Miłosz. All the more so because he writes in Polish, and that is not a serious language."

"How so?" asked Kalistas.

"You need to write in one of the major languages — French, English, or German. Perhaps Italian or Spanish if necessary, but better one of the first three."

"I write in Lithuanian," said Almantas.

"Such a pity," said Sartre. "And at your age, it's hard to learn a new language. But there might be a future in exporting this type of food. It is very satisfying. Perhaps a restaurant?"

BOB KNOCKED ON my door to let me know the guests were leaving, and although we did not line up to shake their hands on the way out, we were there to nod and smile at them as they left.

Just as they approached the exit, Tomas Klimas, my former British agent, the lover of blancmange, appeared out of nowhere.

"Vive la France!" he said loudly with real emotion in his voice, and then he repeated it. I was not sure how he'd even made it into the restaurant during a visit from important foreigners. Sartre stepped away from his party and beckoned for his translator to come with him. He took Klimas's hand between his.

"My friend, I appreciate your kindness, but you should not praise France too much. It is a bourgeois nation. Let me say, therefore, in response, vive la Lithuanie Sovietique!"

He was turning to leave when I heard someone say, "Vive la Lithuanie libre."

Had Sartre heard that? He did not look back. I was not even sure I had heard it, but there must have been a few French speakers around because a number of the guests were studying their coffee cups carefully, the way one does if someone at a reception has broken wind.

The Seaside Café Metropolis

OF THE PARTY, only Kalistas stayed behind a moment after first looking to see if any of his friends were in the café at the front. None were, and the place began to empty as the KGB-appointed seat fillers stood up to leave. The regulars would be back soon enough, and poor Klimas retired to his habitual corner and ordered his habitual carafe of cognac.

"You should have heard the conversation," said Kalistas when he came up to me. I almost admitted that I had.

"Was it good?"

"Scintillating. The philosopher was fascinated by our country and said our language sounded very musical to his ears."

"Didn't you speak mostly Russian during the lunch? After all, his translator was Russian."

"Of course we spoke Russian, but he has heard others speaking Lithuanian. He has a very fine ear, attuned to the world around him."

"I see. And did he tell you anything of note about his philosophy?"

"He did, but I can't tell you about it."

"Why not?"

"Well, first, you might tell others, and I would lose my advantage. And second, I like to mull over my writing projects rather than talk about them. Every barroom raconteur can spin a tale, but serious writers save their best work for the page."

"I thought you were a philosopher, not a writer."

"Not a writer as a scribbler of mere verses or novels. But obviously, philosophers write."

"And how did he and his wife like the food?"

"His wife? He and Simone de Beauvoir are not married. Marriage is a bourgeois institution."

"I was asking about the food."

"I didn't notice. I don't think either one of them did either. To speak of food is irrelevant, don't you think?"

I didn't think so at all. And the hungry young man had often talked about nothing else.

I looked for Alina both in the café and out on the sidewalk, but she had disappeared after dropping off the boxes of her late lover's photographs and negatives. I didn't think about it much at the time and went downstairs to the kitchen. Niko stopped speaking to a chef as soon as he saw me, and then he crossed his arms and waited, and the others stood behind in anticipation, like white ghosts in the steam of the place.

Naturally, I paused for effect.

"Brilliant!" I said. I applauded him, and the staff did too, while Niko nodded happily and dabbed at one eye.

"Did he say anything about the meal?"

"He praised the food, I understand, and then exclaimed that there can be no philosophy, no art, and even no politics without a solid basis of food."

"Of course he's right. No wonder he's a famous philosopher. Food is the éminence grise of emotion and achievement. When you are reaching the pinnacle of insight, or seeking the warmth of friendship, you have been primed by the quality of the food on the table before you. The kitchen, the chefs, we are the handmaidens of culture and of progress. No one really knows it. No one really acknowledges it, and that is fine. We serve in silence, and our hearts are satisfied."

I had never realized Niko was an orator as well as a chef.

The staff broke into applause once again.

I asked Lucy to step upstairs, and she came to my office.

"What happened to Mona?" I asked.

"Marcel took her away."

"Do you know if it was anything serious? Maybe she just bit

her tongue by accident, or an infected tooth erupted."

Lucy gave me a skeptical look. "You're speaking hopefully. She coughs often, right? Have you noticed that in the past?"

"Not really, no. Everybody coughs sometimes."

"Not regularly. She does. And she's a bit pale and thin, don't you think?"

"I haven't thought about it."

"Of course not. You're a man. You don't notice things."

"Do you think it's serious?"

"It's hard to tell. Wait and see, I guess."

"And how is it that you noticed her in the first place from across a room when no one else did?"

"I keep my eyes open."

"Yes. And come to think of it, when we were discussing this meal, how is it you knew so much about wine?"

"Like I said, I read. At various times of my life, I had to wait a long time, and I filled that time with reading. Antiquarian bookstores are full of cheap old books."

"What do you mean, you had to wait?"

"No higher school would take me after I finished high school. I wasted a few years before I got into technical school. It wasn't my first choice."

This was code for something in her background that made the authorities forbid her entry into a good school. Maybe she had a relative who lived abroad or had spent time in the gulag like Genius. To me, she was a gem being wasted as an assistant downstairs. "I want you to move up here," I said.

"What, and be a waitress?"

"Maybe."

"No, thanks. I haven't learned all there is to learn downstairs yet. Niko is a thinking chef. I want to be around him a while longer."

I was astonished to have my offer turned down.

"The money is better if you serve. You get tips sometimes."

"I'll reflect on it. But not too fast. And by the way, I see a big, fat book on the shelf behind you. Is that a cookbook?"

"*Larousse Gastronomique*. Pretty rare."

"A cookbook?"

"In a manner of speaking. More the French history and philosophy of food."

"Do you think I could borrow it?"

"It's in French. You wouldn't understand it."

"Do you speak French?"

"Not really, but I can get by. I'm a Canadian. We get some French in high school."

"I thought you were Argentinian."

"No."

"So can I borrow the book?"

"Do you have a French dictionary?"

"I can find one."

I took the massive book down from the shelf and set it on my desk, flipping it open to an illustration of a platter of prawns with oysters set along the rim. I forgot about her for a moment as I studied the image, and she must have forgotten about me because our heads bumped slightly and then we jerked back.

"Sorry," I said.

"We don't have those kinds of foods here. Are those clams?"

"Oysters. No, we don't have them, but we do have freshwater crayfish in place of prawns, and they are very good."

"The world is so full of a variety of good things, but we have so few of them here."

She was right, but it did not do to dwell on it.

"Keep the book for a while. And keep my offer about working upstairs in mind. You shouldn't look a gift horse in the mouth."

The Seaside Café Metropolis

"I'll let you know if and when I am ready."

I let her go with some regret, both because she had turned me down and because I had offered her the position in the first place. I didn't want to come across as "the boss," one who preyed upon the female staff. I did take an interest in her, but I had no intention of preying upon her.

Cold Borscht

1 litre kefir or buttermilk
1 glass water from boiled beets
500 grams good beets, boiled, peeled, and grated
2 cucumbers, peeled
1/3 bunch dill, chopped finely
2 chopped hard-boiled eggs
1 bunch spring onions
Sour cream (optional)
Salt
Traditionally accompanied by boiled potatoes

Boil the beets in lightly salted water until tender, about an hour or longer, depending on how fresh the beets are. Reserve the water, and then peel and grate the beets (or julienne them finely) and put them in a large bowl. Reduce the water in which the beets have been boiled by half, and then strain and add about a glass of the liquid to the bowl, depending on the texture you will seek later and depending on how salty the liquid is. Peel the cucumbers and chop them finely, or julienne. Add them to the bowl. Chop the dill finely and add it. Chop the eggs very finely and add them. (Some recipes call for sliced eggs to be added later. Usually Poles do this for some reason.) Chop the green parts of spring onions and add them. Now add the kefir and stir thoroughly. Add salt to taste, if necessary. Put aside in a cool place for an hour or more to let the flavours meld.

To thin the soup, pour in more of the beet liquid or add a few ice cubes to both chill the soup and thin it a little with the melted water. To thicken the soup, you may add sour cream. The soup is served very cold, but the side of boiled potatoes should be hot.

Some diners put the hot potatoes into the cold soup. Some leave the hot potatoes on the side. The choice is controversial and leads to many arguments. To preserve peace, watch what the others are doing and do the same. If you are using leftover boiled potatoes, they may be fried up before serving.

Zeppelins (Big Meat Dumplings)

For the dough:
12 raw potatoes
8 boiled potatoes
Salt
Lemon juice (optional)

For the filling:
500 grams minced pork, beef, or veal (or a mixture of all three)
Salt
Pepper
Finely chopped onion (optional)

For the topping:
100 grams bacon cut into bits
1 chopped onion
Sour cream

The Seaside Café Metropolis

Grate the raw potatoes as finely as possible and then, using a tea towel, squeeze out as much of the liquid as you can and save it in a separate bowl. Let it sit for a while. Mash the boiled potatoes, then mix into the raw grated potatoes. After the raw potato liquid has stood for a while, pour off the liquid on top into the pot you will use to boil the dumplings. Potato starch will have settled into the bottom of the bowl. Incorporate this starch into the raw and mashed potato mixture along with some salt, and then mix and knead the mixture thoroughly.

Combine finely chopped onion and minced meat (the onion can be fried first) and add salt and pepper and mix well.

Take about a glass of dough and flatten it out in your palm. Add about a soup spoon of meat in the centre and then fold the dough over the meat, making a Zeppelin-shaped dumpling. Press the edges very tightly.

The Zeppelins should be cooked in salted boiling water for about twenty-five minutes. The water must be kept at a gentle boil at all times. If the dough has not been mixed properly, it will fall apart in the water and you will be left with a mess. Sometimes, the dumplings darken or even turn purple if the potatoes are a little old. You can avoid this by adding a little lemon juice into the dough mixture, if you can find a lemon.

Once the Zeppelins have been cooked, drain them well and serve with a topping of fried bacon bits and fried onions mixed with sour cream. How much you drain the bacon fat before adding the sour cream is up to you. If you expect heavy drinking at the table, be sure not to drain the bacon fat at all.

−8−

Herring and Onions on Warm Potatoes

SOME DISHES ARE iconic for certain places in the way that apple pie is iconic for America and croissants are iconic for France. In Lithuania, herring was a mainstay at every celebratory meal, and common at ordinary meals too. You could be sitting in the cramped kitchen of a friend and find before you a small plate on top of a larger one and an extra fork because the flavour of herring is very strong and you want to remove the first plate and fork before moving on to a main dish.

Why bother with such a fussy, malodorous food? Tradition. Catholics used to have a lot of meat-free fast days and Jews ate no pork, and anyway, there was not always enough food to go around. At the Royal York, we served almost no herring except for a salad of herring and apples, but in Lithuania, such a dish would have been considered a strange mixture of first course and dessert, like serving trout with apricot jam.

I had come to love the simple Lithuanian dish of both the rich and the poor — always a small dish, an opener and not a main course, in which the slight remaining saltiness of the herring contrasted nicely against the thin slivers of pickled onion and a bit of oil, moderated by the blandness of warm boiled potatoes beneath the fish. No wine could bear up with this, and it was best eaten with beer or a shandy, although in Lithuania, adding lemonade to beer was looked upon as idiocy, wanton destruction of good suds.

Why make such a point of this dish? Because it was the only thing Mona would take when Marcel brought her in, and we ate together at the front of the café. She was pale, but in a surprisingly beautiful way, making her skin seem alabaster, and she was slim, but not in a manner that would make it seem that something was wrong.

"So you are sure it's tuberculosis?" I asked.

"Sure as sure can be," said Mona. "I'm lucky to be here at all. They were going to send me straight to the sanatorium. I had to avoid that, but I don't think I'm putting anyone in danger of infection as long as I keep my distance. Except for Marcel, of course. He's a darling, and he won't go away no matter how hard I push."

"But why didn't you do as they said?" I asked.

"I wanted to straighten out a few things before I go. I wanted to see you and explain what's happened. I would like to come back and work here after I get well. This place has a good atmosphere. It makes me feel free as soon as I step inside the doors."

She looked vulnerable. She claimed she needed us, but really she was a star, an attraction at the café. I needed her professionally as well as wanting to help her personally.

"You'll always find a place here with us, but you have to heal yourself first! I understand the sanatoriums do well at treating people with tuberculosis. Take a long rest, and your lungs will get better."

"It's not as simple as that," said Marcel. "We've come here for your help."

"Let me know, and I'll do everything I can."

"The sanatoriums for tuberculosis patients are hellholes. They send people there to die."

"That can't be true anymore. Not so many people get sick of tuberculosis these days."

"They still do, but it's a state secret."

"Aren't there drugs for the illness?"

"Yes, penicillin, but there isn't always enough, and it depends how far the disease has progressed. What we really need is to get her into a good sanatorium with a good doctor and a steady supply of medication."

So it was all about contacts. In other countries, you could pay for first-class treatment, but in the Soviet Union, everything depended on who you knew. If you belonged to the higher class, the nomenklatura, you could get access to better food and medications. But if you didn't belong, you needed to know someone who could pull strings for you.

"Why did you order herring and potatoes?" I asked as she kept picking at the food.

"During the war, I was always hungry. People used to die of hunger back then, falling right down while walking along the street. But the man who found me and trained my voice had resources. I was faint and weak, and he nursed me back to health, mostly with potatoes and onions. Herring if we could find them. He had some dried apples as well. They saved my life. I remember the flavour so well, and the hope the dish gave me."

I recalled how young she had been during the war. "What happened to this …" I searched for the right word. "… *patron* of yours?"

"The Germans put him in the Stutthof prison camp."

"What for?"

"Who knows? They didn't need reasons."

"And after the war?"

"The Soviets deported him to the north. I haven't heard from him. I suppose he's dead."

"You don't sound all that sad about it."

"Well, a lot of people died. As for him, he got what he wanted, and I got what I needed, and as far as I'm concerned, I didn't owe him anything after that."

I watched this woman calmly speaking and eating herring and potatoes as if we were catching up about familiar acquaintances, chatting about old times. Marcel was the one who looked distraught, restlessly shifting in his chair, running his fingers through his long hair and peering closely at her face.

"Marcel, you must know somebody with pull."

"I don't."

"What about your friend Kalistas? His father had enough connections to get him into a meal with a French philosopher."

"I know that, and so does the rest of the city. He doesn't let anyone forget it. But I can't go to him."

"Why not?"

"We're not speaking."

"You're best friends! What's the issue? It can't be anything so important that you wouldn't make up for the sake of Mona."

"I would. I'd humble myself in front of him and ask, but he won't speak to me. If he sees me coming, he turns away. If I phone him, he hangs up."

I thought of the microphones somewhere nearby. I began to drum my fingers on the table, knowing that all the connections were poor and the noise might help muffle our words. Not that I expected any great revelations.

"And what did you do to earn this anger of his?"

"I told Kalistas he was a traitor to his country and an unprincipled turncoat."

The Seaside Café Metropolis

I laughed, which offended Marcel. I drummed my fingers a little louder. "I'm sure you've called him many things in his life. Why was this so bad?"

"Because this time it was true. He sold out. He used his celebrity after that little lunch with Jean-Paul Sartre to insinuate himself into a place at the university."

"Lucky him! A job in the academy at last."

"Teaching Marxism-Leninism."

There it was. Kalistas had been a radical young man until he caught sight of a secure university position. But was he selling out? That was what young people thought; that was what Marcel thought. Although I was relatively young, I suppose I was thinking like an older person who reasoned you had to make a living, and you had to pay lip service. Maybe you even intended to make the world a better place, but you could only do that from within the system rather than from outside it. Of course, once you were inside, you might forget all your good intentions and simply do whatever it took to climb the career ladder. One compromise makes further compromises easier.

I saw no need to keep on drumming.

I later learned that in the West, Marxist-Leninist philosophers would become very chic in the sixties and seventies, but in the Soviet Union, teachers in that field tended to be people who were unsuited for anything else, the kind of position you gave to an aged-out sportsman or your brother-in-law. Still, any university professorship came with certain privileges and prestige, and Kalistas could count on a reasonably nice apartment in Vilnius and two weeks' summer vacation in a suite at the academics' beach house on the Baltic coast.

"We were hoping you might know somebody," said Marcel.

"Not really." I was uncomfortable with the question. I was not part of the party system in the Soviet Union. Admittedly, I was in a privileged niche, a place where the authorities let me be in order to create a kind of fantasy café of freedom. I had no protector unless it was Dominic, who had hired me, but he struck me as the opposite of a party man. Of course, that didn't mean that he wasn't one. The only real party man I knew, the only one I imagined to be a hard-core party man, was Piotr Zorin, who ran the listening post inside the café. If I went to him with this sort of request, I might actually succeed, but then I would be in his debt, and in debt to the forces behind him. It was an unpalatable thought.

But what if my discomfort, my principles, kept Mona out of a good sanatorium? I could be high-minded, or I could help a woman in trouble.

I looked over at the two young lovers across the table from me. Marcel was sitting in front of a cold cup of coffee and fiddling with a cigarette that he held in his hand for a while and then put back in his breast pocket, only to remove it absent-mindedly a little later. He was trying to quit smoking for the sake of her lungs, but the reflex to reach for the cigarette was still there. As for Mona, she was calmness itself. She had had many close calls in her youth — just a child when the war started, an orphan who survived by singing her way among the bombs, the hunger, and the predatory men who wanted to use her. Now she would do her best and then take on whatever came next.

"I don't think I have any solid connection," I said, "but give me a week, and I'll see what I can find."

"Could you make it four days?" asked Marcel. "I'm nervous about dragging this thing out."

I went downstairs after this conversation in order to start a negotiation with Zorin, but I could not stand the thought of capitulation before exhausting other options. I froze before reaching his door, and I stood and surveyed Niko's kitchen realm.

The Seaside Café Metropolis

Down the hall, the children were seated at their little table under the staircase, where they were eating crepes someone had prepared for them. The kitchen itself buzzed with activity, knives flying over vegetables and steam rising from cauldrons stirred by white-hatted chefs. I noticed Julia go to Genius for something while he was sorting mushrooms, and she touched his shoulder to get his attention. He turned and smiled at her, and I envied this ray of warmth. And then, to my astonishment, she gave him a peck on his cheek.

Lucy glanced at me from where she was boning a chicken. I suppose I had stood for longer than I'd intended because Niko finally looked up from a notebook he was studying and raised his eyebrows.

"Were you wanting to say something?" he asked.

"I'm just admiring the operation."

"My staff are self-conscious under your gaze. You don't have enough to do?"

"I was actually wondering about the children down the hall, Monika and Ona."

Parents have ears finely tuned to not only the laughter and cries of their little ones but any mention of them in any way. Without seeing them directly, I could feel the parents' eyes on me at the periphery of my attention as I looked at Niko.

"They pose no problems for us here, if that's what you mean," said Niko. Such a good man, protecting the interests of his staff.

"Bob tells me he has a grandson at loose ends. What happens if we have three children down the way?"

"I see no problem. Do you think we have a problem?" asked Niko.

"How many children are too many children?"

"Good question. You'll have to do something to accommodate them."

Yes, I would have to do something. But what? I went back upstairs to my office.

WHEN I WENT to look for my mother, I found her room empty, which is to say she wasn't there, although her things still were. I couldn't imagine she would be out for long, so I put on the kettle and surveyed the room, its habitual mess, her sweaters and shirts badly folded and stacked on open shelves, the pillow on her bed still unfluffed from last night's sleep. I emptied her ashtray and washed a cup and a plate in the basin.

It occurred to me that she would be happier with her son if I had taken up teaching Marxism-Leninism instead of running a restaurant. I thought that she probably looked upon me as the one who had sold out. But I couldn't be what she wanted me to be. I had a calling, not exactly an exalted one, but a calling nevertheless. I wanted to be in the heart of society, in the hustle-bustle of life, involved in a café that was as much a stage as it was a restaurant.

She wanted to make the world a just place, a better place in her own manner, as my father had tried to do. I did too, in my small way, even though it looked from the outside like I was just doing a job. And what would my father have thought of me in my present role? I wasn't sure, but the odds were his opinion would be closer to my mother's than to mine.

In my darker moments, I believed I was letting down both the living and the dead, to say nothing of the huddled masses, longing to be free.

When I finally made the tea, sat down at her table, and reached for the sugar bowl, I saw a scrap of paper with some handwriting upon it and picked it up.

The Seaside Café Metropolis

Sudden invitation to visit a collective farm. I'll be gone a couple of days.

The note was so much in the style of my mother. Not addressed to me, not put out where I would be likely to see it, and not dated. She could have departed that morning, or she could have left two days ago.

As it turned out, she must have just left. I kept stopping by her room because she had no phone and there was no other way to check up on her. When I finally did come upon her, it was three days later, and she had just come in herself and was unwinding a scarf from around her neck. She was smiling, not because of me but because of something she had been thinking.

"You look awfully happy," I said after we'd greeted one another. "Did you have a good time?"

We sat down over tea.

"I don't like to display my emotions to you, but the truth is, sometimes I begin to wonder if I've made mistakes in my life."

"Oh?"

"I look around here, and this must be one of the best places in the world, and I see misery on people's faces, and I see poor transport and stores short of goods. I get a little depressed. I wonder what I'm doing here. How am I contributing to the growth of worldwide socialism? And let's face it, I haven't contributed so much as observed things since I got here. But that's okay because I thought at least I could bear witness. I thought I could record the progress being made here and maybe write a book about it, I mean the wonders I've seen. But the world here was short on wonders. Until now."

"You found social progress on a collective farm?"

"Yes. They were pouring the concrete for the third silo because the herd has gotten so big they need more silage."

"What is silage?" I asked.

"I don't know. But the cows need it. I think they eat it."

"I thought cows ate grass."

"Don't make me digress from my point."

"What point?"

"About socialist progress! I was telling you about the expansion of the silos. And then the two barns were huge. I spent an evening at the community centre, where we ate pork grown and slaughtered on the farm, and bread from rye grown on the farm. The sugar in the tea came from sugar beets grown right there. And the songs by the farm collective's choir! So full of hope."

I loved my mother. I wouldn't have been there if I did not. I'm not even sure she knew what a Potemkin village was, and given that I wanted something from her, I wasn't going to explain. Instead, I let her speak, and I listened for some time. Eventually, though, I got around to my point. That surely she must know important people. Surely she must know someone who could get one of my employees into what was called a spets hospital, *spets* being short for *special*.

"Those places are an abomination!" she said. Her mood turned as quickly as the sky when a cloud has passed in front of the sun. "They should not even exist. Are you trying to make me depressed again, after everything I've said to you? I'm sure that a regular hospital is just fine, and she should be grateful if she's been offered a place in a sanatorium. If she lived in a capitalist country, she would need to pay, but here she won't. I hear those places are as good as spas."

THERE WAS NOTHING left for me to do but to abase myself before Piotr Zorin. Even if he was unable or unwilling to help me, the

The Seaside Café Metropolis

very fact of my asking would reveal my vulnerability and give him leverage over me.

I made it downstairs, ignored my staff, and walked down the corridor toward the door to Zorin's office. I stood outside it for a while, and as I did, I finally heard the children's voices, which had been there for some time but had been inaudible to me in my distress. I turned to see that there were now three children at the low desk under the staircase: a small boy had joined Monika and Ona. It had to be Bob's grandson. They noticed that I had noticed them, and they fell silent, expectant and unsure.

I couldn't bring myself to knock on Zorin's door. I walked back into the kitchen, where the staff, in particular Genius and Julia, watched me with the same intensity the children had shown a moment ago.

I turned to go back upstairs, and as I went, I heard the quiet laughter of the children from back in the hall. Clearly, they were relieved that I was gone. The same was probably true among the kitchen staff as well.

I was unlocking my office door when Marcel tapped me on the shoulder and, without waiting to be invited inside, told me that Mona had found a place in the best sanatorium in Lithuania.

"Come inside," I said, "and we'll have a cup of coffee."

He sat down across from me, and I ordered the coffee. I was very pleased, delighted she had found a place and I hadn't needed to compromise myself. Marcel, on the other hand, looked sadder than I had ever seen him before.

"Are you sorry to lose her from Vilnius?" I asked. "Don't be! That's the best place for her to get well, and when she does, you can start your lives together all over again."

"That's not true. I had to lose her to save her."

"What do you mean?"

"She went back to her editor, and he's the one who got her the place in the sanatorium."

"I thought he hated her for leaving him."

"A needy, repentant woman is very appealing to a certain kind of man."

I offered him a cigarette, but he turned me down.

"What's the point of quitting smoking if she's gone?" I asked.

"I'm going to get her back. Let the editor cure her first, and then she can abandon him again."

"Don't you think he might have expected a tactic something like that, a false return to him for the sake of his connections?"

"So? What if he did?"

"Mona probably had to make promises to him. She'll be in his debt."

"Promises mean nothing to true love," said Marcel. "Love is stronger than promises."

I didn't have much bible knowledge, and Marcel certainly had less, but he was unknowingly paraphrasing the biblical line about love being as strong as death. I was pretty sure he didn't know the second part about jealousy being as cruel as the grave.

Having made his declaration for me to ponder, he left in an impotent rage. Love is strong. Yes, love is strong, both for good and for ill. We like to romanticize it, but love can tip into obsession, obligation, and even hate. Sometimes love is not as strong as death. Sometimes love is not stronger than the sight of the next pretty face.

After Marcel left, I looked in the niche behind my desk where I had put Alina's boxes of photographs and their negatives. She had disappeared somewhere, and I would need to store the boxes more permanently until she returned. I opened one of them and saw the photographs were simply strewn in there, as if packed in haste. Right on top was a photo of Alina and Lokys, the two of them lying on their backs with him looking up at the camera. Her eyes were closed as if she were sleeping with her head tucked into the arm he held over his head as he stared up aggressively. She was wearing a white T-shirt and had her thumbs hooked into the belt loops of her pants, while his white shirt was rolled up at the sleeves and knotted at the waist. It was practically a fashion photo, but something more too. I thumbed through various other photos, some of them nudes of Alina, one in which she sat with her head on the palm of her hand and looked at the camera through an open window.

They were very powerful photos. The camera loved her, and the atmosphere was haunting somehow, maybe because I knew how Lokys had ended up. But I had no idea what had happened to her or why she had entrusted the boxes to me, a near stranger. I'd have to do something about those photos eventually. They were too good to be left unseen in some storeroom. I wasn't really sure what one did with good photographs.

Melancholy crept up on me, and I went downstairs to the kitchen to speak to Niko, but he was busy instructing one of the chefs on how to make a nest of sugar threads. Lucy was at a counter at the back with a massive half-full bag of washed carrots on her left and an equally large basin half full of chopped carrots on her right.

With her hair back in a bun and tucked under a white cap, she was focused on her work, but she must have felt my eyes on her because she turned around.

"Checking up on the help?"

"Don't cut yourself."

"I'm a professional. I could do this with my eyes closed."

"Cocky."

"But accurate."

"How is your French coming along?"

"Well enough. I've reached the letter C in *Larousse Gastronomique*. Have you ever heard of a man called Curnonsky?"

"No."

"It's a pseudonym. He is French, born in 1872, a great gourmand. They say eighty restaurants held a table for him every night in Paris between the wars, just in case he showed up. He ate out every lunch and dinner of his life and had something to say about all kinds of food."

"Like what?"

"Like, 'Good cooking is when things taste of what they are.'"

"Very insightful. But the French also say, 'The sauce saves the fish,' which means the opposite, don't you think?"

"Well, if you're going to get competitive with quotes, I could add, 'Hunger is the best sauce in the world.'"

I thought about this for a moment, and of course I knew she was right. The war and the Siberian exile were quite recent in Lithuania, so the memory of hunger was still in the air. But I couldn't let her off so easily.

"Was this Curnonsky a chef?"

"Not really. He ate more than he cooked."

"So why should I take him seriously?"

"Because he was a philosopher of food, not a glutton. Books need readers and theatres need audiences, and the best among them can be critics, if they're not jaded and bitter. But what about an audience for food? What good would it do to devote hours to a special dish and then serve it to someone who didn't care, or someone who had no taste, or someone who gobbled up whatever was in front of him? An informed diner rewards the labour of the chef."

"Who are you quoting now?"

"Nobody. I just thought that up."

"How old are you again?"

"None of your business."

"You admire this Curnonsky."

"The French certainly do, or did. I don't know if he's still alive. That book of yours came out in 1938. But can you think of a Lithuanian who is admired for what he had to say about food? All we have in our culinary history is a vegetarian intellectual who said he refused to eat corpses, meaning meat."

"Life here is provincial," I said.

"Not if you're from here, like I am. Vilnius is the capital. It's no province to me. To you, maybe, with your fancy pedigree."

"Fancy pedigree? I grew up the son of a chambermaid in a place referred to as Hogtown. And anyway, who is being pretentious? You're quoting from a French book. How is it even possible you have reached the letter C? You don't speak French, and you have no training in it. You probably have to look up every single word in the dictionary."

"I do, but only the first time I see it. I am good with languages."

"But you work long hours here."

"I study in my free time."

"Don't you have a boyfriend?"

"That's none of your business either, but the answer is no."

I didn't know what to say to fill the silence that followed. Soviet workplaces were hierarchical, and the staff normally didn't talk back to their superiors, but if they ever did, they would be slapped back down to their appropriate places. Thrown off kilter, I fell back on my earlier offer to have her work upstairs.

"The answer to that remains what it was before, no."

I was getting a little exasperated. "Do you always answer every question with *no*?"

"It depends on the question."

Once again, I heard the laughter of children from down the hall. Lucy smiled at the sound, and I had the uncomfortable feeling she was smiling at me as well.

I SHOULD HAVE felt the happiest I had been since my arrival in the Lithuanian Soviet Socialist Republic. My café continued to be the epicentre of both fashion and freedom and the height of culinary achievement. Well, frankly, the competition was not all that strong, but my achievement had to count for something. Still, my itch to escape the Soviet Union, ever present but moderated by my need to take care of my mother, began to return, and some nights I dreamed of the Royal York Hotel, with its high-beamed lobby and its grand ballroom painted in gilt.

Through that lobby streamed travellers off the trains from Montréal and New York, Detroit and Chicago. Some had rolled all the way across the country from Vancouver and points in between. The best performers, the latest fashions, the newest turns of phrase all appeared on that stage.

I now resided in a reasonably good world with the brothers John and Joe holding the outside at bay at the door. My Seaside Café Metropolis was inhabited by older, successful customers in the back and an evolving cast of young bohemians at the café up front along with Tomas Klimas hustling potential traitors or KGB talent with his carafes of cognac. New people came and went along with the regulars, providing an amusing and changing cavalcade. Bob oversaw the main floor of the café for me while I arranged orders in my office, and downstairs Niko and his team laboured and Zorin listened.

I had all I could possibly want given the circumstances I lived in, yet something was missing.

MARCEL SHOWED UP again some weeks later. He had not been at the café since Mona had rejoined the editor, and I had had no word of what had followed that reunion. As usual, Marcel appeared at my office when he needed something. He was wan and dishevelled, and his fingertips were yellow, which showed that not only had he taken up smoking again, he was doing it with a vengeance.

"Do you have access to a car?" he asked, leaning forward with his hands on my desk like a general calling for more armour at the front.

"It depends. Why do you need a car?"

"Mona is very sick. She sent word that she wants to see me."

"Where is she?"

"In a clinic in Birštonas."

Hardly anyone or even any enterprise owned a car in those days, and the café was no exception. But I had contacts in the Ministry of Agriculture, and I began to work the telephone. Marcel sat across from my desk, chain-smoking all the while, tapping his foot, sighing, and otherwise making his impatience felt. It took me a couple of hours, but I eventually got a car for four bottles of white Moldovan wine. They even let me drive it myself for the addition of the gift of a bottle of Armenian cognac.

"I thought there'd be a driver. You're going too?" asked Marcel. He never was one to waste his reserves of gratitude.

"She is my employee, and I love her almost as much as you do."

"Everybody loves her, but not as well as I do."

"I know that."

Birštonas was an old spa town a couple of hours away, the Baden-Baden of Lithuania with the requisite mud and salt baths. Between the wars, it had been a major tourist centre, and now it was something like a town for invalids, those who needed long-term rehabilitation. The residences and hospitals lay in a pinewood park on the banks of the slow-moving Nemunas River, a very pretty site.

Mona was to be found on the terrace of the Tulip Hospital, seated in a wheelchair with a wrap over her shoulders and a blanket on her lap although we were in full sun and the day was warm enough for shirtsleeves. Before her, the river flowed in its calm and indifferent way, and a fisherman was anchored near the opposite wooded bank.

She was sleeping when we came upon her, and Marcel did not want to wake her, so we pulled up chairs and waited. Her face was very pale, but the illness had not diminished her beauty in any way. She seemed calm while at rest, but she still held a handkerchief in the hand that lay on her lap. The handkerchief was lightly streaked with blood. Her other hand lay on the armrest, and Marcel eventually reached forward to put his own hand upon it.

"It's very cold," he said of her hand, and he looked at me in alarm. But I could see her chest rising and falling steadily, albeit slowly.

"Don't be skittish. You've come to visit her, not to frighten her. How did she get word to you?"

"By letter."

"So that was a couple of days ago. Maybe she was in crisis then but she's gotten better now."

Marcel examined her face. "You must be right," he said. "She looks very well. She must be on the mend."

"Of course I'm on the mend," she said, opening her eyes and turning her hand over to squeeze Marcel's hand. He reached to embrace her awkwardly in the chair.

"Are you sure you feel better?" asked Marcel.

"Yes, silly. Don't be so alarmed."

"But your letter."

"I just missed you. I wanted to see you, and I thought you might not come otherwise. I'm sorry for frightening you."

"It's all right. I'm just happy to see you. Have they been treating you all right here?"

"Very well."

"I'm sorry I couldn't provide you with this. I feel terrible that you had to return to that monstrous editor to get this sort of treatment."

She patted his hand. "Don't blame yourself for what you don't have. Remember, I love you for what you are, not for what you have. But I want to ask you a favour."

"Anything."

"First, use his name."

"Whose?"

"The man you call the editor."

Marcel bristled for a moment and then calmed himself. "All right. What is it?"

"Adam. An easy name to remember."

"I'll call him Adam. But why does this matter?"

"Because I want the two of you to be friends."

He let go of her hand. "What? This is all too strange. Mona, you're asking too much of me. How can I be friends with the man who treated you so badly in the past, the one who lords over you now?"

She sighed.

"You know, Marcel, I have had some hard times in my life."

"I realize that. And it's so unfair you have to be sick now. But you are getting better, right?"

"Yes, yes. Sure. But the other hard times I went through were chaotic: there was gunfire, and there were bombs. There were marauding men, and there was hunger so long and relentless I could hardly think of anything but where I could get my next bite to eat. But this time, I've been able to think. I've looked at the flowing river for days, either out here or from my window, and it's made me feel peaceful. I want others to be at peace too, and that's why I want you and Adam to get along. Do you think you could do that?"

As Mona said this, she looked over at me in a manner I couldn't understand. I was used to being the man in the background, not much more than the stage manager looking on from the wings. She wanted me to know something, but I didn't understand what it might be.

"Mona, please. It's not an easy thing you're asking. When you get well, will you go to …" I could tell Marcel had intended to call him the editor but paused to correct himself. Yet he could not bear to utter the man's real name.

"I promised I would return to Adam, yes."

"So then how can I get along with that man?"

"For my sake? I thought you loved me."

"Of course I love you. That's the whole point."

"Then promise you'll do it."

"Why is this so important to you? Why can't you just forget me? Isn't that what you do with old lovers? And don't the old lovers have the right to be bitter because of their loss?"

"You have that right, but I'm asking you." She was going to say more, but she was overcome with a short fit of coughing. To my relief, no more blood appeared on her handkerchief.

"Marcel, dear, could you go inside and get me a glass of water?"

I was about to rise and do it for him, but she made a small gesture with her hand, which I read as a signal for me to stay.

"The water should be tepid. Neither too hot nor too cold."

He bounded off like a man after a bandage for his lover's bleeding wound. She turned to me then.

"I don't have much time because he'll be back soon. It takes forever for the water to run warm from the tap here, so that should slow him down."

"Is there something I should know?" I asked.

"Yes. Listen, I'm not just talking about peace and brotherhood for the sake of some lofty goal. I have Marcel's interests in mind. He's young and passionate, but he's reckless, and he'll ruin his career through romantic obstinacy. Yet he has talent. And Adam likes to have protegés. Marcel could be one of them if only they'd get along."

"Mona, you're sick. Why are you doing this? Think of your health, not Marcel's livelihood."

"I don't have much time."

"Nonsense," I said, but just then Marcel returned with an aide dressed in white and carrying the glass of water with the care of a priest carrying a chalice.

"He insisted on coming along," said Marcel.

"Here is the water for the patient," said the aide, "but I must warn you that she is contagious. No one else must even touch the glass. Actually, you should keep your distance as well."

He set the glass down at her side and waited, and Mona took a sip to please him. Nodding at us all, the aide walked away, and Marcel sat down beside her.

"Well," she said. "Can you do what I'm asking? Can you be friends with Adam?"

I watched Marcel struggle with the idea. He wouldn't say it out loud, but after a time he looked down and nodded.

"I take it that means yes."

He nodded again.

"Good. Because Adam is here. He's been waiting for you to arrive as I knew you would. I've spoken to him too, and he's going to come out here a little later."

Marcel looked up at her. "Why are you doing this? Why do you want to make me suffer?"

"It will be better in the end. Listen, I can't talk anymore for a bit. I'm very tired. Let me rest for an hour, and then I want us to meet here again. I'll ask Adam to be here. All right?"

"I suppose so."

"Don't sulk. I've been very sick, so you need to be kind to me."

He nodded and then joined me, and we walked to the far end of the terrace where we stood for a while, watching the water flow by. A broad promenade ran along the riverbank, and Marcel walked with me there. The sunshine was pleasant. Over the river, clouds of gnats hovered in their mating dances, and further along the walkway sat a few wheelchairs with their occupants facing the sun.

"She was lucky to get a place here," I said.

"No thanks to me."

"Completely thanks to you. You didn't want her to settle for second- or third-best. And you're the one who permitted her to approach Adam to take her back."

"I hate using his name."

"But she asked you to."

"I know, I know. But some things are just unbearable. Why does she want me to be his friend?"

I could say nothing, so I just shrugged. We walked for a long time to the sound of songbirds and the gentle swishing of the trees in the park beside us when a breeze came up. We sat for a while at the end of the boardwalk and then began our slow return. As we approached Mona's terrace, I could see she had returned, and tall Adam stood beside her, bending down from time to time to speak earnestly with her. When she saw us approach, she beckoned with some desperation.

"Come quickly," she said as soon as we were in earshot.

Adam turned to look at us, an elegant man in black with equally elegant specks of grey across both temples. But his look was far from elegant. It seemed as if he had been weeping.

"She is very ill. I have been trying to get her back inside. Please get an attendant to wheel her back in."

But Mona was holding one of the wheels of the chair so she could not be moved.

"I won't go," she said breathlessly. "The two of you must shake hands."

Marcel was in a panic, confused, but his impulse was to obey and so he thrust his hand forward, and Adam took it in his.

"Now will you go in?" asked Adam.

"Not yet." She could barely speak. I could hear gurgling from inside her lungs, and bits of pink spittle were coming up.

"Promise that you will love each other as brothers. Promise that you will help each other."

"But I have nothing to offer him," said Marcel.

"Say his name."

"I have nothing to offer Adam," said Marcel.

"One day you will. And Adam, as for you …"

But she could not go on. She was seized by a fit of coughing that rattled her body, and then she leaned forward and vomited what seemed to be an enormous amount of blood on the blanket that covered her knees. Adam took the initiative and wheeled her quickly to the sanatorium door, where he was met by an attendant, and the two went in.

Marcel was going to follow, but I held on to his arm because he would only get in the way. He stood there, stunned, and then turned to me with anguish written all over his face. And then he looked down at the place where Mona's wheelchair had been, where the blood lay splattered on the tiles. Her side table still stood there too, along with the glass of water she had drunk from earlier that day. In a movement so swift and unexpected I could do nothing, Marcel reached forward and took the glass and drank down the contents before turning and looking at me, the glass still in his hand, his expression one of rage and defiance.

MONA DIED TOWARD evening, having suffered from an unstoppable hemorrhage that drained the last of her strength. The three of us had been sitting in a waiting room, not saying much. Once, Adam had gone out with Marcel for a cigarette.

"I didn't know you smoked," I'd said to Adam.

"I don't," he'd replied.

Now, after a long spell of silence, Adam finally spoke.

"She went through so much in her life! She was such a survivor. How cruel that something like this took her down."

"How cruel," Marcel echoed.

"Will you permit me to make the burial arrangements?" Adam asked.

"I'd like to help, but I have no money."

"That doesn't matter. I know she would have wanted both of us there."

We sat in silence for a long time. After a while, a nurse came out in her white cloth cap and a white gown speckled with fine dots of red.

"Go home now," she said. "There is nothing for you to do, and the body is being prepared to be sent to Vilnius."

"One more look?" asked Marcel.

"Absolutely not. You don't want to see her now, and the doctor is doing an autopsy. It's better to remember her as she was."

As it turned out, Adam had been dropped off in Birštonas by a Ministry of Culture car, but the driver was not able to return until the next day, so I offered to take him with us. Marcel sat in the front with me, and Adam was in the back. The sun had set by then, and the road was not good or familiar to me, so I drove along slowly, the headlights jerking down sharply whenever I hit a pothole. I slowed to a crawl.

"You know, Marcel," said Adam, "I happen to be aware that

The Seaside Café Metropolis

the Ministry of Defence is putting out a call for applications for a big historical painting for their main boardroom. Do you think you might be able to come up with something for that?"

"I'm sure I could do a very fine painting. But there's no chance they'd accept a proposal from an artist like me."

"Let me worry about that."

It was dark inside the car, but I could make out Marcel's face a bit even in the dimness. It seemed to take a few moments for the offer to sink in, and then his face became slightly more alive than it had been for hours.

"Thank you," he said. "I'll put something together after the funeral."

"Yes, good. But don't wait too long."

Herring and Onions on Warm Potatoes

2 medium herrings
1 kilogram potatoes
1 medium onion
1 glass water
4 soup spoons vinegar
1–2 soup spoons sugar
Pepper
Cooking oil
Milk (optional)

Salted herring from the barrel must soak in a few changes of water or milk overnight or longer. Cut off the heads and skin and bone the fish (saving the roe or milt to be fried as a separate dish for unwanted visitors) and cut the filets into delicate pieces. Cut the onion into rings. Submerge the fish and onion rings in the water, vinegar, and sugar mix for an hour or more.

Pour off the liquid. Spoon herring and onions onto warm boiled potatoes. Drizzle oil on top. Season with pepper.

If the dish is served at home, the host must watch carefully to make sure no guest chokes on any of the missed small bones. It is not recommended to eat this dish alone.

Burnt Crepes with Sweet Cheese

A SERIES OF small difficulties presented themselves to me on a cold winter morning and then began to cascade as the hours progressed. It was a day when no one wanted to sit near the frosted front window, when every opening of the door brought a swirl of frosty air to nip at the ankles of the diners, and when we received a surprise shipment of two hundred kilos of butter, arriving in a pair of massive upright blocks.

They were packed in flimsy crates, like the coffins of frozen paupers, set upright to save floor space.

In the land of shortages, these sorts of appearances were uncommon gifts; if you happened to receive a sudden opportunity to lay your hands on rare items such as arabica coffee or beluga caviar, which could be kept on a shelf or in a storeroom (locked up to deter thieves!), you were in luck, but the gift became a white elephant if the product required refrigeration. And of course our kitchen cold room was uncharacteristically full.

This small difficulty grew a little bigger when a note from the assistant deputy minister arrived, saying that the minister of agriculture himself had seen to the gift of butter, and he would be curious to find out what we had managed to do with this sort of wealth.

I had my two tall crates of butter set in the loading area out back because the weather was cold enough that the butter would not come to any harm and no clever crows or industrious vermin were about. To save space, I left them upright but leaned them against a wall so they would not tip over.

"Any ideas?" I asked Niko.

"We could reduce the volume by making clarified butter, but the product doesn't have quite the same taste as fresh butter. And Lithuanian butter is so good it would be a shame to do that. I understand Polish tourists sometimes take Lithuanian butter back home with them in order to compare it with their own local butter."

I gave him a skeptical look.

"Well, what do you think they might want to take home as a souvenir from this blessed Soviet republic? The heart of their historic hero Józef Piłsudski is buried in the cemetery here, but that stays. What else is there to take home as a souvenir?"

"Let's let the crates sit for a while until we think of something. The weather doesn't look like it's changing, but I want to make sure some scavenging dog doesn't show up."

Little problems never come alone. They multiply like mice, which are nuisance creatures in the singular but horrifying in the plural when you see them streaming out of your box of biscuits.

As I was talking to Niko, I heard the habitual high voices of the three children down the hall, amusing themselves while their parents worked the restaurant. Their chatter came to a halt when Zorin's door came flying open. He looked first to the children, who froze under his stony glance, and then over to me, where I was standing with Niko. He came over directly.

"Comrade Argentine, I have borne your insolence for too

The Seaside Café Metropolis

long. Those brats down the hall interfere with the work my colleagues and I carry on in the office. Their presence is intolerable."

"How, exactly, do the children interfere with your work?"

"We are sound engineers. We cannot have squawks and screeches distracting us."

"Distracting you from what?"

"This is none of your concern. Those children must go, and they must go immediately."

"To move the children now, I'd need to send them home with three of my staff. I might as well close the café in that case, and the minister of agriculture is expected soon. I'm sure he wouldn't be too pleased."

"Your minister of agriculture is like some kind of trump card you choose to play again and again. I sometimes wonder if he isn't mythical. I have never seen the minister here, and anyway, you are not the minister, and I remind you that my minister of communications takes precedence over yours. Furthermore, I have called the workplace safety committee office, and they are on their way to investigate this dangerous situation."

"Dangerous to whom?"

"To both the children and the workers. Get them out, and get them out now."

I was pretty sure the threat of the impending workplace safety committee inspectors was false. But even if it wasn't, in the sludgy bureaucracy of the Soviet Union, it would take weeks for the inspectors to arrive. Still, one could never be sure.

"Give me a little time."

"I said immediately."

"That's how long immediately seems to be around here."

"Are you disparaging the Soviet Union?"

"I never mentioned the Soviet Union. Are you the one who is implying an insult?"

Zorin was enraged, but he chose not to challenge me on the delay. He stormed back into his office, and when I turned around, I could see the whole staff had frozen to watch the exchange. Julia was already beginning to untie her apron to take her daughter home.

"We are busy," said Niko. "I can't really afford to lose the help."

"I'll see what I can do."

I went upstairs with the intention of finding someone to look after the children for a little while, just to put them somewhere else for a few hours until Zorin cooled down or left at the end of his shift. But as Niko had said, the restaurant was busy. Unusual circumstances call for unusual solutions.

Sitting alone at the front of the café was Sarunas, the sculptor, the last of my young bohemians. The rest had managed to insinuate themselves into the academy or into the press, but poor Sarunas was finding that sculptors were harder to place. His luckier and more prosperous friends had left their perches at my café, and now Sarunas sat there alone like a bird whose flock had already migrated. I had come up intending to ask Bob to help out with the children, as after all, one of them was his grandchild, but he was useful to me, and Sarunas probably needed something to do.

"Why me?" he asked, flabbergasted, when I told him he was to take care of three small children for the next couple of hours. It was as if I had asked him to step in to pilot an airplane. He tensed and put out his cigarette, and the look of terror was almost comical.

"I chose you because I have no one else," I said. "I have done you favours, and now you can return one."

It never occurred to him he might repay a debt from the past. Instead, he tried to capitalize on the present.

"What's in it for me?"

I thought for a moment. "A dinner."

The terror evaporated, and the calculation of what he could get out of me set in.

"A dinner for two," he countered, "so I can invite a girl."

I was about to agree when he upped the ante.

"With wine."

"In that case, you have the children for the entire afternoon."

That took care of the short term, but I needed to take care of the longer term. My staff were my family, and I couldn't merely throw their children back at them. I needed to help out. I told Sarunas to use my office but also to take the children out for a little while, for a kind of recess, with their small bodies well wrapped, though, against the cold.

I went back downstairs to ask Niko for a cardboard box, a bottle of wine, a good knife, and the loan of one person for fifteen minutes.

"We are very busy," he remonstrated.

"It won't take long."

He nodded toward Lucy, and she took the knife she already had in hand. I carried the cake box and bottle of wine, and we went outside.

"Did you want to get a coat?" I asked her.

"It will just distract the chef if he sees me pass by again. What did you need me to do?"

The crates of butter were upright. Why they should be packaged in such an unusual manner was a mystery that I couldn't explore at the moment. The crates were flimsy, and, good with a knife as always, Lucy found the blade was enough to pry open the front of one of them. Before us stood a golden pillar of butter almost as tall as a man.

"This is fantastic!" said Lucy. "There's a deficit of butter across town, and you have enough here to melt down and bathe in it."

"Yes. I need to cut the top off the butter, a piece about the size of a cake, and put it in this box."

Lucy looked at me oddly but began to use her knife to do as I'd asked. It's not easy to cut such a mass of butter, but Lucy did it without causing too much damage. I laughed a little as she went about her work.

"What so funny?" she asked.

"Back in Toronto where I was born and lived, we had an agricultural fair every November. It was a favourite of schools to send children out to learn about farm animals. We'd all buy soft apple cider and pretend to get drunk on it."

"And what does this have to do with butter?"

"There was an annual butter sculpture kept in a refrigerated display case. Amazing detail! I recall the sculpture of a cowboy, from cowboy hat all the way down to six-gun."

"It sounds like a waste of good food."

"Not a waste. The butter was put to use later."

When I had what I needed, she tapped the front of the crate back into place with the butt of her knife. I asked Lucy to do me a favour and look over Sarunas in case his babysitting got out of control. As for me, I had around four kilos of butter in a cake box and a bottle of wine, and I set off to solve one of my bigger problems.

I DIDN'T KNOW much about children in general and even less about children in the Soviet Union, but one of the claims the state was starting to make was that both parents would soon be free to work because daycare nurseries were arriving in Vilnius.

Almost twenty years after the end of the Second World War, there were still pockets of ruins all throughout the centre of town, which had been "liberated" building by building. The fleeing

The Seaside Café Metropolis

Germans had set some of the buildings afire, and the attacking Soviets were enthusiastic users of new flame-throwing devices.

Nurseries were beginning to be built atop the rubble in some spots. But as with everything else, there was a shortage, so grandparents, maiden aunts, and even bachelor uncles ended up taking the overflow. I didn't have any of those available, unless my own mother, and she had done an indifferent job with me.

You needed to know the right people to get a spot in a new daycare, or be high up in the party apparatus, or find some other way to get in. I was in the category of those trying to find some other way.

The only daycare I knew of was ten minutes away, a complex in a pretty location overseeing the river Neris, which wended its way through Vilnius. The building was low and broad, postwar stucco, but relatively well-kept because it was so new. I had noticed it in my rambles in the past but had never had a need to go in. This time, I opened the gate and walked around the back to find a pleasant if small playground. It was empty now in the cold weather. I returned to the front and came in to a very large room that was part cloakroom and part corridor, but again, with the typical heedlessness for wasted space so common in the USSR. There was no space anywhere for people to live, yet official buildings, schools, and daycares were full of dead space where you could have set up ten tables for a billiard hall.

I walked through a large, empty classroom, then a playroom, and finally entered a dormitory where a few dozen children lay sleeping on tiny cots against opposite walls with a broad aisle between them. Even toddlers were obedient in the Soviet Union, and these children napped with hands crossed on the blankets over them or tucked under their heads if they slept on their sides.

I came across my first adults in the staff lunchroom, where half a dozen women in cardigans sat around cups of tea, smoking and chatting. The children's nap hour was their break time, and they didn't greet my interruption with much enthusiasm, but they did steer me to the director's office down the hall.

Hair dye in the Soviet Union came in shades never seen in the West, and Madame Director had chosen an orange hue that looked like a cross between the colour of a brass spittoon and an automotive emergency flare. She would have made an excellent tour guide because her head was as bright as the lamp on top of an ambulance, so a distracted tourist would see her easily whenever he glanced over to find his group. On top of this, she was burly and packed tightly into a severe grey business suit.

She had me figured out the moment I walked in.

"Cake and wine," she said. "It must be someone's birthday, or else you want something."

"Not cake, just a little something I brought along as a gesture of respect. It's butter, actually. I have the good fortune to have stumbled into an excess. But it needs to be kept cold."

She showed a flicker of interest. Since there was a deficit of butter, she could probably use it, but as far as bribes went, my offerings were small potatoes. Still, never one to waste a bribe, even if it was insufficient, she called over one of her assistants to put away the butter and the wine.

"You have come for a reason," she said.

"Yes. I am the director of the Seaside Café Metropolis, and three of my most important employees have children that require daycare. Not for long, though. A couple of them will be ready for elementary school soon."

"Not your problem, is it?" she asked.

"Yes, it has become my problem."

"But not mine."

"No. Yet I was hoping you could be a solution."

"Let me explain something to you," she said, and she went on

The Seaside Café Metropolis

to list a series of requirements for entry into a daycare, beginning with registration a year ahead of time, health checkups, residence in the local neighbourhood, references from employers, and many other details I chose not to pay any attention to until she came to two final stumbling blocks — a shortage of funds due to cuts in allocations and a shortage of room. She started off this litany with a grimace but finished it with a wide smile of contentment, having proven her case.

"You have some problems of your own, I see," I said.

"Who doesn't have problems?"

"If I could solve your problems, maybe you could solve mine."

"Maybe. But it seems unlikely. Would you like me to return your gift of butter and wine?"

"Those were just a down payment. I will bring you much more to make it worthwhile to take in the three children I named."

"Why bother? What you want is impossible."

But she remained mildly interested, maybe more curious than convinced I could actually do anything to change her mind.

I asked for the use of a telephone, and she obliged.

THREE HOURS LATER, from fifty metres away on Lenin Prospect, I could see Bob standing outside the Seaside Café Metropolis, looking up and down the street. I didn't hasten my step. Whatever new problem lay in front of me could be handled in due course.

"You're finally back!" said Bob.

"That's true. What is it?"

"The minister of agriculture is standing out on the back dock along with Sarunas, the children, Niko, and even Zorin."

Along with the problems of the day, people were accumulating in startling numbers and unusual combinations. If I'd been in an Old Testament frame of mind, I might have been wondering why God was testing me.

What Bob didn't tell me, and what I discovered on arrival at the back, was that Lucy stood there with the others, holding a bowl filled with butter shavings. I'm not quite sure why I noticed her first when the rotund minister of agriculture was beaming over the scene while Zorin stood aside, clutching his hands together like a villain in a melodrama.

"Mr. Argentine, you have exceeded my expectations. You probably don't even know how many problems you have solved for me."

"No," I said. "I'm not sure what problems I have solved at all. I'm just grateful for the gift of butter."

"But what you've done with it is outstanding."

I looked to see that the front panel was off the pillar of butter and Sarunas had carved a bust into the top, a lovely likeness of a Soviet agricultural hero of some kind, a young man with a determined face and buttery eyes looking up to the future.

I looked at Lucy.

"I told him what you'd said about the winter fair in Canada. About the butter sculpture."

"The kids were driving me crazy," said Sarunas. "I took them out here to distract them."

"It's too cold out here," said the minister. "Let's all go inside, and I'll explain something to you."

"What about the children?" I asked.

"Bring in the children too. I love children. Give them something nice to eat. Don't you like children?"

I looked to Zorin, who shrugged.

Downstairs in the kitchen, the minister sat at the family table, a real working man among the working classes. I don't want to give the impression that he was all jolliness and support. He could roar when he wanted to, and even Zorin, for all his disdain for the Ministry of Agriculture, kept up a respectful mien until the minister gave him a look, making it understood his presence was no longer required, and Zorin retreated to his office. The minister asked that Sarunas join us over a cup of tea.

"Very good likeness out there, young man. Do you think you could carve more figures?"

"Yes, of course. I've been trained," said Sarunas. "I could do Bernini's *Ecstasy of Saint Teresa* in butter."

The minister had never heard of Bernini. He let it pass. "I imagine a full-size woman with long tresses and a country dress."

"I could do that. No problem. I'd just need a cold room."

"Then you're hired."

"I'm hired?"

"We're going to break into the Polish butter market. Their tourists love our butter, but there aren't enough of them, and we need to do something with excess production once this deficit is over. Poles have butter of their own, of course, but not as good as ours. There is going to be an agricultural fair in Warsaw next fall, and we need to make an impression. I have visions of not one sculpture but a whole panorama of dairy production. Are you up to the challenge?"

One must always agree with ministers, and Sarunas agreed without quite grasping what it all meant. The minister sat back in satisfaction and looked fondly at the children down the hall, now out of their winter clothes and drawing pictures at the low table.

"I'm trying to find a better place for those children," I said.

"Yes," the minister agreed, though his thoughts were clearly elsewhere. "But I'm sure there's no rush. Let them be until you find the right spot."

I wished Zorin were there to hear the words, but I could quote them, and they might buy me some time. As for Sarunas, it looked like our bohemian sculptor had found his ticket out of the doldrums.

AS FOR MY own ticket, Dominic the architect had been willing to discuss my idea, and his charm and connections were enough to eventually bring the carrot-headed daycare director with us into the massive front cloakroom of the daycare centre.

"I don't understand what you propose," she said.

"A children's café should be clear enough," said Dominic.

"I've never heard of a children's café."

"Neither has anyone else. It will make you famous."

"I don't want to be famous. I just want my daycare to do well."

"And it will. You have an excellent and scenic setting. We will institute a café here where only children, or parents with children, will be permitted to visit. We will cover the walls with art suitable for children and bring in small tables, and you will become a thriving centre."

"I'm already a thriving centre."

"Yes, but short of cash and panache. The children's café will help to supplementarily fund the daycare at the back, and it will bring you praise from the ministries."

"Which ministries?"

"Does it matter?"

"Your idea is outlandish. I need permission. I can't do anything without the approval of my superiors."

"Of course, but I'll take care of that."

"And if it's a café, we'd have to feed them."

"Children's food," I said. "Crepes, cheese dumplings, cinnamon toast and tea. My own café could help to keep you supplied."

The Seaside Café Metropolis

She let this information sink in and then turned to Dominic. "I don't understand. Why are you doing this? Why make more work for yourself?"

"I am doing it because I am an architect. I design spaces, and this will be a wonderful new space."

She wavered, but it looked like she might agree.

"Just one thing," said Dominic. "There are three children we need to get into this institution in the coming days. Sooner would be better."

The redhead looked at him wryly. She knew how things were done. What he offered was good, but there would be a price. She was willing to pay it.

IN SUBSEQUENT YEARS, the children's cafés of Vilnius and even of Kaunas would go on to gain great acclaim. They polished the reputation of the somewhat gritty Soviet Union. Dominic was already quite well regarded for his design of the Seaside Café Metropolis, and this children's version eventually made him beloved of parents. The cafés went on to feature murals and mosaics, and they were used in television documentaries for propaganda purposes in the West.

As for our sculptor, Sarunas, he was well on the path to success, having taken the first steps in butter. Maybe *steps* is the wrong word. Let me just say he had begun to carve out a buttered role for himself.

IT IS EASY to forget the instruments of our success, the people who make things happen. Many days later, after Sarunas had been launched and the children had been placed in the daycare, I asked Lucy to come to my office.

"You made this all happen," I said. "If not for you, Sarunas never would have started to carve the block of butter."

She shrugged. "I was just a link in a chain of events," she said. "You were the one who told me about the butter sculptures at the winter fair in Canada."

"But you were a link in my chain of events, all with a happy ending. I'm grateful."

"Thank you very much," she said as she turned to go away, and while I should have been happy with all the outcomes, I didn't say anything more, and yet I felt as if there was something I had forgotten to say.

Burnt Crepes with Sweet Cheese

As the ancient Lithuanian proverb tells us, the first crepe always burns until you get the pan to the right temperature. Children love sweet cheese crepes, but if your resources do not permit you to waste flour, or if you should suffer the misfortune of a simultaneous deficit of both butter and cooking oil, remember, you are still obligated to feed the children. You may serve them cheese dumplings instead, which require neither oil nor butter and will help build sturdy socialist bodies.

Cheese Dumplings

1 egg
500 grams farmer's cheese
1 glass flour
2 soup spoons sugar
A pinch of salt

The Seaside Café Metropolis

Bring a pot of salted water to a boil.

Beat the egg and mix with the farmer's cheese, salt, sugar, and flour until well blended. Take a handful of dough the size of an egg and roll it between your hands and onto a cutting board to make a snake the thickness of your ring finger if you are a man or your middle finger if you are a woman. Cut pieces of dumpling from this and the other snakes in a uniform size. Drop the dumplings into the boiling water, and make sure they do not stick to the bottom. After they rise to the top, let them boil for two or three minutes more. Drain and serve.

For the topping, use jam or sour cream or both, or, if you have finally found some butter, you can use that.

Buckwheat Groats

THE CLIMATE IN Vilnius was similar to the climate in Toronto, and so by June, all of nature was bursting out and the scent of spring turned my head for a moment when I stepped outside in the morning. I sighed and went to work. I loved my work, but it was all indoors, and sometimes I felt like I was missing something, although I was never sure what it might be. A hike in the mountains? There were no mountains in Lithuania, and I owned no shoes appropriate for a hike. I dismissed the moment of romance.

As the seasons changed, my problems evolved as problems do.

Buckwheat had been unknown to me before I went to Lithuania, and it never really made an impression even there until I started to work in Lithuanian restaurants and the customers there asked for it. Buckwheat is a nutty seed eaten widely in Eastern Europe because it can grow on poor soil and in cold climates, and it is so nutritious you can practically live on it if you have nothing else. Imagine a very nutty brown rice. Even after I did find out what it was, I didn't pay much attention to it because it is a modest food, like barley or corn grits, the sort of food that is necessary but banal and even irrelevant to establishments aiming for sophistication.

But diners want a combination of novelty and familiarity, so we served buttered buckwheat groats alongside pork medallions, a dish that Russian visitors liked very much, and we had a lot of Russian visitors. Moscow still oversaw most of what went on in Lithuania, whose locals could be *somewhat* trusted to manage their socialist utopia according to directives but who needed to be checked upon frequently, *just to be sure.*

Linas was Piotr Zorin's eyes and ears in the kitchen. A fresh-faced country boy if ever there was one, he wore a broad smile and eyes that looked innocent of any sophistication or knowledge beyond the surface of things — and sometimes barely the surface. He was wearing this good-natured stupid look even as I found him in my office, standing there as if lost in thought.

"What are you doing here?" I asked.

"I came in to ask you a question and was waiting for you to get back."

"How did you get inside?"

"The door was unlocked."

That was not true then or ever. With the listening device I had in my closet, I could not afford to let any passersby examine the room without my knowledge. I was sure that Zorin's men came in regularly even so, but an intrusion in the middle of the day was a brazen contravention of unwritten rules — the spies pretended not to follow us, and we pretended not to notice when they did.

"I was looking for an order for buckwheat. We're almost out."

"Since when do you concern yourself with orders? Do you realize you could be fired for this? Who gave you permission to enter this room? If anything is missing, I will not only have you fired but call the militia as well."

Linas looked as if he were somewhat penitent, but he did not look quite sorry enough. He had been sent by Zorin, I was sure, and thus was protected. I made him follow me and led him downstairs to the kitchen, where Niko was looking over the menus for the week.

"Did you send this man into my office in my absence?"

"I never said he did," said Linas, but I wanted a bit of a spectacle, and sure enough, the sous-chefs and line chefs all looked over through the smoke and steam to see what was going on.

"I would never send anyone into your office in your absence," said Niko.

"And what would you think of a man I found in my office without permission?"

"I'd say he was a thief," said Niko.

The word was echoed by a couple of the staff.

"I'm no thief. I just wanted to see if there was an order for buckwheat on your desk. I was trying to do a favour for Gene."

Genius, my nervous electrical engineer. He was peeling onions and looked up at the sound of his name. His eyes were moist, not unexpectedly.

"I didn't ask you to do anything for me," he said. Julia was down in the kitchen, and she sensed something. She walked over and stood beside him.

"No, but I see you eat buckwheat like there's no tomorrow, and you even take it home when there are leftovers."

"It's policy to permit leftovers to be taken home," said Niko.

"But he's so crazy about buckwheat I wanted to do him a favour and make sure we had enough in stock."

"Did he ask you to do this?"

"No. I did it out of the goodness of my heart."

"And do you concern yourself with the tastes and needs of anyone else in here? Have you found a source of anchovies for me? Grapes for Lucy? She seems to like them. Perhaps candied almonds for our director? No, of course not. The idea is ludicrous.

You are a liar," said Niko, "and you must have been in there looking for the cash box."

"Leave the poor boy alone," said Zorin from the door. "Look at that face, will you? He's incapable of telling a lie." He had come along through the corridor, now empty of the children who used to play there. I missed them, their presence a kind of atmospheric antidote against Zorin's grim cloud.

Zorin was the éminence grise of the Seaside Café Metropolis. He was always around but usually invisible, like a rare bird that chose to show itself infrequently. Or a predatory bird that might swoop at any time. Everyone knew he was there, of course, and everyone understood what he did, but all of us acted as if he was just some sort of technical person. And that was how he liked to play his role. So for him to step out to help Linas in this way meant the young man had to be important to him.

"The real question," said Zorin, "is why this friend of Linas, this Genius, likes buckwheat so much."

"He's not my friend," said Genius.

"So is he your enemy? And if so, why?" asked Zorin.

Genius turned red in the face and put his hands behind his back. I guessed they must have been trembling.

"He's just a colleague," said Julia, "neither a friend nor an enemy." I was a little surprised at just how vulnerable Genius was. He must have suffered a great deal in the past to be so nervous now.

"You still haven't told me about your taste for buckwheat," said Zorin.

Niko intervened. "Isn't there some food you like, friend Zorin?"

"I eat what the state sees fit to serve me, and I am grateful for the sustenance. So I must insist on an answer. Why does Comrade Genius like buckwheat beyond reason?"

What Zorin asked was preposterous, but he was saying it for some purpose I could not divine. He was using a leading question, and I had no idea where it was going. I just knew that we needed to be careful because Zorin was setting a trap of some kind. A moment of awkward silence followed.

"Because he is getting ready for the buckwheat festival," said Lucy, walking toward Genius so he would be flanked by a woman on each side. She had been near the back of the small crowd and stepped forward though the steam, hands on her hips and sure of herself for all her youth and all the loose strands of hair that slipped out from under her white chef's hat.

She looked at me, and I understood immediately that I should follow her lead. I felt she knew what she was doing, and I trusted her.

"Don't hold me for a fool ," said Zorin. He had been moving in for some kind of kill and was irritated by Lucy. He turned to me.

"What is this nonsense?" he asked.

But Lucy went on. "The details about the varieties of buckwheat are in the French book of culinary history, *Larousse Gastronomique*. In Normandy, they make buckwheat galettes, so that is something new, something we haven't tried here. The boss was going to do a festival to promote new interpretations of a staple food grown right here in our Lithuanian Soviet Socialist Republic."

"Yes," I said. "I was going to honour the memory of the visit of those French philosophers some time ago."

"Comrade Niko," said Zorin, suspicious and probing, "what other dishes did you have in mind besides this so-called Norman specialty?"

Niko did not hesitate at all.

"Buckwheat bake, a kind of casserole made with chicken; buckwheat and cheese; stewed buckwheat and vegetables for tender stomachs taking a break from meat; buckwheat cutlets; buckwheat soup ..." He rattled off another half-dozen recipes as I listened in amazement. I was particularly impressed by the recipe for vegetarian buckwheat. No one was ever tired of meat in Soviet Lithuania because the supply of meat was irregular and Lithuanians would eat it every chance they got. I'm not sure the word *vegetarian* had ever been used in the country before.

"And Genius has been tasting the buckwheat in preparation," said Niko.

"What is there to taste in buckwheat anyway?" asked Zorin.

"Whether it's toasted or not, and to what degree. Charred buckwheat is horrible," said Genius, finally picking up the thread.

"So in the end, if you do need buckwheat," said Zorin, exasperated but defending his apprentice, "Linas was doing you a favour after all by checking to make sure you had enough."

The argument was weak, and I needed to press the point.

"Maybe so," I said, "but I'll tell you this. He was being presumptuous. If I ever find him in my office again, or if I ever find him doing anything in the least irregular, I will have him out of here faster than he can take off his apron."

Zorin shrugged. "Of course. But I don't expect he ever gets out of line." Zorin walked back down the hall.

"So when is this buckwheat festival supposed to happen?" Linas asked brightly.

"You'll find out when we choose to tell you," said Niko.

SO MANY LIES said so quickly, practically a four-part jazz improvisation following Lucy's thematic lead. It was amazing what storytellers we had become. But we needed to keep our stories straight. I managed to get Niko and Lucy into my office after blocking the listening device at the edge of my desk. But to be

The Seaside Café Metropolis

safe, we sat in chairs in a far corner, and I turned on the radio.

"You are brilliant, Lucy. I'm grateful. But how did you ever come up with the idea?"

"I sensed something was wrong, and I just followed my instincts. It's lucky, though, because buckwheat in French is *sarrasin*. I haven't gotten to the letter *S* in the *Larousse Gastronomique* yet. But under the letter *G*, I came upon the recipe for galettes de sarrasin, and the main ingredient was buckwheat flour."

"A lucky strike. But how did you ever think of a buckwheat festival?"

"It shot into my head. We have Pancake Tuesday once a year, so why not Buckwheat Saturday?"

"Are you friends with Genius that you wanted to defend him?"

"Not particularly. More with Julia, who just wanted to protect her man. And he's a nice man. They were going to pick on him, but he's timid, so I thought someone had better stand up for him."

We talked for a while, and then I let her go and continued with Niko alone.

"You are as brilliant as she is," I said. I saw his look. "All right. More brilliant, but she is much younger and more beautiful. Yet the whole business of buckwheat mystifies me. Linas was lying, all of us were lying, but the fact remains that Genius is a fan of buckwheat. What does that mean, and why does it matter?"

"Buckwheat was the food of political prisoners in Kazakhstan, where he was imprisoned," said Niko. "Some people come to hate the staple of their past, and some people remember it as the nourishment that saved them. I guess he must be in the second group."

"Poor man. I'm surprised, though. Tastes evolve. There were things I hated in my childhood that I adore now, like fish, eggs, and mushrooms. And I would never want to eat prison food once I was out of prison. It's inexplicable to me."

"Like the human condition," said Niko. "Who we love, what we love, and what we dream of."

De gustibus non est disputandum. The Latin phrase tells us we are not supposed to question taste, but how can we not? I would save that subject for another time. We had solved a problem for Genius, and we had to look to what came next.

"You know Genius's father is still in the gulag?" said Niko.

"How could I know that?"

"He mumbled about it to me one time. His father is going to be released soon and wants to come back to Lithuania, but the local authorities might not want him here."

"Why not?"

"Vilnius is a small town. It's embarrassing to have someone you denounced walk past you on the street. Maybe they're trying to keep him out of the country."

"But what does the son have to do with the case of the father?"

"If one family member is guilty here, all family members are guilty. Compromise Genius and you've solved the problem of his father for the KGB."

I gave up trying to parse the reasoning. "Now we really will have to have a buckwheat festival," I said.

"Yes, of course. We'll make blinis, but instead of calling them crepes we'll call them Norman galettes and mill some buckwheat into the flour. Easy enough. Most people here don't know what a Norman is, let alone a galette. But never mind that. Leave the recipes to me. On another matter, let me give you a little piece of advice."

"Please, be my guest."

"You chastised Linas, but not enough. Remember where you are. You must lay into your victim. You must make him fear not only for his job but for his physical safety too. Maybe even the physical safety of his family. You must rage and rage and tear such a strip off him that he will be terrified."

"Why would I want to do that?"

"Because you are in the land of Nikolai Gogol, not Norman Rockwell."

"Obviously. But what does that even mean, and how do you even know who Norman Rockwell is?"

"Even in our profound ignorance here, we have glimpses of the ideal lives the Americans live over there. Here superiors must kick down in order to maintain order. Serfdom lasted longer here than anywhere else in Europe. You are too American in a way, using an iron fist in a velvet glove. There is no velvet here. Czars, Nazis, and various Soviet overlords have terrorized this place for a very long time, so you must learn how to act more in line with what's expected of you in this place."

"I don't want to be cruel."

"Have you seen people smile here?"

"What? Of course I have."

"Yes, but not the way they smile in American movies. I mean wantonly, to strangers on the street. In photos. From over here, all of those smiling American faces look moronic. Here, you smile at friends, not at strangers. If you do, they think something is wrong with you. Perhaps you are weak or have a mental defect. People admire strength here, and so you have to demonstrate your strength from time to time by terrorizing people."

"Why would I terrorize my friends?"

"Not your friends. Your enemies. And keep in mind, any stranger is a potential enemy."

"In Canada, we quote an Irish poet who says there are no strangers here, only friends we haven't met yet."

"Ah yes, the Irish. A peace-loving people, right?"

"Not exactly."

"Of course not. They say one thing and do another. You have to learn to dominate your enemies."

"It sounds like mafia behaviour."

"Linas won't respect you unless he fears you, especially with Zorin protecting him. And anyway, the buckwheat festival is the least of your problems. They seem to be after Genius."

"Because of his father, right?"

"Maybe. There's no wondering why in this place. They need to destroy someone from time to time to demonstrate their power. You have to protect Genius if you want to keep your electrical engineer and demonstrate your own strength. And you'll have to get rid of Linas somehow."

"We need a plan," I said.

"Yes, we do."

"What about Lucy?" I asked.

"What about her?"

"What do you think of her?"

"We're not talking about Lucy."

"Now I'm talking about Lucy."

"Why are you talking about Lucy?"

"Because I have chosen to talk about her. So tell me, what do you think of her?"

"A young enthusiast. She might turn out to be a good chef if she keeps up the research and sharpens her kitchen skills. I mean, she's exceptionally good with a knife, but her assembly and sauce-making abilities are elementary."

"What do you mean, she's good with a knife?"

"She can bone a chicken in record time and not tear the skin."

"Ah."

"Is there anything else you want to know about her?"

"No. Why?"

"You seem interested."

"How could I not be interested in a mind that saved Genius and saved me and protected the whole Metropolis family?"

"So you admire her on behalf of the collective?"

"Of course."

"You know, Emmet, you are talented far beyond your years, but in matters of the heart, you are an adolescent."

I was stunned and paused to drink from a cup of coffee on my desk. "It is unprofessional to speak of personal matters when discussing a member of the team," I said.

"So ask her out beyond your professional environment."

"I wasn't planning on asking her out anywhere."

"Exactly. That's the problem, your failure of imagination. Now I've solved the problem of Lucy for you. Let's consider what we can do about Linas."

THE YOUTH GARDEN was a park down near the bottom of the city, the former orchard of the former Bernardine monastery. It lay in an oxbow of the charming Vilnia River with the castle hill high on the right bank of the stream and on this side, the left bank, a couple of nearby churches, one Gothic brick and the other baroque. How did I know these things? A very thorough tour guide had taken my mother and me around the city when we first immigrated.

Even among the ruins from the war, you could see the place had once been beautiful and still had some good bones. Maybe someday it would be beautiful again. Mother was more interested in factories and new architecture. She liked the idea of sweeping away the past whereas I loved best the things of yesteryear, from architecture to food.

To my mother's regret, the statue of Stalin had been taken down in the park, and instead we had a fountain sculpture of three dwarf elephants shooting water from their trunks.

I had never seen Lucy in clothes other than kitchen whites, and she seemed like another person altogether in a flower-print summer dress with her light brown hair down to her shoulders and a woven bag looped over her shoulder. She looked very beautiful and Niko must have read my character correctly because I was briefly at a loss for words when I saw her at our meeting place in front of the park gates. At work, I would have had none of this hesitation. Now I was outside of my usual self, somehow, aware of my own awkwardness.

"What's in the bag?" I asked her after we'd said hello.

"A blanket, a small loaf of bread, two apples, and a bottle of mineral water. I thought that since it's a beautiful day and we're going to be in the park anyway, it might be nice to sit in the sun. The fine weather is so short here, I want to take in every moment of it. And besides, all my work is in the kitchen basement, so I want to get out a bit."

"I wish I'd thought of that," I said, feeling like a man who'd forgotten to buy his date a corsage.

"Don't worry. You can buy us coffee somewhere later on."

I was a little shy and never would have proposed sitting on a blanket together because it seemed forward, the kind of thing you might do with a proper fiancée or a high-school girlfriend. But I was older than that, and so was Lucy. I searched for words again.

"The cat got your tongue, Mr. Director?"

"It does, but I wish you'd forget about work while we're out here. I'm just Emmet."

The park was laid out like a formal French garden, with gravel paths and symmetrical flower beds, and we came upon it as the roses were in bloom, filling the air with their sweet scent.

"How is it that a Canadian finds himself in Vilnius?" asked Lucy, and I told her the story of my mother, which she took in without the comments I usually received about being a dutiful son.

"And what about you? Are you from Vilnius?" I asked her.

"Oh no. I grew up in Šiauliai, but my mother, sister, and I came here right after the war."

"What about your father?"

"He was taken away for being a nationalist in the first wave of arrests after the war. My mother wanted the whole family to flee west as the Soviets were approaching in 1944, but my father said he was just a farmer and had done nothing wrong and he wasn't afraid. Once they arrested him and deported him, she brought us here because it was safer to be in a new place where nobody knew us."

"Is he still alive?"

"No. He died a long time ago in one of the work camps. He was a bit too old to work in a mine, but no one asked for his opinion, and I guess the labour wore him down."

"I'm sorry."

"I'm starting to forget him. That makes me a little sad, to tell you the truth. But it strikes me we come from opposite sides of the barricades. Your father was a communist and mine a nationalist."

"I hope that doesn't matter."

"It doesn't matter to me, but you see, the authorities here don't forget. I had plans to go to university, but there was no way I could get in with a 'criminal' father, so I had to settle for technical college. And it took me years to get into one of those. If you ever wanted to get rid of me, all you'd need to do is denounce me to the authorities as the daughter of an enemy of the people."

"Denounce you? Please. I never have and never will denounce anyone. The opposite. Technical training was your second choice?

But you seem such a natural in the kitchen. As if you were born to it."

"I wanted to study medicine or, failing that, chemistry. I had other ideas too, but this was the best I could get."

"Do you regret it?"

"Not anymore. I know the terrible world I live in, but I've found a refuge. I love food, and I love learning about it. The café is a kind of oasis in a very big desert. That book you lent me is a treasure, and it makes me want to learn more. I want to read Brillat-Savarin, and Carême, and Escoffier. Do you know where I can get my hands on their books?"

"I don't. Not in this country. But I have a friend or two I've kept in touch with back in Canada. I could write and ask for something."

"Thank you. I would love that."

"Is it your ambition to be a great chef?"

"I'm not sure about greatness. I just want to know all there is to know. I want to be very good at what I do."

We walked for a while among the flowers and later along the bank of the river, and then Lucy saw a spot of dappled shade on that warm day and we sat down on her green felt blanket. She took out a paring knife with which she cut us slices of bread and poured sparkling water into two glasses.

"Why is it again that you came to the rescue of Genius?" I asked.

"He's Julia's boyfriend for one thing, and he's on my team. He's like me, or my father, I guess. An enemy of the people. We hide out in basements like the kitchen at the café, but the KGB comes looking for us, or sometimes not even the KGB. Some disgruntled idiot thinks you're getting above yourself and wants to cut you down to size and denounces you. My neighbour was denounced because someone with a jealous nose thought she was eating pork cutlets too often."

I laughed. "How is that even a problem? It's ridiculous."

"Of course it's ridiculous, but someone thought it was suspicious that she had access to so much meat. You're the one who chose to come to the land of ridiculous. I can barely understand that."

"Because of my mother."

"She's an adult, and so are you. Why are you so attached to her? She could have ruined your life."

"She had a hard time raising me, and I feel loyal. But in the end, she brought me here, and look, I'm speaking to you, a beautiful woman on a lovely day."

"Hmm."

Lucy took out the two apples and began to peel them, cutting one slice at a time and then offering every second slice to me on the tip of her knife.

"You're a funny one. So driven at work, but so tentative out here. You're a bit shy. Have you been attached to your mother too long? You're a little bit charming and a little bit naive, somehow. Maybe that's why I've told you about myself. I don't normally reveal so much, even to people who've known me for a long time. You now know more about me than any of my colleagues in the kitchen."

"Everyone is so tight-lipped about their personal lives in this country."

"Because your personal life could get you into trouble at the drop of a hat."

"So you trusted me?"

"I did. I hope it was justified."

"Oh yes. There are just a couple of things I want to say."

"Yes?"

"First, I hope to see you again?"

I had become more comfortable with her as the time passed, but my question gave me a small knot in my stomach. She responded without a pause.

"Sure. You're fun in your own way, so different out here from the confident Mr. Director at work."

"That's the second part. At work, we'd still have to act professionally."

"Our lives contain compartments here in the Soviet Union. We learn to have multiple personalities, so I'll have no problem being the director's employee at work."

We talked of food and then hotels, about which she knew nothing because she had never even been in one. And then we packed up her bag and walked in the direction of the Užupis neighbourhood, where I promised to buy her coffee. On the way, I reached for her free hand, and she let me hold it without any hesitation. I felt as happy as a child.

The Užupis quarter lay close to the park and the picturesque city centre, but it was not a good neighbourhood, and I'm not sure why I chose to go that way to look for a café or why Lucy let me. It was late afternoon on a Monday, and the shadows were getting longer, but it was far from dark, and the neighbourhood appeared more miserable than sinister, with littered streets, sooty windows, and crumbling stucco making the streetscape look like something out of a Dickens novel. We turned down a lane and were met by a man who came out of nowhere with a brick in his hand. He was a coarse type, stout and unshaven and red in the face with liquor breath projecting all the way out to us.

"I have a brick for sale," he said. "I'll sell it to you for three rubles."

Lucy let go of my hand. "I think you'd better buy it," she said.

The Seaside Café Metropolis

I'd heard of street gangs, and I'd heard of muggings, but I'd never been mugged myself. Vodka cost three rubles a bottle, so it wasn't hard to figure out why he wanted the sum.

Discretion said it was wiser to pay, but first Niko and then Lucy had made me seem less than manly. If I'd been on my own, I would have paid and been done with it.

"I don't need a brick," I said.

"You'll get it one way or another — in your hand for the cash or in your face, and then your lips will be too swollen to kiss your girlfriend."

Now I was irritated. "Absolutely not."

He lunged at me then, but he had been drinking, and I knocked aside the hand with the brick that was coming for me. He caught me by the collar with his left hand, and I lost my balance and fell. I knew immediately that I was in a very bad situation with a man with a brick standing over me, but as I scrambled to get up I heard a yowl of pain and saw the brick fall to the ground. When I was finally on my feet with my heart pumping and my fists up, I saw our mugger was holding his left shoulder with his right hand, and blood was seeping through his fingers. Lucy was standing with her bag at her feet and the paring knife in her hand.

"What did you do that for?" he asked.

"I can bone a chicken in three minutes, and it wouldn't take me much longer to bone you. So get out of here."

I brushed off the knees of my pants. "You heard the lady," I said.

"My name is Karl," said the man. "Remember that. I'll come looking for you."

"You don't even know who we are," scoffed Lucy.

"It's a small town. I can find you, and you'll be sorry I did."

And he turned and lumbered away down the lane.

"I think I owe my life to you," I said once I'd composed myself.

Lucy calmly held the knife with its blade away to keep the blood from dripping on her dress.

"Don't exaggerate. I saved you from getting a bump on your head. But why didn't you just give him the money?"

"I thought I was protecting you."

"Very gallant, but this damsel has seen a few things. She can take care of herself."

"And of me as well, it seems."

"And of you as well. But I know you'd take care of me too. I mean, you tried. Now let's find a tap somewhere. I want to wash the blood off this blade. Who knows what filth is running through that brute's veins?"

PIOTR ZORIN DESCENDED on me as was his habit, out of the blue in the middle of the afternoon while I was working at my desk. I was more than ordinarily irritated by him after the exchanges about Genius.

"What is it?" I wanted to know.

He seated himself without an invitation and leaned forward.

"Trying on an old suit?" I asked, as if he were a friend. He ignored the comment. "It smells of naphthalene. Lean back a bit, will you?" He still ignored me, and I let it go. It was not good to push things too far.

"I have an important matter to discuss with you," he said.

"Well?"

"It will take some time. It's a difficult subject. I will come at this hour tomorrow, and I want you to be sure to be here."

"What's wrong with telling me now?"

"Now is not a good time."

"All right, but tomorrow afternoon is not a good time for me."

"Why not?"

"Business."

"What sort of business?"

"None of your business."

"Postpone whatever it is. My matter is of utmost importance."

"If it's of utmost importance, tell me now. If not, tell me two days from now when I will be a little less occupied."

He squirmed, the worm. He was trying to intimidate me, to have my anxiety grow in expectation of his news. Zorin left without agreeing to come two days later, and I made a point of being absent the following afternoon in case he showed up on his schedule rather than mine.

When I did walk in two days later, the Metropolis was humming in the best way. The café in the front was full of young and beautiful people, some in love and some not, but all of them animated or louche or sullen as their characters and their hormones dictated. The water in the small fountain in the intermediate space splashed merrily with the bartender looking on, and the various professors with their pipes and their cigarettes discussed linguistics or the latest gossip in the restaurant at the back. Andrius and his jazz band were not playing at the time. We saved the music for evenings to mark a kind of atmospheric change in the place, to set the evening aside from the day. Besides, musicians didn't make much of a living and needed to maintain day jobs or go to school.

I sat myself in my office and waited for Zorin, and to make his point, he arrived an hour and a half late. So much jousting to show who was in charge, but I let him have his moment.

"The Ministry of Communications has given me the responsibility of bringing you an important message." He sat back and waited for me to respond.

I, in turn, sat still and waited. When he saw I was waiting, he made me wait some more, so I reached into my drawer and took out a package of cigarettes, removed one, and lit it without offering him anything. I did not normally smoke, but the package came in handy from time to time.

Finally: "The ministry is concerned with the decline in public morals."

I said nothing. I waited some more.

"It has come to our attention that some of the young women here are arriving bare-legged, with short skirts but no stockings."

He sat back as if he had made some kind of point.

"It's warm outside now. Maybe stockings are a deficit item," I said. We had shortages all the time. My implication that our glorious socialist system was not working as well as it could seemed to bother Zorin.

"There is no shortage of stockings. But there is a shortage of public morality, and this place is encouraging it."

"Go ahead. Spell it out."

"You are permitting women to come in here without wearing stockings."

"And?"

"And you will forbid that from now on."

I had never heard a rule quite as stupid as this one.

"How will I do that?"

"Put up a sign."

"But modern stockings are practically invisible. How can we be sure of who's wearing stockings and who isn't?"

"That's not my problem. Have someone feel their legs if you have to. I will be making sure this directive is followed. Mark my words."

BACK IN TORONTO, a festival required all sorts of advance advertising. There, you needed to promote an event to get people to come out, but in Soviet Vilnius, so little was new that all you needed to do was let out the word that a special menu was here, and the crowds arrived unbidden. The appearance of three new dishes —buckwheat galettes, buckwheat cake, and buckwheat soup — was magnified by the news that the band would be playing new French jazz, although the music was from Django Reinhardt, who had died in 1953. Anyway, it was new to a lot of people in Vilnius who didn't keep track of music trends.

That was all we needed to make a memorable Sunday. I increased the anticipation by planning to keep the café closed in the afternoon to prevent people from arriving early and staying for the new menu at dinner.

A week before the event, I invited Linas to speak to me in my office. He came in bearing his halo of socialist realist happiness, a glow of good health and innocence.

"They tell me you have been doing well downstairs," I said to him as he stood before me in his apron.

"They have?"

"Yes. And I think it's time to expand your horizons. Do you own a suit?"

"I do."

"Well, make sure it's in good shape. On the opening evening of the buckwheat festival, I want you upstairs."

His regular glow practically became a beacon. "I'm honoured. But doing what?"

"Mostly just observing so you get an idea of what goes on in the rooms upstairs. I may need to assign you somewhere, but at the beginning, just stand by the bartender in the middle room where you can see what's going on both front and back. Perhaps Comrade Zorin can give you some tips."

THE BUCKWHEAT FESTIVAL launch was turning out to be a sensation. As I had expected, the very idea of a "festival," though it was no more than a notion, fascinated the locals, and there was a rush for places. The street outside had many young people in their best clothes, hoping for free places to open up. I had saved a booth for a special guest, but the place was otherwise full.

As a general rule, dancing was not permitted in the Seaside Café Metropolis, but that evening some of Django Reinhardt's jaunty music carried from the stage in the back to the café in the front, and two couples stood up to dance, glancing nervously over their shoulders as they did so. Bob looked to me, and I nodded back at him to allow a little dancing, but not too much. Just two couples and just one dance.

Zorin appeared from time to time, moody as a late autumn day but mollified somewhat to see Linas standing in his badly cut but exquisitely pressed suit and wearing a tie with a crooked knot the size of a woman's fist. Bumpkin-like, Linas scanned the rooms, agog at the finery, the beauty of it all. He must have seen this as his reward for being an informer, a gift permitting him to spy on the people who were beautiful but anathema to the spirit of the revolution. Or did he even have enough depth to think these thoughts? Maybe I was projecting, enjoying my ability to use a long word, even if only in my mind.

The Seaside Café Metropolis was buzzing shortly before six when I took Linas aside and told him I was going to permit him to watch the door. He seemed proud to receive this new assignment, but slightly nervous too. I gave him detailed instructions and relieved my regular doormen brothers, John and Joe, and sent them downstairs to eat at the staff family table in the kitchen.

And then I waited. It did not take long.

My special guest, the minister of agriculture, was a punctual man. I had managed to secure his attendance as well as his wife's.

The Seaside Café Metropolis

I'd known them for some time from back in my previous restaurant job. They both loved food — it showed on their stocky bodies — and I was glad for their enthusiasm.

Ministers were not usually known for being jolly, but these two were a pair of bon vivants within the constraints of the rather puritanical Soviet Union. Their position was too elevated for them to be frequent guests at the Seaside Café Metropolis, but they did appear occasionally, a Michelin Man and a Michelin Woman, plump, in clothes too tight, but good-natured within limits. This was, as Niko had reminded me, the Soviet Union, not Happy Valley. To be happy too often would mark you as a fool.

Zorin chose this time to come upstairs and make one of his rounds through the café, but I did not want him anywhere near Linas at the front door, at least for a little while. I stopped him in the middle of the restaurant by the fountain.

"Can I buy you a drink, friend Zorin?"

He eyed me suspiciously.

"Why the sudden camaraderie?"

"We are having our buckwheat festival, and that's a kind of celebration, isn't it?"

"I always found the notion ridiculous."

"Perhaps, but we are colleagues, after all. We work in the same place, and this is a special moment. Let me get you a cocktail."

He reluctantly permitted me to draw him toward the bar.

"I am not really sure what a cocktail is," said Zorin.

"They are not popular here, but there is a great variety of them in the West. Will you try a Manhattan?"

"Why not?"

I had the bartender do the best approximation possible under the circumstances. We used Starka, a local flavoured vodka, in place of bourbon. To this he added a dash of 777 to replace the red vermouth. There was no way to get Angostura bitters, but the local bitters were called 999, so we added a splash of that. The two liquors did make me wonder why there was no drink called 888. Maraschino cherries did not exist, and a bit of orange peel would have been nice but there were no oranges to be had at the moment. Finally, the bartender added ice, gave it all a shake, and poured it into a small glass, since we had no martini glasses.

Zorin had softened. "Well, bottoms up," he said.

"No bottoms up! You must sip a Manhattan."

"Sip?"

"Yes, sip."

"Why wouldn't I just drink?"

"To prolong the sense of pleasure."

"The sense of pleasure comes from the alcohol, and the quicker the alcohol gets into the system, the quicker the pleasure."

"Try sipping."

"I only sip hot soup."

"Please."

He did as I asked. And grimaced. "Bad liquor has adulterated the good." He held his nose and swallowed the contents of the glass in one gulp.

I was wondering if I would have to make conversation with him, and if so, on what subject. His childhood? I could not imagine Zorin as a child. He must have been born an apparatchik. Luckily, the minister of agriculture and his wife came to the rescue.

I DID NOT see the minister and his wife arrive, but I heard them.

The shriek from his wife followed by a torrent of abuse from the minister himself was so loud that the sound carried to the back of the café, and the music stopped momentarily before going on. Musicians know the music must go on, even if a ship is going down.

I made my way to the sidewalk beyond the front door, where the red-faced minister was tearing into Linas from not more than three inches in front of his face. The young man leaned back against the outside wall of the café, pressing against it as if he hoped it would give way and he could flee. The minister's wife stood with her arms crossed, expressing her wounded nature by holding her chin high and staring up at the street lamps.

"Minister, I am sorry, but what has happened?"

He turned on me, full of rage, but not quite as hot as he had been a moment before.

"This young dolt pinched my wife's leg."

"I felt like a piece of pork, the way he moved his fingers," the woman said.

"But I was told not to permit women inside if their legs were bare, and her stockings were practically invisible," said Linas.

"So you touched her leg?" I asked.

"I pinched a little skin to see if there were stockings upon the flesh."

"Idiot!" I said. "The representative of the minister of communications told us to check, but who said you should be pinching women's legs?"

Linas looked to Zorin, whose face had turned to stone.

"The minister of communications told this young man to touch my wife's leg?" asked the minister of agriculture.

"Not the minister himself but his representative here, Piotr Zorin."

I looked around. I saw nothing but Zorin's back as he retreated to the rear of the café.

"I want this man and that other one both punished," said the minister's wife.

"I am terribly sorry," I said. "I can deal with this fool, but Comrade Zorin was appointed from above. Please, come inside, and I will ask the waiters to bring champagne to ease the insult."

I turned to Linas. "Go home now. Immediately. When we need you, we'll call you back."

He tried to protest, but I would have none of it.

It took some work to get the minister and his wife to calm down, but their bon vivant natures soon took over. The buckwheat galettes were a hit with them, and the champagne eventually worked its magic.

For all his ubiquity, Zorin was nowhere to be found that evening.

AS IT TURNED out, the minister of agriculture's wife could not be mollified unless the man who had touched her legs was fired. She never wanted to see him again, and she certainly intended to come back because she was fond of the galettes and wanted to eat them once more, but not if she had to look at that ridiculous young man.

As for Zorin, he disappeared as well. Then the assistant to the deputy minister of agriculture called me to say that nobody's legs would need to be touched any longer.

So that was the end of Zorin, at least for a time.

But of course, it was not the end of the KGB. The basement room continued to be staffed by a variety of listeners, but the man who seemed to be their superior was bald and sullen and never greeted me, and I returned the favour in kind.

As for Genius and Julia, the potential crisis seemed to heighten their solidarity. I started to see them coming in to work at the same time after dropping off their children at the nearby daycare. I once even saw them holding hands in the most charming way possible.

Buckwheat Groats (Kasha)

Gently simmer toasted buckwheat groats in salted water for about fifteen minutes in a ratio of 2:1. If you want to put in additions, use your imagination. If you have none, just add butter.

–11–

Pheasant Under Glass

IT WAS CUSTOMARY in Lithuania to commemorate the anniversary of a loved one's death, so I was not entirely surprised to see Marcel and Adam, the latter previously known only as the editor. They were sitting in the back of the café in a booth rather than at a table in the front. I was happy to find them together, reconciled after Mona's death as she had wished. They were lounging after a meal, drinking coffee, and so I ordered three glasses of Armenian cognac on the house and joined them.

"To the memory of Mona," I proposed, and they raised their glasses. We drank, and I ordered another round.

"How have you adjusted?" I asked Marcel.

"My life has been a horror. I think of her every day, and I go to her gravesite often. It's a wonder I made it through this year."

"And you?" I asked Adam.

He sighed. "My wife has moved back into the apartment. We are attempting a reconciliation. But some sort of spark has gone out of my life."

We sat in melancholy silence for a while before Adam spoke again.

"I will have to go to Moscow for a few weeks for a Soviet-wide session of the art journals. The conference runs only three days, but I will stay on after that as long as I can. Maybe even some months. I can lose myself in Moscow better than here, and my wife and the children will stay behind. Moscow is vast, and I have no memories of Mona there, whereas this place is so small, so provincial, that I think of her on every street corner. But here's a happier bit of news. I'll be taking along with me a good reproduction of Marcel's latest painting. I think we might be able to get a print deal, and if that happens, reproductions will get sold across the whole Soviet Union."

I was very pleased that my aspiring artist had finally done so well. "What is this painting that Marcel has done?"

"Quite a success," said Adam. "It will be featured among paintings of the year. The subject matter is a bit conservative, but the execution is excellent. I wouldn't be surprised if he wins a Soviet Union–wide prize for it."

"What's it about?"

"It's called *The Village Peasants Sign Up for the Collective Farm*."

Marcel looked deeply into his second glass of cognac and said nothing.

"Well, congratulations," I said. "I imagine there will be membership in the All-Soviet Artists' Union after this, and likely a teaching job at the Vilnius Art Academy."

"That's right," said Adam.

"Whatever happened to the painting you were working on for so many years, *The Parting of the Red Sea?*" I asked.

"Another potential success, but still in process," said Adam. "It is a massive historic diptych showing the strategic parting of the Red Army during the siege of Moscow. Then came the deluge right after that as the Nazi forces were enveloped and drowned when the Red Army came out from behind Moscow in wave after wave. But it's now called *The Red Deluge*."

"*Après moi, le déluge,*" said Marcel, finally looking up at me a little defiantly and drinking his second glass. I wasn't sure what he meant, exactly, because the quote was from Louis xv, who didn't care what disaster happened after his reign. And in Lithuania, the Deluge sometimes referred to the sacking of the Vilnius by the Russians in 1655. I thought I'd probe a bit.

"Care to explain?" I asked.

"I mean what I mean."

That was that. Marcel had once been a charming and heedless young man, but the set of his jaw now reminded me a little of Mussolini's, as big as the Rock of Gibraltar, defiant and unfortunate. He was having great success, but he and I both knew that the Marcel of years ago would have despised the new version of the celebrated Soviet artist he was becoming.

"Ah. Well, then. I am sorry for the loss of Mona. I loved her too, and congratulations again on your successes. But tell me this. You used to belong to quite a group at the café out front, with Kalistas, Sarunas, and Rudy. I never see you four together anymore."

"We've gone our separate ways."

"Whatever happened to Rudy?"

"He married Angela and became the editor of the *Pravda Youth*."

It was the newspaper for young people, an arm of the Communist Party.

"Married?" I asked.

"Yes."

"Angela worked for me for some time, and Rudy was a regular. I thought I might get an invitation to something like that."

"So did I."

"You weren't invited?"

"No."

I had always imagined I was a kind of godfather to my aspiring bohemians, but they must have thought otherwise. I was part of their disreputable past. It disheartened me. To have been a Falstaff to a king, to a captain of industry, to a genius, would not have been so bad. But to have been Falstaff to a hack made me feel like someone who had run the Ford Hotel café instead of the more illustrious one at the Royal York Hotel.

"I happen to stay in touch with Sarunas," said Adam.

"Ah, yes," I said and smiled at the memory. "Our master butter sculptor."

They both looked at me like I was out of my mind. I suppose Sarunas kept that part of his life a secret.

"He is doing pretty well. He has received a commission to cast bronzes of the Red Army liberators. They're going to put the statues up on the bridge across the Neris."

And so that was the end of my struggling bohemians. Each of them had become a success. But I missed their younger selves, the slightly wicked youths who used to linger over coffee in the front of the Seaside Café Metropolis. Now that they had achieved acclaim, I imagined them a little less happy than they used to be, but one thing was for sure. They could now afford to eat whatever they wanted whenever one or another showed up alone or with a companion. Potato trumpets became the historic food of their youth, but popular still with a new generation of aspiring bohemians that was beginning to appear.

That class of heedless young artist matures and gives up its wilder youth, but a new generation arises, never quite the same but sharing similar dreams of freedom and success, not realizing that the two rarely go together.

The Seaside Café Metropolis

I FORCED MY mother up the castle hill on a long, steep walk through the park to the red brick tower that overlooked Vilnius. She did not seem all that happy to go up there with me. Although the day was fine, she complained almost non-stop about the steepness of the hill.

"I'm out of breath already!"

"You have been talking. Stop talking and you'll have more air to breathe."

"I don't care for picturesque views. They bore me."

"You smoke too much. I'm surprised you can breathe at all."

"Smoking helps me to concentrate."

There were now gaps between her sentences as she gulped at air.

"Concentrate on what?"

"I am bearing witness, remember? The socialist experiment is long, with many ups and downs, and I am focusing on every moment for the sake of posterity."

"Are you writing down these observations of yours?"

"I am making notes."

"In sentences?"

"What business is it of yours?"

"I'm trying to figure out if you're actually doing anything or just stewing in your cellar smoking cigarettes day and night."

I had annoyed her, and she did not speak for a while after we had reached the top of the tower. Medieval Vilnius lay to our left, with its church spires and red tile roofs, all charming at this distance with none of the grit and wartime ruins and crumbling stucco I saw at street level. A little further over was Lenin Prospect, lined by ornate wedding-cake buildings raised toward the end of the Czarist period. My own Seaside Café Metropolis was on that street, but of course, the seaside was far, far away. The Neris curled its way through the view, and on the far side of the river were the new neighbourhoods springing up, full of five-storey walk-ups called Khrushchevkas after the leader of the Soviet Union.

Traditional as always, I admired the old city, but once my mother had caught her breath, she had eyes only for the newly constructed apartment buildings. There was a bit of a breeze up on the tower, and she clutched at the knot of the scarf on her head to keep it from blowing away.

"Why do you wear a scarf like that?" I asked.

"Silly question. To protect my hair and my head."

"Only pensioners wear scarves like that. You're still in your fifties, but you look like somebody's grandmother."

"I feel a hundred years old sometimes. And besides, I could be a grandmother by this point if you were a little more advanced in your baby-making career."

She had never said anything remotely like that. Our talk was mostly practical, sometimes philosophical, but rarely personal. I felt as if this might be a gentle signal that a new phase of our relationship was opening up.

"Well, I have been seeing someone."

The smile froze on her face as she surveyed the apartment blocks. She was trying so hard to keep smiling that the effort prevented her from being able to speak.

I went on. "She's a charming young woman who works at the café. I've only gone out with her a few times, but I think we might have a future."

"If you fall head over heels," she said, "never forget who you are."

"What?"

"Don't become a fool. Remember your obligations."

"My obligations?"

But she didn't specify, and I knew what she meant anyway.

The Seaside Café Metropolis

TO SAY I was surprised to receive an envelope with an American stamp upon it would have been an understatement, and to find within it a letter from the mysteriously absent Alina was stranger still.

>Dear Mr. Argentine,
>
>As you can tell by this letter, I have found myself after many complications in the United States of America, where I received permission to go and take care of an elderly aunt in Brooklyn.
>
>Life has not been easy, but I have begun to adjust.
>
>I thought of you often and of the photos you so kindly put aside for me. I fear many years will pass before I can see them again. I have become interested in them for a particular reason.
>
>I was at a candy store here that has a kind of snack bar, and it turns out it is a place where some Lithuanian expatriates meet. One of them was a photographer who happened by as I was showing some of Lokys's photos to my girlfriend.
>
>His name is Jonas Mekas, and he is a photographer and an artist, and it turns out there is a world here not that different from the world Lokys and I inhabited back in Vilnius. There is an art group here called Fluxus, and they do many strange and wonderful things that some people call art.
>
>Mr. Mekas was taken by the photos I showed him, and he asked to see more. I had some with me back at my room, and I brought them the next week, and Mr. Mekas liked these photos even more. He was very excited by them all and said we must have a New York show of these photos. But I don't have many with me.

This offer is all very sudden and I have not adjusted to living here and I don't think I am ready yet, but poor Lokys will be forgotten unless someone works on his legacy. I wonder if you could send me a few of the negatives you'll find in the boxes?

But only a few! It's dangerous to send the only negatives that exist in case something happens to them and Lokys's genius is then lost forever. Perhaps you could look to see if any photographs of the negatives are mixed in because I don't fear losing photographs as long as the negatives are safe.

On second thought, just hold on to them. The fear of their loss is making me nervous.

I am particularly interested in the series of village photos Lokys made, the ones of his relatives with severely lined faces …

How had she managed to get out of the Soviet Union? I was absorbing this information at the desk in my office when Bob came in to tell me there was a taxi idling outside the main door of the café.

"Is there something special about this taxi?" I asked.

"Yes. It has plates from Minsk, in Byelorussia."

"I know where Minsk is." The city was well over three hours away by car. Why would someone take a taxi across that distance?

"Who's on the door?"

"John."

"Why didn't he tell the driver to leave?"

"He was going to, but he saw there was a distinguished older man in there with a big wrapped gift box on the seat beside him, and John was afraid he might be some kind of high official. Are you expecting a delegation?"

The Seaside Café Metropolis

I wasn't, and I could have had the car moved along, but my curiosity was piqued, and I went outside to see what was going on. I found the scene just as Bob had described it, with an elegant-looking man sitting in a suit with the window opened a crack as he smoked a cigarette in an amber holder and sipped what I guessed was coffee from a thermos cup. He had a white goatee and a pocket square in his suit jacket, and he held the cigarette holder as if posing for an ad for a European movie. I tapped on the window, and he rolled it down, and I could tell immediately that it was not coffee he was sipping from his cup.

I explained who I was.

"Then maybe you can help me," he said. "My name is Yevgeny Nazarov."

He stopped there and waited for me to react, but I didn't recognize his name. Once he understood that, he added, "The poet."

"Ah," I said, as if my memory had been jogged. "Just a moment. I'll be right back."

I went downstairs to the kitchen to look for Niko but came upon Lucy bearing a loaf of black country-style bread the size of a cemetery headstone.

"Country bread from the market," she said. "So much better than the stuff we get from the bakery, and cheap too. Do you want to try a slice?"

"Niko lets you do purchasing?"

"He trusts me."

"I do too. Bread tastes better in the cold room."

"Of course." She set down the loaf and cut a couple of slices, and I followed her into the cold room. She dropped her slice on a shelf as soon as the door closed behind us and wrapped herself around me and kissed me hard.

"Too bad it's so cold in here," she said when we finally pulled apart.

"It's warmer in my flat."

"After work?"

"After work. I am getting fonder and fonder of you."

"What did you say? What is that word? *Fonder?* You sound like my uncle. Tell me you love me."

"I do love you. I even told my mother about you."

I was not sure why I said that, and she seemed a bit surprised too. She picked up the slice of bread she had dropped.

"And what did your mother say?"

"Not much. I think she might be a little jealous, to tell you the truth. She says I should go out on dates more often, but she looks frightened whenever I do."

"My, my. And how is the process of cutting your apron strings coming along?"

I don't think I had ever felt so foolish as at that moment. I wasn't sure how to respond. Niko did not look surprised at all when he saw us come out of the cold room together, and I told him about the man in the car outside.

He froze. "Did you say Yevgeny Nazarov is sitting in a car outside the restaurant?"

"Yes. He seemed a bit eccentric to me and a little drunk."

"He's Byelorussia's most beloved poet. A hellraiser in his youth, barely tolerated by the government and adored by everyone else. He fills auditoriums when he reads. You let him sit in a car outside? Bring him in. I have some smoked sturgeon I was saving in case the minister of agriculture showed up, but this man can have it. I'll want to take a look at him from the doorway."

"Should I introduce you?"

"I'm too shy."

"You?"

"Great art intimidates me."

"What could he be doing here?"

"Ask him."

I went back outside to the car window.

"Won't you come inside?" I asked. "The chef has some nice smoked sturgeon he'd like you to try."

"I'm not sure I'm at the right place, though. I was hoping to meet your most illustrious Lithuanian poet here. This is the kind of place he would go to. I left Minsk without bringing along his phone number or address."

"You came from Minsk in a taxi without a phone number or address?"

"I received a fantastic payment for a series of translations of my books into Uzbek, Kazakh, and Georgian all at once. What should one do with a windfall except spend the money on friends?"

"What's your Lithuanian friend's name?"

"I'm not sure. It was a very late night we spent together in a bar in Vitebsk where he told me not only that he was Lithuania's most important poet but that Lithuania was the most advanced culinary capital in the whole Soviet Union. It was a wonderful night, and I brought him a gift to pay him back."

"Come inside and we'll track him down."

"I want to make sure he's still alive. He lived hard and might have died since I saw him last."

"Well, describe this Lithuanian poet to me and I'll see if I recognize him."

"All right. He's around my age."

I guessed in his dissolute fifties.

"He likes cognac."

That included almost everyone in the nation.

"He has a limp."

"Does he carry a cane?"

"Maybe. Let me think. Hmm. With an ivory knob at the top, I believe."

"That must be Leonidas Gilys," I said. "Does that sound right?"

"Maybe. Is there another poet with an ivory-topped cane?"

"No."

"You're sure?"

"Come inside. I'll call him, and we'll get him here."

"I don't want to risk losing the cab. I'll wait until he arrives."

I went inside. Getting a phone number in Soviet Lithuania was not an easy matter if you did not already have the number. There was no phone book — or rather, there was, but you had to go to the post office and beg the guardian of the book to let you look within. Instead, you had to rely on the human phone book, so I went inside and asked around among the guests, and eventually I ran across one of the pipe-smoking professors who had the number I wanted.

I have spoken of the regular professors before, but not as much as I should have, having concentrated on the younger customers at the front of the café. They were not all real professors, of course, but accomplished men and a few women, some of them just partiers and some of them hard-core alcoholics and all of them admirers of wit and jollity and needing some escape from the glum regime that ruled us.

If the atmosphere of the Royal York Hotel that I had come from was restrained British with a dash of American insouciance, the convivial Seaside Café Metropolis atmosphere was light-hearted Lithuanian with a dash of Russian exuberance. No police force was listening to what diners said in the Royal York Hotel, although they kept their voices down. My café was bugged by the KGB, but my diners were louder and more theatrical and behaved in public as if they did not have a care in the world. People needed to have a little fun even under a tyranny and looked for it wherever they could.

The Seaside Café Metropolis

Leonidas Gilys was far from being Lithuania's greatest poet, but he had once been popular and had accomplished friends. He had written a few hymns to Stalin in his day, but nobody much considered him guilty because of that. What choice did poets have in those postwar days except to lay bouquets of praise at the feet of their Soviet conquerors? As far as I knew, Gilys had not written a new poem in years. He was indeed a partier well along the road to alcoholism, but his wife tried to keep him away from travelling too far down that route. I finally reached him by phone and explained who was in Vilnius looking for him.

"Oh no!" he said.

"Do you not want to come?"

"I do, but my wife has gone out and has taken my shoes and my trousers with her."

"Taken your shoes and trousers?"

"She's trying to keep me from going out too much. Never mind. I'll get there."

He showed up in slippers and a housecoat. Even the best-laid plans of wives go awry. He wore socks halfway up his calves, but his knobby knees were exposed. His white hair was uncombed and his eyes were red, but he had the energetic movements of a young maverick that had possessed an old man's body.

The Byelorussian poet in a smart suit and pocket square threw his arms around the dishevelled Lithuanian poet whom he loved but whose name he had not remembered. There was laughter and happiness right there on the sidewalk. Nazarov took a handful of banknotes from his pocket and thrust them out to the taxi driver, telling him to wait, and then he reached inside for the wrapped gift, and I had John take it from him and bring it inside to one of the big booths at the back of the café.

Two old poets who liked to drink had managed to create a vibe, a sort of electricity that lit up the back room. Word went out across town, and soon more and more "professors" gathered at the back. There was loud talk and much hilarity, and through all this Nazarov kept his wrapped gift, rather large, the size of four shoeboxes, sitting on the floor at the side of the table.

They ate smoked sturgeon and caviar, beefsteaks and chicken Kievs. Niko created an impromptu torte out of sponge cake infused with brandy sauce and layered with whipped cream and preserved plums. They drank champagne and cognac. They declaimed poetry — their own and that of others — and sang a little, and the afternoon turned into evening and then turned into night while these men with incredible stamina, preserved in alcohol, kept up their merriment.

Finally, around ten, Nazarov asked me to the table. Their booth was overcrowded with men and women, and people stepped out from the nearby booths as well. Andrius and the band onstage stopped playing so Nazarov could speak, and some of the guests from the front of the café crowded around the middle area by the fountain and the bar to hear what was going to be said.

"My friends, I have come to this famous restaurant because I understand you are inventive. I understand you love good food. I come for your illustrious company as well. But most of all, I come with a challenge. You are the closest thing we have to a French restaurant in all the Soviet Union, so I have brought you a French gift. I would like the Argentinian to open the box."

"I'm a Canadian," I said, but this correction was lost on the crowd. We were playing comic roles, like something out of *It Happened One Night*, so I did as Nazarov asked, removing the ribbon that held the wrapping paper and then opening the lid of the box.

A frog jumped out.

There was shock and there was laughter, and then two more

frogs jumped out, and as I looked down into the box I saw there were another half-dozen rather dry and depressed frogs that did not have the energy to follow their compatriots.

"Mr. Argentine," said Nazarov. "Will you take these frogs and make frogs' legs for us tonight?"

It was a playful and ridiculous challenge. Frogs' legs were never served at the Royal York, and they were no more than a fearful rumour in Lithuania, as frightening as the idea of eating snails. One man's delicacy is another man's horror. I looked to Niko, who was standing in the doorway. He was alarmed.

Master chef or not, he was an admirer of Nazarov, but he was not eager to butcher frogs for their legs.

"We do not kill frogs in Lithuania," I said. "We free them from their constraints. Let's get these dried-out dears to a pond."

Of course, there was no pond nearby, but we had a fountain with a basin, and some wit took up the call of putting the frogs into the fountain. Before I could reflect on it, the boxed frogs went straight into the fountain, and a guest caught two of the three frogs that had previously jumped out and put them there as well.

A little silliness is a good thing, but too much is too much.

"Andrius," I called, "we are having some fun. Do you have any music appropriate to the moment?"

He did. James Scott's "Frog Legs Rag." I had never even heard of the tune. How was it possible that this young Lithuanian had it in his repertoire? It was an old tune, sounding like something a pianist might play to accompany a silent movie. It made for good atmosphere, though, as if we were living in a farce.

Slowly, Bob and John began to usher people out of the café. We closed at eleven, and I was not going to permit the party to run all night, famous poets or not. There was much movement of people getting their jackets and settling their bills with the servers.

I was standing by the bar on the far side of the fountain, watching the frogs peering out at the crowd from the edge of the pool, when a shabby but powerfully built man came striding forward, moving in against the flow of guests who were mostly moving out.

He came straight for me, and John from the door was nowhere to be found at that moment. The man carried a knife in one hand and bore down on me before I could fully understand what he was doing.

But he stepped on the lone frog that had not made it into the fountain.

A frog is a slippery creature, all the more so when it is squashed underfoot. The man's feet went straight from under him, and he fell down, banging his head on the edge of the fountain pool before he hit the floor.

The frogs in the pool ducked under the water, and the knife in the man's hand clattered across the tiled floor. He lay inert, stunned. Again, it took a moment for the mass of people to comprehend what had happened, but I remembered him now and stepped forward to look down upon his glazed eyes.

"The name is Karl, if I recall correctly," I said. Even in his dazed state, he managed to search around with his right hand, seeking the knife. But I stepped on his wrist, watched him writhe in pain, and asked John to call the militia.

ONCE THE MILITIA had taken away Karl, the writers still had enough alcoholic energy to permit them to go to the basement bar at the nearby writers' union, a place that never closed but one whose steep steps had caused the deaths of more than one drunken writer. John had put the surviving frogs in a sack and carried them down to the Neris to let them go.

The Seaside Café Metropolis

Some of us lingered to decompress and talk over the events of the evening. I invited Genius and Julia, but their children were home with her parents that evening and it was already very late, and the kids would get them up in the morning. By this, I deduced they were living together.

Lucy sat down beside me at the table and gave me a look. I put my arm around her shoulder, and this seemed to satisfy her, but she tapped her finger on her wristwatch to remind me we had a date. Niko and Andrius noted the move, and I was glad they did.

"Now I will be able to tell my friends and grandchildren I once served the great Nazarov," said Niko.

"You know," I said, "poetry seems to play a far more important role here than I recall it doing in Canada. I mean, we had coffee houses with poetry readings, but I can't say we had a national poet that everyone knew."

"It's because you have too much of everything in the West," said Andrius. "When you are free and rich, your life is full of important and unimportant things, and you can't tell one from the other. When you are living in a lie as we are here, you need to have someone who expresses the truth, and a great poet does that."

He snapped his mouth shut and looked at me in alarm.

"Don't worry," I said. "I saw the basement crew leave when they took out Karl."

"But they might be recording."

"I doubt it."

"So that's one benefit to living in this police state," I said. "At least you get good poets and pay attention to them."

"I'd give up my poets and I'd give up my jazz for a taste of real freedom," said Andrius.

"You would? Or would you just want to travel, to visit places, like London and New York?"

"I'd get out. All of us would if we could. Jews in particular."

"Why Jews?"

"Don't get me started. Do you think this place is heaven for Jews?"

"Well, the Soviets saved you from the Nazis."

"And then kept us locked down."

"Niko," I asked, "would you emigrate?"

"You know that was my intention at the end of the war. I just wasn't fast enough. You are the one who's the mystery, the one who came here."

"You have all heard about my mother."

"Yes," said Lucy. "And now the regime trusts you somehow. That makes you suspect. You could be a highly placed spy."

"You know me well enough to recognize that's untrue. As for me, I thought I had seen all I ever wanted to see of this place long ago. I thought I'd get out too, if I could, but I don't think it's possible. My mother and I were a propaganda coup for the regime. How would it look if we left?" I looked to Lucy, who felt warm under my arm. "What about you?"

"I have a family here. I love my country. I have a mother not getting any younger and a sister I'm close to. It would be hard to leave them behind, but does that mean everyone has to stay where they are for their entire lives? The whole history of the world is about people moving. I'd like to eat ice cream in Naples and choucroute in the Bofinger restaurant."

Niko and I looked at one another and then looked to her for explanation.

"Bofinger is an Alsatian brasserie in Paris. Very famous, in a quiet way."

"But why are we all talking of leaving?" I asked Niko. "Wasn't this one of the best nights ever?"

"It was fun," said Andrius. "There may be tyranny outside, but here, in this café, we have real freedom."

Niko harrumphed and turned to me. "Do you know the dish pheasant under glass?"

"I've heard of it, but we never made it at the Royal York. Have you?"

"No, but the freedom he says we have here in the café is like pheasant under glass: covered, restricted. A cooked bird forbidden to fly."

"Better somewhere than nowhere," I said. "We get to experiment with dishes here, to make moments of joy. And think what fun we had tonight."

"Some fun with a man with a knife coming for you," said Lucy.

"But look how it ended up! And by the way, if you remember, you're the one who cut him first, so why did he come after me?"

"Must have been a gentleman," said Lucy.

"I told you she was good with a knife," said Niko.

AS IF HE had heard us discussing it all, Dominic appeared from the front door. It was very late.

"What are you doing here, and how did you get in?" I asked.

"I designed this place, remember? I have a key to every door in the building."

"But the hour!"

"I heard about the adventures and thought I'd come in to make sure there was no damage."

"None at all. Would you like a drink?"

"Coffee, I think. We're too close to morning to carry on with alcohol."

For all his proprietary interest, Dominic was not a frequent guest, but he was around enough to be familiar with those of us sitting at the table. Niko went off to make coffee, and Dominic wanted to hear about all that had transpired. We gave him the details, by which point Niko returned with a tray of coffee.

"All of you have done so well," said Dominic. "I was hoping that this café could be the first of many islands. Eventually, there would be more places with modern music and modern ideas. I thought we might change the world in some way by loosening up, putting on a human face, having a little fun, eating good food, and losing the stultifying atmosphere of the old days. But I might have been optimistic."

"You have the children's café to your credit."

"I do. That's something." I had taken my arm off Lucy's shoulder when he came in, but now I reached for her hand under the table, and she held on to mine. "How long have you been running this place?" Dominic asked.

"You know as well as I do. You can count the years yourself."

"I was an optimist then. I thought there would be more and more islands like this. Instead, I see that the level of the ocean is rising."

I wished he would be a little less enigmatic, but he did not elaborate. He sat with us a little longer and then he left and we closed up and went our separate ways. Lucy came along with me.

"What do you think it means?" she asked.

"I don't know. But it's not good news."

"And I was just starting to learn so much."

It was late. Our footsteps echoed in the empty streets.

"Do you think the café will be closed down?" she asked.

"I don't know. But I do know that even if it is, I'd like us to be together."

"At another restaurant?"

"I'm trying to say I love you!"

"Then you should be a little more adept at it. Do I have to do everything myself?"

"What do you mean?"

"You should be kissing me on the street now in one of the darker spots between street lights."

I took her advice and did as she directed me. Then we went on to my flat.

Pheasant Under Glass

This is a ridiculous idea. Do not attempt to do this. A glass dome can break easily in the kitchen, and the sight of the dish will enrage socialists.

-12-

Potato Kugel

I HAD TWO chairs in front of my long desk for guests, and a couple more further back if we needed more seating. The new downstairs listening boss came in for a chat, and although I offered him the chair to the left of me as I faced him, he took the one to my right, the one closest to the microphone. He must have wanted to record his directions clearly to me in case I failed to follow them. Regimantas Pikas was his name. He was neither tall nor short, old nor young, fastidious nor sloppy. A functionary going about his functions.

There were times when I'd thought I had worked out a *modus vivendi* with Zorin over the years. Zorin had continued to eye poor Genius as if the man were a morsel over whom he kept licking his chops, but now that Zorin was gone, this new KGB man seemed to be worse than the old KGB man. His range of potential victims was broader than that of his predecessor.

Many forms of repression, some mysterious and some explicit, dogged various of my café guests over the years. Several lost their jobs without explanation, and two were arrested. One even died in an unsolved hit and run while she was crossing the street. It bothered me that some of my Seaside Café Metropolis patrons might have betrayed themselves unwittingly at the restaurant.

But how could I have protected them? Everyone knew or should have known the unwritten rules of secrecy in Soviet society. But alcohol loosened tongues, and alcohol flowed through the café like a river whose current could carry the unwary all the way to the gulag.

"I have come to alert you about an impending VIP visitor," said Pikas. "The guest who is coming to dine here is named Albert Dumbras, and he will be in the company of the deputy minister of culture, the deputy minister of education, and the president of the journalists' union along with his wife. The guest has made a special request."

"Some kind of food that he wants?"

"Yes. I will come to that. But more important, he would like your mother to join the party at dinner."

"My mother doesn't know any Albert Dumbras. Where is he from?"

"Waterbury, Connecticut."

"In the United States?"

"Do you need education in geography?"

"She doesn't know anyone from Waterbury."

"Apparently she does, and now on to the details."

"POTATOES AGAIN," SAID Niko when I went down to fill him in. "What is it with you Lithuanians and your love affair with the potato? Pork, potatoes, cabbage, carrots, onions, and apples, and that's all you need to keep a Lithuanian happy except for the most basic bread and butter."

"Liquor and beer too," I added, and he conceded with a nod, "but I'm not Lithuanian. I'm a Canadian."

"Not Argentine?"

I sighed. "Why not? I don't know why I've insisted on this all along. I can be anyone I want and anyone you want, so feel free to identify me as a real Argentinian. It wouldn't be the first lie told about me."

"You are more exotic locally if you let them think you are Argentinian."

"Canadians are not exotic?" Niko reflected for a moment but declined to respond. "I didn't want to hide behind the name."

"Oh, come now. Everyone hides something. Don't you?"

"Don't ask."

"So explain to me why a pudding of finely grated potatoes and onions mixed with eggs and bacon fat should even exist in this restaurant? We are a café, a metropolitan café in the sense of being worldly, if not a seaside café. Why would we want to serve peasant food?"

"We don't ordinarily, but this is intended for a special guest, an American."

"Americans eat this food?"

"Not many. The Jews have a version with schmaltz instead of bacon fat, but this man wants the Lithuanian version."

"And why is that?"

"Because he came from here in his childhood before he went to America."

"Ah, childhood food again. But why should we care about a tourist's childhood food?"

"Let me remind you there are no normal American tourists in the Lithuanian Soviet Socialist Republic. American tourists go to Moscow or Saint Petersburg. The tourists in Vilnius are usually from Byelorussia, Ukraine, and Russia. This is an unusual guest, a political guest. He immigrated to America before the war, and he has been running a communist newspaper in Waterbury since then."

"In Connecticut?"

"How can you know that?"

"I paid attention in school." Niko reflected for a moment. "I see. So he is cut from the same cloth as your mother. The difference is that he loves communism at a distance."

"Yes."

"He and your mother are a whole category."

"Yes."

"And how do you feel about this?"

"What are you, a psychologist? We are not here to discuss my feelings. We are here to discuss what we are going to serve him."

"You call it a discussion, yet you come and tell me what to make for him. Anything else?"

"Yes. Apple pie."

"What is this *pie*?"

"How can you know geography and not know this? It is an American dessert, like apple strudel, but with a difference."

"Ah yes, my German officer loved apple strudel. At the time, it was hard to get sugar, but sugar is in good supply now ever since we became such good friends with the Cubans. I make a very good pâte feuilletée."

I hesitated but went on. "The apple pie uses a simpler crust, often employing lard, and the apple filling is very deep, three or four centimetres and thickened so it doesn't run."

"All right. I will rein in my imagination and follow your directive. And does the American like cinnamon?"

"How could I possibly know that?"

"You seem to know everything else."

"You exaggerate. Again, why do you ask?"

"You have been here long enough to know that whatever is not permitted is forbidden, so I am asking to find out if cinnamon is permitted."

I told him it was not only permitted but required.

The Seaside Café Metropolis

AS PROPAGANDA FIGURES, my mother and I had long ago ceased to be novelties, and as a result, our lives in general and hers in particular had become very quiet. She had not been out to a dinner like this for a while. We received fewer and fewer exclusive invitations, and those that came were to events for the second or third tier of VIPs. I had the café, at least, but my mother was a fading star.

I had forgotten she could actually pull herself together when she went out rather than wearing her sackcloth-and-ashes revolutionary garb. She had on a kind of suit I did not know she owned and even wore an amber pendant over her white blouse. Was she wearing makeup? It was hard for me to tell, but she had a glow on her of some kind or another. Rouge or high blood pressure?

"Why did I never know about this man?" I'd asked her after I'd delivered the invitation. Before answering me, she got up and emptied her ashtray. I should have noticed the action at the time, but I only remembered it later.

"You never met him, but we corresponded because he was a colleague of your father's."

"I didn't know you knew any Lithuanians in America."

"He's lived in the United States for thirty-five years, so he's practically an American. He published the communist newspapers until he was hounded out of business during the McCarthy years. Now he imports books from the Soviet Union."

"Bestsellers?"

"Ideological works and cultural magazines."

"And he finds a market for these things in Waterbury, Connecticut?"

"You'd be surprised how well the working class is educated in class struggle there. And besides, it's not all that far from New York, and comrades make special trips to his store."

"So you haven't heard from him since Dad died?"

"Oh yes, I have. We kept up our correspondence until I moved here." She hesitated and then went on. "Back then, he asked me to move to the United States, and I thought about it but chose this instead."

"You considered moving to the States for a man you'd never met?"

"Who said I never met him? I'm dropping the subject."

"Are you blushing?"

"I don't blush."

"Then you should check your blood pressure."

MY MOTHER WAITED in my office while Mr. Dumbras and his party of escorts completed the day's tour of a model collective farm, a broom factory employing the blind, and a children's choir rehearsal at the Young Pioneers' auditorium. Was it possible she had never visited my office before? I pointed out the good leather couch and coffee table and office furniture. I pointed out the fine lithographs on the walls. I even pointed out the bas-relief of Marx and Lenin on the wall behind my chair, but none of it made much of an impression on her. Something was on her mind. When Bob knocked to say the party had arrived, she and I stepped out to the middle of the restaurant by the fountain and the bar.

Albert Dumbras was a slightly stocky figure in a tweed jacket, sweater vest, and tie. He had plenty of thick, white hair, his most dashing attribute, but otherwise he looked like a vice-principal nearing retirement from a public elementary school.

"Jenny," he said.

"Al. It's been a while."

This in English before they switched to Russian.

After I was introduced, I handed over direction to Bob and his team and retired back to my office.

They had called each other by their first names. How was that possible? Comrades did that sometimes, but it was slightly affected. These two had sounded natural, like old friends. I sat in my office with a glass of brandy, mulling over what I had seen. I'd thought I knew her as deeply as it was possible to know anyone, but it turned out I didn't know her at all. And if I didn't know this, what else didn't I know?

After a while, I went to my closet, turned on the light, and pulled the door mostly shut behind me, just so I could hear if anyone knocked at my office. I hit the switch and heard the clatter of utensils and the clinking of glass and crockery. It took a while to untangle the voices from the background noise.

"I was so surprised to find out you were here," said my mother. They were speaking in English. Her Russian was terrible, for all her revolutionary fervour, and she had no Lithuanian. Meanwhile, no one else at the table spoke English, as far as I knew. Maybe not even the listeners in their basement office, but they might have had tape to present to some sleepy translator later that night.

"I only came here because of you."

I could hear the others speaking rapidly in Russian to one another, alarmed by this turn of language. They were panicked but keen not to be rude, yet anxious to know what was being said.

"That can't be true."

"I'm saying it is. How have you found life in this place?"

"Inspiring."

"Really? I was born here, but I hardly ever come back. Ever since my parents died, I miss nothing but the food because it reminds me of my childhood."

"And how goes the revolution?"

He sighed. "The times are not what they were. There's less hope now, and the ones who have it are looking to China and Mao."

"What do you think of his revolution?"

"I don't know."

"Al, has some of the fire gone out of you?"

"I'm still spreading the message. People buy the books. The universities in particular like Marxism, and some of the new wave of students do too. Maybe the younger generation will get the revolution done."

"What about you?"

"I hope for a better world, but I don't think I'm going to be the one to make it happen. Ah, look! Kugel! Honestly, they make this in America too, but it just doesn't taste the same. I wonder if the potatoes are different."

Once the hosts got over their shock at the two speaking privately in English, they began to ask Albert questions directly in Russian. I went out to make a tour of the restaurant and show myself, but there was nothing I needed to see except how close to one another they were sitting. There was actually some sort of matron between Albert and my mother, but she was being squeezed as the two kept leaning over her to speak to one another. I noticed my mother was not smoking. I had never seen her not smoking. It troubled me.

I returned to my closet and threw the switch again.

"Apple pie!" said my mother. "I haven't ever seen this thing here. Albert, they must consider you the guest of honour to have come up with this."

"Maybe your son had something to do with it."

"Maybe."

"Jenny, you never told me why you didn't take me up on my offer."

"I was still mourning. I thought it would have been disloyal to Leo."

"He'd already been dead for quite a while."

"To the memory of him."

"I see. And how do you feel now?"

I couldn't hear her answer. The damned crockery was clinking, and the matron between them let out a gale of laughter based on a Russian joke being told across the table. All I managed to glean was that he wanted to see her again.

"ARE YOU WEARING makeup? At home?"

"I might be going out later."

"Why does this place look so neat? And where's your ashtray?"

"Is it a crime to clean up? I quit."

"You quit smoking?"

"I did."

"I don't remember you without a cigarette. You must have smoked as you breastfed."

"I only took it up to keep your father company."

"But your new boyfriend doesn't like it."

"Don't be ridiculous. He has asthma. And he's not my boyfriend."

"Sure. Old friend. Friend of my father. Family friend. What do you want me to call him?"

"My fiancé."

I sat down.

"You'll wrinkle the bedclothes."

"He's moving back here?"

"No. I'm going to Waterbury. He has important work to do with his bookstore there."

I could barely gather my wits enough to take in this information.

"I'm pretty sure hardly anyone reads his communist books in America."

"Some do. More will. Revolutions happen a little at a time."

"But not romances."

"Aren't you going to congratulate me?"

"I'm delighted."

"Your care for me always was half-hearted."

"What about me?"

"What about you?"

"I came here to support you."

"Thank you very much. I am no longer in need of support. So now that I'm leaving, do you intend to stay or will you return to your life of servitude in the Toronto hotel?"

"It wasn't servitude. I'm still in shock. I'm not sure what I should do."

"Take your time. I'll be happy for you no matter what you do."

"You'll be happy for me?"

"Sure. Why not?"

GETTING OUT WOULD not be as easy for me as it was for her. The Soviet Union had welcomed us with open arms, and then it shut its arms tightly around us. My mother would be going out with her old flame in order to continue the worldwide struggle for Marxist revolution through a bookstore in Waterbury. So the Soviets would let her out, and if she married an American, the Americans would have to let her in.

And what was I going to do?

"Do you want to go out with your mother?" asked Niko.

"I think I've followed her long enough."

"I thought you were rather too attached to her. Some men of a certain kind devote their lives to their mothers."

"Thank you very much for that. But I couldn't get into the USA easily after my sojourn in the Soviet Union. My mother's fiancé has citizenship, so if they marry, the USA can't keep her out. I, on the other hand, will look like a Canadian enthusiast for communism. Besides, I'm not entirely sure I want to go there."

"Strange. I always thought you were looking for an exit strategy. I'm flattered. This is a very fine place, there is no doubt, but nothing lasts forever. I should know. These several years will already be written up in the memoirs of your young bohemians decades from now, but they will be telling stories encased in amber. The past stays the same forever. You have to look to the future. Would the Royal York Hotel take you back?"

"I don't know. It's been quite a while since I was there, and half my contacts have probably died or moved on. As you say, nothing lasts forever."

"There are some very fine restaurants in other cities such as New York, I am sure," said Niko.

"But how to get there?"

"Try to see if you can do it. How do you know you can't if you don't try? But take Lucy with you. She's too promising to be wasted here."

"And who says I would go along with him anyway?" asked Lucy, coming from around the other side of the counter.

"I just praised your culinary potential to the boss. Shouldn't you be grateful?"

"It's not my culinary skills I'm talking about. Yes, I'm ambitious, but to ride out on the coattails of my boss would be demeaning."

"Don't be a fool," said Niko. "Life offers us very few opportunities. Seize his coattails if they are available and fly with him to a better place."

"Do I have a role in this conversation?" I asked. They both looked at me. "If I do get out, it would only be with you, Lucy," I said.

She crossed her arms and looked at me hard. "Go on."

"What more is there to say?"

"You mean you consider that a proposal?"

"Very poor form on his part," said Niko.

"Here is what I want you to know," said Lucy. "Suddenly your mother is leaving, and now you want me. That's a bit suspicious to me. I'll be no mother to you."

"If you knew my mother, you'd know she wasn't much of a mother to me either."

"That's not my point, Mr. Argentine. I expect words of love. I expect a little action on your part instead of reaction to my prodding."

"Lucy, will you marry me?"

"What, just like that? I just said you need to woo me more."

"But if I'm going to apply to emigrate, you have to marry me first so we can apply together."

"Yes, you have to keep the practical realities in mind," said Niko.

"Okay, okay. I'll put a provisional yes on that," said Lucy. "But you have to promise to woo me in the future."

"That's all?" Niko asked, grinning. "You should lobby for more."

"I intend to. I want to be sent to the Cordon Bleu school to learn proper technique, and I want an unlimited book budget when we get out so I can read up."

"That's it?" I asked.

"Not quite. If we succeed, we'll have to try to get my sister and mother out. I love this country, you know, though I'm willing to leave it for a career opportunity. But I'd miss my mother and sister too much if I left them behind."

"You make no mention of your fondness for me. Am I just a ticket?"

The Seaside Café Metropolis

"You have certain charm. It's growing on me."

"Well, Mr. Argentine," said Niko. "She drives a hard bargain. Do you agree?"

"What are you, my referee?"

"No, but this country does have a tradition of matchmakers. Call me a matchmaker. And Lucy, you remember you might not get out of here at all if he can't get out either. What happens if you marry him and you are stuck with him here?"

"There are worse places and worse men."

"Well," I said, "that was a little understated, don't you think? I could use a little wooing of my own."

"If you insist, I might say I do love you," she said.

"That's it?"

"Isn't it enough?"

"You should both quit while you are ahead," said Niko.

Potato Kugel

10–15 potatoes, preferably old ones

2 eggs

2 soup spoons melted fat

A splash of milk

Salt

Pepper

For the topping:

80 grams bacon bits

1 chopped onion

A quantity of sour cream

Heat the bacon bits in a baking tin or casserole until the pieces are cooked. Remove them, but leave their fat in the tin and swirl it. You may also soften the onion with the bacon, in which case set both aside for later.

Remove the eyes from the potatoes, then peel and grate to the finest degree possible. Avoid grating your fingertips into the mix because they spoil the colour and flavour of the finished product. Add salt, pepper, melted fat, and beaten eggs as well as a splash of milk into the mass, stir well, and pour into the metal tin that has been coated with the grease. The mass should be about five centimetres thick. Bake in a hot oven for half an hour and then reduce the heat to medium and bake for another forty minutes or more.

Cut the pieces of kugel into serving portions and serve hot, topped with bacon bits and fried onions with sour cream on the side.

Note: For enriched kugel, some recipes double the bacon and onion. Half of the bacon/onion mixture is blended into the kugel itself and baked together with it, while the second half is used as topping as described above. This enriched kugel is particularly appreciated by student fraternities when they play drinking games.

Tree Cake

I HAD JUST started the long and bureaucratically painful process of getting a marriage licence and an exit permit for Lucy and me when I received a note to make an appearance at the Ministry of the Interior at a certain hour at a certain place.

I walked into the drab office to find a familiar interlocutor sitting across the desk from me.

"Comrade Argentine," he said.

"Comrade Zorin."

He had thickened, as if from eating too many potatoes rather than the finer food at the Metropolis. His collar was so tight I wondered how any blood was making its way up to his brain.

"Please have a seat. I am afraid we cannot offer you coffee here. This is a government office, not a restaurant."

He seemed very happy to see me. Somewhat like a cat delighted to meet a mouse who'd once got away.

"I thought you worked for the Ministry of Communications," I said.

"Oh? I wonder how you got that impression."

"I see you have landed on your feet here," I said.

"Yes. An office job with regular hours. It makes my wife very happy."

"You have a wife?"

"And children. Those of us who sacrifice ourselves for the nation have private lives as well."

"What a surprise."

"And it seems to me that you intend to have a private life as well."

"I'm getting married, yes."

"Congratulations. I hope your marriage will bring you great happiness as you help to build socialism within the Lithuanian Soviet Socialist Republic."

"But I have also applied to emigrate."

"Exactly. And I am here to say that you have received the honour of being designated a necessary worker. Thus you will not be allowed to leave but will be expected to continue in your work to build a rich and varied culture in this city. Your marriage, of course, is no problem. You may get married and stay here to enjoy the fruits both of your labours and of your loins."

SO THERE WAS my reward for staying loyal to my mother. She could emigrate, but I could not. How did I take all this? Well, I was getting Lucy, and she was not entirely unhappy to stay in the country where the rest of her family lived. And there were worse places than the Seaside Café Metropolis, and let's be frank, many of them were in Canada.

It would be a vast understatement to say bureaucratic affairs moved slowly in the Lithuanian Soviet Socialist Republic. Neither my mother nor I could get married quickly, and her marriage arrangements took an exceptionally long time. Although Mr. Dumbras was a friend of the communists, he still had to follow the myriad of rules in a state where everything that was not explicitly permitted was forbidden. He had to leave the country as his visa expired, and then he needed to request a new visa after having put in the request for the civil marriage ceremony. Actually, a civil ceremony was the only kind available.

Lucy brought me the news that Julia and Genius had decided to get married as well, and she'd invited them to do it on the same day and join in the reception afterward for us and for my mother and Mr. Dumbras. Lucy didn't seem all that amused when I said we should declare a marriage festival at the café, something in the manner of the buckwheat festival. We could invite all the couples getting married that day to party along with us.

"Don't be ridiculous. That would dilute the sense of family."

"Isn't that what you're doing already?"

"Genius and Julia really are part of the family here. We need to have a big group, a tribe, a clan, so we can protect one another."

"We could invite the whole country to get married that day, and then we'd have a whole nation."

She didn't answer that, and I didn't push it. To tell you the truth, I didn't mind Genius and Julia joining us. But I was finding I was agreeing to everything Lucy said all the time, and bachelors of a certain age need to put up a little resistance. But not too much! You wouldn't want to lose the woman you love, but on the other hand, it is good to remind her occasionally that you have thoughts of your own, even if you have only two or three.

As the weeks and months rolled by, my mother managed to stay off cigarettes and began to undergo a transformation I would never have imagined possible. She found a swimming pool where she could get a little exercise. She joined a local women's choir in order to accustom herself to being out in society. She even started to come into the café to meet with Niko from time to time to learn how to cook the traditional dishes Mr. Dumbras might like his wife to prepare for him once in a while.

Love for my late father had turned her into a revolutionary, and now love for Mr. Dumbras was turning her into … what, a housewife? I could not imagine that was true, but what else could I think?

"I thought you despised conventionality," I said.

She was wearing a flower-print blouse. My mother in flowers! I could barely believe my eyes.

"People evolve, and besides, his bookstore is still working toward a socialist future. I am facilitating that evolution."

"And this move here all those years ago. Do you think it was worth it?"

"You certainly did all right, didn't you? Didn't you meet the woman you love here and get to act the big boss?"

"But not in my home."

"Rightly so."

She had a point. The other point I chose not to articulate to her was that I had always been the one who wanted to get out, and now she was leaving and I was stuck where I was. Or not stuck, depending on my point of view at the moment. I had my café and I had Lucy, and I loved them both.

I also had a modest apartment of my own, and Lucy moved in with me well before we got married. I liked to think her move had been motivated by love alone, but I suspected that living in a two-room apartment with her mother, sister, and uncle had something to do with her desire to move in with me.

I had never lived with anyone since moving out of my mother's house back in Canada, and I had become used to doing things a certain way.

"If it wasn't for me, you'd turn out to be one of those fussy bachelors by the time you were middle-aged," Lucy informed me.

"I'm not fussy. I'm just discerning."

"Finicky."

"I'm exacting."

"Prissy. And if you let this exchange carry on this way, my words will get worse. You have directoritis."

"What is that, exactly?"

"You have been a director of an establishment for a long time. You're too used to getting your own way, like some kind of president for life. Any boss who has been boss for a long time becomes bossy."

Lucy pointed out certain personal shortcomings I had not been aware of. My bedclothes were too worn, and my lack of good kitchen utensils was a defect even though both of us ate virtually all of our meals at the café. I had a record player but no records.

"I give all the albums I get to Andrius and the band."

"Your public life is fine, but now we'll have a private life as well, and we need to have some music in the home."

Lucy was willing to improve the place if I accepted all of her suggestions. As I said, I accepted most. Was she bullying me? Should I have stood up to her?

I liked her just as she was.

I WAS TERRIBLY proud of everything I had achieved at the Seaside Café Metropolis despite there being no seaside and no metropolis. The name was aspirational, an invitation to dream a dream and to live a certain version of bohemian life, if only for a few hours or, in my case, a number of years. Not truly bohemian, of course, but light-hearted, free, as if the worries of everyday life and the much greater monstrosities of human politics and tyranny did not exist. It had been a safe port in politically dangerous waters, as long as one avoided the traps of the hidden microphones.

Having initially made the decision to leave, I had grown a little sentimental about the place. I had started looking upon my regulars with fondness, and I smiled to see new young people scraping their kopeks together to be able to pay for coffee and potato trumpets.

And my sentimentality grew. I found I was proud to be the director of such a fine place. I was proud to have such a good team, and with a new wife soon joining me, what else, after all, could I possibly want?

Lucy and I could continue to work in the café and hope the political winds did not blow upon us too severely in the future. With my mother in the United States, we would have a reliable source of books. Lucy would be able to extend her education by reading Carême and Brillat-Savarin.

WE HAD PLANNED our triple wedding. My mother had no objection because a communal wedding felt properly communist to her. We had our weddings on the same day and a combined reception at the café, inviting closer friends to the back room and leaving the front open for those regulars without formal invitations but wanting to wish us well.

The cake to end all cakes in Lithuania is the tree cake, so called because it looks like a miniature golden Christmas tree about a metre high. It is made upon a spit in front of a fire. The pastry chef pours batter on the spit and turns it. Once a thin layer bakes, the chef pours on yet more batter, and eventually "boughs" begin to form from the dripping mixture. The chef works it so the base is broad and the tip much narrower, and when the finished product comes off the spit hours later, it stands glorious and proud. The taste is like that of a very dense and rich pound cake, the batter having contained many eggs and a couple of pounds of butter.

This was the centrepiece on a table by the fountain. Andrius

The Seaside Café Metropolis

and the band were playing light music from the stage including a little Dixieland because even the stodgiest of old patrons had heard of Dixieland. One whole swath of guests included old communists come to bid farewell to my mother and her new husband as they set off to spread the good news of socialism out of Waterbury, Connecticut.

Most of my staff were working, and my former young bohemians were all there, each of them fatter and more satisfied than he had been a few years before. They now had wives, including Marcel, whose wife was a close match for Mona in looks but whose character was shrewish. Still, he seemed happy. As for my Lucy, the staff of the restaurant from the waitresses to the kitchen staff fussed over her as one of their own, and she was radiant in her own ironic way.

We sang the wedding songs and we cut the tree cake, and people wandered around, drunk and happy on cheap bubbly wine before the hangover kicked in. Out of the crowd appeared Adam, the former lover of Mona, the former editor, whom I had not seen in some time. He asked to see me in my office, and although I told him I should stay out in public on my wedding day, he said I might like to hear what he had to say.

"HOW IS LIFE in the art world?" I asked him once we were seated across from one another with a glass of cognac in front of each of us.

"Oh, I have left the art magazine. Actually, I've been working in the Ministry of Culture for the last year."

"And how is that?"

"Very good indeed. I have been handed an interesting project, but a difficult one. I thought I might consult with you."

"Consult with me? In what, the culinary arts?"

"Not at all. Let me give you a little background. There has been a new push to promote the arts of the various Soviet socialist republics abroad among the capitalist countries. I will get to travel abroad as a result."

"Congratulations."

"The thing is, we need to show something abroad, and since folk dancing is passé and our chamber music orchestra is already famous, I needed something new, and a project has fallen in my lap."

"This is all very interesting, but I was married today, and my bride is alone outside."

"I'll cut to the chase. There has been a sharp rise in interest in photography, and in particular in the photography of a certain Lokys, whom you might remember."

"I do. Poor man. But what does this have to do with me?"

"His wife emigrated soon after his death and has managed to raise a firestorm of interest in New York. She had only a hundred or so photos with her, and there is a gallery interested in putting on a major show. But she needs the archive, which she says you have, and she wants you to bring it to New York. I would go along, of course."

"You would let me go to New York?"

"Obviously. Alina insists you be the one."

"But the Ministry of the Interior told me I was a designated essential worker who would never be allowed to leave the country."

"That was the Ministry of the Interior. The Ministry of Culture agrees you are essential and says you must be sent out to New York."

"With my wife?"

"Even that might be arranged. What do you think?"

What I thought was that Adam was eager to travel to New

York and would be happy to send me if he could ride on my coattails. It was a good opportunity, but I did not want to give away my thoughts until I had spoken to Lucy.

"I'll think about it," I said.

"You know, there is a new restaurant in New York that everyone is talking about."

"How would you know anything about New York restaurants?" I asked.

"This country is not as provincial as you think. We have eyes and ears, you know. Have you ever heard of the Four Seasons Restaurant in New York?"

"No."

"It is very chic. I think I can lay my hands on a copy of the article in the *New York Times*. I'll get it to you."

"You read English?"

"Of course, doesn't everyone?"

THE PARTY WAS lively, with dancing and much drinking, and near the end of it all, my mother, the new Mrs. Dumbras, was sitting with her husband and Lucy and me in a booth by the stage. Andrius's band had called it a night, and soon we would be moving on home. I told them about the offer that Adam had made to me in my office.

"So we might be emigrating after all?" asked Lucy.

"It looks like it could actually happen."

"We'll be happy to visit you in New York," said Mr. Dumbras. He was a gentle man, after all. My mother would do well with him. I looked to her for a reaction.

"Well, yes," she said, "you could probably find a job in New York. It will save you from going back to that terrible job you had in Toronto."

"Terrible?" asked Lucy. "He always talked about how grand it was."

"What?" my mother asked. "Do you mean he described the Ford Hotel as grand?"

"Mother," I said. "It was the Royal York. I'm sure you've mixed up the names in your memory."

She shrugged. What did it matter? We had completed one epoch of adventures in our lives. Now we were going to move on to another.

Tree Cake

If you cannot commit, do not attempt this recipe.

This festive cake should stand about a metre high and look like a golden New Year's Eve tree (remember this is a socialist secular holiday with no relation to earlier superstitious traditions) with shorter branches at the top and longer ones toward the base. It is a traditional Lithuanian wedding cake, firm, yet moist when fresh. Like a good marriage, it also lasts a long time (but not that long). After some weeks, it will be as crumbly as a biscuit, but still very good.

1 kilogram butter at room temperature
1 kilogram sugar
40 eggs, separated
1 kilogram white flour
1 litre thickened heavy cream or sour cream (at minimum 30 per cent butter fat)
5 teaspoons vanilla sugar

The Seaside Café Metropolis

Apparatus:

Linen cloth

A long pole, preferably metal, preferably with a handle at one end (A spit, do you understand? Some people call this a spit cake, but this name is revolting.)

A steady fire for four or five hours

Another pair of hands, or more pairs if available

Mix the butter and sugar together in a large bowl until they are well blended. Add the vanilla sugar and mix well. Slowly add the egg yolks and mix until smooth. Then blend in the flour. Slowly mix in the thickened cream. The egg whites should be beaten until light and added gently in several batches at this point until the batter becomes smooth and slightly lighter.

Butter a linen cloth generously both inside and out and wrap it on the centre of the pole. Set the spit in front of the fire with a pan underneath to catch the drips. Begin turning the spit and use a ladle to pour small amounts of batter on the pole where you have put the cloth. Turn as the batter cooks upon the spit. Once the first layer seems ready, repeat the process. Pour more on one end than the other to form a narrow end and a broad end. Keep turning the spit! A moment's inattention will waste half a day's work. The cake will not develop branches unless you turn the spit quickly at certain moments. Also, depending on the heat of the fire and your distance from it, the cake will either burn or remain insufficiently baked. Once the batter has all been used up, let the cake cool and remove it carefully from the spit. Rush now, and you will have wasted half a day's work. Do not leave the linen cloth inside if it has adhered to the cake. The first attempt at this recipe is often a failure. The measure of the baker is her ability to get it right in the long run. Either the person turning the spit or the one pouring the batter tends to singe the hairs on the backs of their fingers and hands. Keep these out of the batter. Do you want to spoil the effect?

Remember the cake is special and used for happy occasions. It is your obligation to be happy upon presentation and consumption of this cake. Indeed, happiness is part of the recipe for the cake to succeed.

List of Recipes

Apple Compote ... 18

Chicken Kiev ... 48

Mushroom Trumpets ... 71

Blancmange ... 88

Napoleon Cake and Champagne ... 104

Riga Sprats ... 133

Cold Borscht and Hot Zeppelins ... 157

Herring and Onions on Warm Potatoes ... 185

Burnt Crepes with Sweet Cheese ... 200

Buckwheat Groats ... 229

Pheasant Under Glass ... 251

Potato Kugel ... 265

Tree Cake ... 276

Afterword and Acknowledgments

My introduction to the legendary Café Neringa in Vilnius, in the Lithuanian Soviet Socialist Republic, came in the summer of 1975. But I didn't yet know the place was legendary.

I was the first of the family to visit Lithuania since my parents had fled the Red Army in 1944, so the trip was packed with latent emotion.

I had been turned back at the Polish border a week earlier due to a visa error and spent seven days trying to get the error corrected in Warsaw. Half a dozen of my Lithuanian relatives bought new bouquets of flowers daily and came to the train station but gave up after a week and went back to their homes in the northern city of Šiauliai. Now I was finally here in Vilnius, and they would soon come to meet me.

But in the meantime, there was the matter of breakfast.

Neringa was a very smart café, with a huge dining room and mosaics with a seaside theme, a middle section with a bar and fountain, and an intimate and charming street-front section. Not at all like the grimy train station cafés I had passed through in provincial Poland and the USSR.

The waitress handed me a thick menu book the size of a newspaper tabloid, with hundreds of items listed. There were many unusual dishes I thought I might try, so I asked first for the chicken in aspic.

The waitress told me they had none.

I looked down the menu and asked for sausages and eggs.

The waitress told me they had none.

This sort of exchange went on for half a dozen items with increasing exasperation on both parts until I came upon the unlikely availability of solyanka soup, a dish I'd never heard of at that time, made up mostly of cold cuts in a broth containing pickle juice. There was no coffee, but I could have tea with honey. The heavy black bread was good.

When my cousin's husband came over to pick me up, he looked around the room with awe.

"What a place, eh?" he said after we'd made acquaintance.

"Sure," I said. "But they didn't have anything I asked for on the menu."

"Did you choose from the checked boxes?"

It seemed that some Soviet menus contained all possible dishes, something like a Linnaean list with many categories and items, but only the ones available were marked by a pencil check in a tiny box. To the waitress, I had seemed like a moron, picking unavailable dishes. To me, the menu had looked like the culinary equivalent of a Potemkin village.

"This is the coolest place in town," said Rimas. He didn't get to the capital much, and he had clearly never been in this place before.

"What's so special about it?"

"It's a legend."

"Legend for what reason?"

"Everybody who was somebody came to this place," he said. "They still do."

I didn't know any of the Lithuanian somebodies in those days, neither the writers nor the artists, the musicians nor the actors. But I did get the idea that this was the iconic café of the city, as important locally as the Café de Flore or Deux Magots in Paris.

The Seaside Café Metropolis

The café had been built in the late fifties during the brief Khrushchev thaw in the Soviet Union. Finally, bohemians and students had a stylish spot to go to, a place with jazz and wicked conversation. It was like all very cool places in the West, with this exception — there was a microphone at every table, and the KGB listened in to what all the bohemians were talking about.

Moscow poet and later Nobel laureate Joseph Brodsky met his local friend Tomas Venclova in that café. Decades later, Venclova pointed out to me the corner table where the turned former British agent Jonas Deksnys used to drink a small carafe of cognac each night. A writer all the way from Minsk once came in by taxi to taste the local atmosphere. Lithuania was like the West to Russians, and it exerted a sort of magnetic pull, and the attraction to Vilnius and the Café Neringa exerted the most powerful force of all.

Iconic places exist in time as well as in geography, so the café was already past its prime when I visited in 1975. But the heyday came back to life in my imagination when I read a book of memoirs about those who had spent time in the café.

This reading was followed by conversations about the place with Aušra Marija Sluckaitė-Jurašienė, a writer later expelled from the Soviet Union with her husband, the theatre director Jonas Jurašas. Gregory Talas, now a resident of Toronto, told me he once played the double bass in the café jazz band. The late Jonas Žiburkus told me about his first mother-in-law who worked there under the direction of a manager called "The Argentinian," an expatriate who gave up his life in South America to return to the budding socialist paradise of the USSR.

The Café Neringa was such an important cultural landmark that when the hotel enveloping it was torn down early in the twenty-first century, the original café part was preserved and the new hotel was built around it.

When my contemporary world locked down during the pandemic, I found myself stranded in Vilnius for six weeks, and the keyboard under my fingers compelled me to start creating the world of *The Seaside Café Metropolis*, a café that became the fictional twin of the historic Café Neringa.

Some of my novel's scenes are inspired by Neringa history as described in *Neringos kavinė: sugrįžimas į legendą* by Neringa Jonušaitė. These include the visit of Jean-Paul Sartre and Simone de Beauvoir in the company of Antanas Sutkus, a fine photographer whose photos of Sartre led to the creation of a Sartre statue placed improbably on a sand dune on the Baltic coast. I also adapted the true story of the tragic photographer Vitas Luckus, who owned a pet lion and who leaped out of his apartment window after fatally stabbing a friend.

Kažkas tokio labai tikro (from publisher Aukso žuvys), a book of essays on historical themes in the Soviet period, had vivid descriptions of bohemian life in Vilnius's so-called Bermuda Triangle. Another important book to give me a feeling of the place at that time was *Déjà Vu. Vilnius,* by Inga Liutkevičienė. Thanks to Inesa Gailienė for finding a way to get that text to me.

Those were real life inspirations, but I had some literary ones as well. The birth of the conceit of bohemia could arguably be traced back to Henri Murger's 1851 novel, *The Bohemians of the Latin Quarter.* That novel was enormously popular in its day, and the stories were adapted into the opera *La Bohème.* The four rapscallion artists and philosophers in Murger's novel have evolved to my four young bohemians in *The Seaside Café Metropolis,* and the tragic death of my Mona echoes the tragic death of Mimi from the opera. I should add that Mona's backstory was based on the astonishing true story of the late Nelly Paltinienė, a Lithuanian singer who lived like a waif through the Second World War in Poland, with her father conscripted and her Jewish stepmother murdered. She went on to become a pop darling of Soviet Lithuania.

How is it possible to live in freedom under tyranny? One must create a sort of fantasy world to shield at least part of oneself from the oppression. And under this shield, people can create alternative lives for themselves, real or imaginary ones.

My thanks to Marc Côté and Sarah Cooper and their team at Cormorant Books, including Barry Jowett, Andrea Waters, and Fei Dong, who once again have championed a novel set in a faraway place in what seems now like a faraway time; to Joe Kertes and Dainius Sileika who read an earlier draft of the novel; and above all to Snaigė, who continues to stand by me.

We acknowledge the sacred land on which Cormorant Books operates. It has been a site of human activity for 15,000 years. This land is the territory of the Huron-Wendat and Petun First Nations, the Seneca, and most recently, the Mississaugas of the Credit River. The territory was the subject of the Dish With One Spoon Wampum Belt Covenant, an agreement between the Iroquois Confederacy and Confederacy of the Ojibway and allied nations to peaceably share and steward the resources around the Great Lakes. Today, the meeting place of Toronto is still home to many Indigenous people from across Turtle Island. We are grateful to have the opportunity to work in the community, on this territory.

We are also mindful of broken covenants and the need to strive to make right with all our relations.